THE VAMPIRE SLAYER'S SURVIVAL GUIDE

SCHOLASTIC

KATY BIRCHALL

THE VAMPIRE SLAYER'S SURVIVAL GUIDE

■SCHOLASTIC

The stakes have never been higher...

Published in the UK by Scholastic, 2022
1 London Bridge, London, SE1 9BA
Scholastic Ireland, 89E Lagan Road, Dublin Industrial Estate,
Glasnevin, Dublin, D11 HP5F

ISBN 978 0702 31833 7

A CIP catalogue record for this book
is available from the British Library.

Printed by CPI Group (UK) Ltd, Croydon, CR0 4YY
Paper made from wood grown in sustainable forests
and other controlled sources.

1 3 5 7 9 10 8 6 4 2

www.scholastic.co.uk

To anyone who has ever worried about belonging.
This book is for you.

PROLOGUE

Under the cover of darkness, a figure creeps towards Skeleton Woods.

A twig cracks under his foot and he stops still, hardly daring to breathe. After some moments of silence, disturbed only by the sound of a trickling stream running around the edge of the woodland, he continues to make his way towards the trees.

Tall and broad-shouldered with a dark, shaggy mop of hair and a wiry, unkempt beard, Grimmwolf is usually easy to spot, but he feels safe in the knowledge that there is no one for miles – save for the inhabitants of a lone, wonky house nearby.

But there are no lights on in the windows, so the

family must be asleep. Hardly surprising considering it is close to midnight. The moon is shining brightly through the clear sky, bathing the trees in a dim, silvery glow, and despite the cold, crisp air of the early January night, Grimmwolf is in a T-shirt with no jacket.

He doesn't feel the cold.

Reaching the woodland, Grimmwolf slowly crouches to the ground, his strikingly ice-blue eyes wide and alert, looking out for anything lurking within the shadows. Amazed that he's made it this close to the woods without any consequence, he takes a long, deep breath as he thinks about what lies beyond these trees.

Skeleton Castle.

For hundreds of years, the secrets of the mysterious castle have been protected, but there has been a rumour circulating that something has recently changed. The woodland is no longer what it was. There has been talk that the treasures stashed away within the walls of the fortress, greedily guarded by the undead creatures who live there, aren't as protected as they once were.

Grimmwolf has travelled miles to see if those rumours are true.

Cautiously, he raises his hand and reaches forward.

His fingertips brush the bark of the tree in front of him.

He waits.

When nothing happens, he stands up tall and reaches out again, this time pressing his hand firmly against the tree trunk.

Nobody comes.

He can sense something about the woodland. Some kind of weak energy force seeping from the trees, bidding him to turn around and leave this place. But he doesn't fall into a trance and run away, like the age-old stories tell will happen should anyone be tempted to get close to Skeleton Woods. Some enchantment lingers. The protective magic is still here, then. But it is severely weakened.

It will not last for long.

A smile creeps across Grimmwolf's lips, revealing unnaturally sharp teeth. He must return to his family to tell them the good news.

Turning his back on the woodland, he begins to run.

As he races away from the trees, his skin suddenly starts sprouting hairs until he is covered head to toe in thick, dark fur. His hands morph into huge, padded paws, his fingernails lengthening into razor-sharp claws.

The tops of his ears sharpen into points and his face transforms into that of a large wolf's, his beard thinning into long whiskers, his teeth sharpening into shiny white fangs.

Stopping at the edge of the field, the werewolf throws his head back and howls menacingly at the bright moon before disappearing into the dark.

It is time for the secrets of Skeleton Castle to be revealed.

CHAPTER

ONE

"VAMPIRE ATTACK!"

A vampire jumps out from behind a tree, her high-collared black cloak billowing behind her. A large-eared bat swoops down from the trees, circling her head. In the dim evening light, I can make out the vampire's long silver hair, alarmingly sharp fangs and threatening blood-red eyes.

But I don't flinch.

Instead, I cross my arms and sigh. "Sharptooth, you did it *again*."

The vampire hesitates, a flash of confusion flickering across her expression. "What? Did I get it wrong, Maggie?"

"Yes," I tell her. "Like I explained before, when you're hiding in the game hide-and-seek, you're supposed to … well … *hide*. I have to find you. You're not supposed to jump out, yell 'VAMPIRE ATTACK', and give away the place where you're hiding!"

"Oh." She looks disappointed, slumping back against the tree while her grumpy bat, named Bat-Ears, lands on her right shoulder, tucking in his wings. "This is a very strange human game. I don't really see the fun in sitting around, waiting to be found. I think my way is better."

Bat-Ears gives a squeak in agreement.

"I'm not sure most humans would agree with you. Vampire attacks aren't really that fun to them," I point out.

"I suppose you're right," she says. "Not all humans have a vampire for a best friend, like you do."

I grin at her. "No, they don't."

I never thought I'd end up with a vampire as my best friend. In fact, when my parents and I first moved to Goreway a few months ago, I wasn't sure I'd end up with any friends at all, let alone one who is, technically, a creature of folklore.

I didn't fit in at my old school in London. Mostly because, after a teeny tiny incident at a sleepover that involved me insisting on everyone watching a horror movie that made them all cry, everyone thought I was a gigantic freak – a freak who claimed to never have nightmares and was obsessed with scary books, supernatural monsters and anything to do with Halloween.

In all honesty, I don't get nightmares. And I *am* obsessed with scary books, monsters and Halloween, so it's not like I could argue with that reputation.

But then my Great Uncle Bram, who I'd never met, died, and in his will he left my parents his old, crooked house on the outskirts of Skeleton Woods in Goreway. Mum and Dad had always wanted to live in the middle of nowhere, so we packed up and moved in almost straight away, which was great because I was able to leave my old school but, at the same time, terrifying, because I'd have to attend a new one.

It's strange to think back on how nervous I was to go to Goreway School, because now I can't imagine being anywhere else. My two best friends in the whole world (aside from my vampire one) made me feel welcome there straight away: Ari and Miles.

Neither of them thought I was weird for being interested in horror and ghost stories – in fact, they informed me that I'd come to live in the right place, considering Goreway had a LOT of famous spooky history, most of it concerning Skeleton Woods, which was very much OUT OF BOUNDS. The reason why? Because no one who entered Skeleton Woods ever returned…

Obviously, as soon as I had heard that, I wanted to go check it out straight away.

Look, I appreciate that may seem an odd reaction, but I never felt scared of Skeleton Woods. I was *drawn* towards that woodland, despite all the folklore surrounding it about ghosts and monsters and vampires. I managed to persuade Ari and Miles to come with me, which wasn't too easy a task – Ari was curious, but Miles took a lot of encouragement.

They had both lived in Goreway their entire lives, growing up listening to the tales of the woods and what happens to those who dare to enter, and Miles took all that very seriously. Eventually, though, he gave in and we made a plan to secretly sneak into the woods in the hope of finding the mysterious Skeleton Castle. Sure, it was a bit nerve-racking thanks to the signs around the woodland that my Great Uncle Bram had put up that read things like:

SKELETON WOODS
HIGHLY DANGEROUS
TURN BACK NOW

But I was determined to go on, even when, with barely one foot in the woods, Ari and Miles suddenly changed their minds and turned back, completely ignoring my calls after them. I made my way onwards through the darkness of the trees, the sunlight blocked out by the canopy of branches and leaves overhead, until I reached Skeleton Castle.

That was the moment my life changed for ever.

Before I went into the woods, I hoped the castle *may* exist and I *might* find it. I imagined *maybe* even coming across some cool, ancient relics, like an old candlestick or something. Instead, I discovered a colony of vampires living there.

Yeah, I know. It was quite the surprise.

Luckily, the first vampire I came across was Sharptooth Shadow, who was, very importantly, a VEGETARIAN vampire, living on a diet of beetroot juice. If I had NOT first come across Sharptooth and instead bumped into, say, Count Bloodthirst, the scary vampire in charge of the castle, or perhaps one of

Sharptooth's fellow vampire students, like Nightmare, Fangly, Maggothead or Dreadclaw, then it may have been a very different story.

But, as I say, luckily I bumped into Sharptooth and, after meeting up a few times in secret, we ended up becoming friends. We were fascinated with each other: I wanted to hear all about the world of vampires and she wanted to know all things human. I introduced her to things she didn't know about like music, fictional books, phones and tomato ketchup, while she entertained me with amazing facts about vampires. I learnt that they have super abilities, they attend vampire lessons on things like cloak-swishing, and they each have a bat to always keep them company.

Count Bloodthirst not only has a personal bat, but he can command ALL the bats.

Cool, right? If you see a bat swooping around the night sky, it's probably delivering a message from Count Bloodthirst to someone.

Sharptooth even explained why Ari and Miles had run away in a trance from the woods: a long time ago, a witch had helped the vampires set up enchantments to protect the castle and keep everyone else out. That way, humans were safe and the Goreway vampires could live there without anyone stumbling across them. What we couldn't work out was why those enchantments hadn't forced me to turn back, too…

It was my parents who ended up telling me why.

It turns out, there was a very good reason why I was drawn to Skeleton Woods, why those enchantments had no effect whatsoever on me, and why I never got nightmares.

I was descended from vampire slayers.

Seriously.

And not just any vampire slayers, but the Helsby Vampire Slayers.

That's my surname: Helsby. I never thought it was a big deal or anything out of the ordinary; it was just my name. But it turns out, my family have produced the best vampire slayers in the WORLD. In every generation of Helsbys there is one "true slayer", and they write down all their wisdom and experiences into a book, which is passed down to the next slayer. My Great Uncle Bram left it behind for my parents. It's titled:

How to Be a
Vampire Slayer

And guess who the new true Helsby vampire slayer turned out to be?

Me.

Not my dad. *Me*. Maggie Helsby.

Talk about a twist. Plain, boring me! A slayer! I'd never done anything exciting in my life. I'd certainly never SLAYED anything before. I'm only eleven years old!

Oh, and, of course, there was also the small issue that when I found out that I was a vampire slayer, I just so happened to be BEST FRIENDS WITH A VAMPIRE.

Life in Goreway was already complicated enough, but then the town mayor got involved and things got MUCH worse. Mayor Collyfleur – or Mayor Cauliflower, as everyone liked to call him – tried to tear down the woods so he could build a private golf course on the land, but I wasn't going to let that happen, and neither were Ari and Miles. By that stage, they were friends with Sharptooth, too, and we couldn't let her lose her home.

Mayor Cauliflower – sorry, *Collyfleur* – did his best to encourage the people of Goreway to be fearful of the vampires living in Skeleton Woods, and he almost managed to get his way, but we kept arguing that the vampires weren't going to harm anyone. They hadn't done so for AGES, thanks to the ancient contract drawn up between the Helsby slayers and the vampires of Skeleton Castle that formed a satisfactory truce: the vampires could stay there with the enchantments in place and live off the animals in the forest, and a Helsby slayer would always live on the edge of the woods to make sure the vampires stuck to their word and the people of Goreway were protected.

Well, it seemed to me that it wasn't just the humans the Helsby slayer had to protect, but the vampires, too. Along with my parents and my friends, we stood between greedy, selfish Mayor Cauliflower and our vampire friends, and refused to let him tear down the woods.

And guess what?

The mayor *lost*. He was chased out of town, never to be seen again! Good riddance. He put himself before anyone in Goreway, and all he cared about was making a luxury golf complex for his own PRIVATE use. According to my parents, his second home – which is not far from us – has already been leased out to a new family. I hope they're nice.

Surely, ANYONE is better than mean, grumpy Mayor Cauliflower.

In a few weeks, the town can elect a new mayor. Fingers crossed it will be someone who really wants the best for Goreway and its residents.

The craziest thing about all the events that happened at the end of last year is that the Goreway community has somehow managed to persuade themselves that they made it all up. Even though they could see a line of red vampire eyes watching them from the woods as Mayor Cauliflower shouted about evil supernatural creatures blah blah blah, they STILL don't believe they were actually real.

"Weren't we silly for believing in vampires!" I've heard people say since.

"For a moment, I really did think they existed!"

"The mayor said there were vampires, and we genuinely BELIEVED him! What were we thinking?!"

"What a clever thing those schoolkids did, putting red lights in the woods, pretending they were the eyes of vampires looking out at us! They protected our woodland! They saved the wonderful, spooky heritage of Goreway! The future of Skeleton Woods is in safe hands!"

It's bonkers.

They've persuaded themselves that the vampires can't be real, without any help from us. This is a good thing, because the more secrecy surrounding the vampires, the better. They can continue living in the castle without anyone disturbing them. Plus, it means my secret is safe, too. I'm not sure that I want people knowing I'm descended from a line of world-renowned vampire slayers.

They might expect me to be able to do cool flips and high kicks and stuff.

But I'm not that kind of a vampire slayer. In fact, I'm not a vampire slayer at all. I've become the opposite, really: a vampire *protector*.

And I couldn't be happier about it.

Although apparently that entails spending my evenings teaching Sharptooth everything about human culture, including all sorts of games, the rules of which she COMPLETELY ignores.

"Shall we try hide-and-seek again after a quick snack?" Sharptooth suggests, her eyes brightening hopefully. "That is, if we *do* have any snacks…"

"I just so happen to have a fresh bottle of ketchup in my ba—"

"I'LL GET IT!" she interrupts, zooming off to where I left my backpack at the foot of a tree a few metres away. She returns with it in the time it takes me to blink.

Vampire speed takes some getting used to.

They can move so fast that they become a blur. They're also super strong, extremely agile, and they have such good hearing that if anyone approaches the edge of the woods, the vampires can hear them from within the castle.

They can't hear *me*, of course. They can't smell me, either. I'm the only human that doesn't have what they (worryingly) call a "deliciously potent" scent. It's all down to the whole vampire-slayer-destiny thing. That's why Helsby slayers were always a threat to vampires – we are the only ones who can sneak up on them.

I highly doubt the Helsby slayers of yore used Sharptooth's tactic and yelled out "HUMAN ATTACK" as they did so, though.

"Aren't you getting a bit bored of ketchup?" I ask, watching Sharptooth happily glug it from the bottle.

"Who would EVER get bored of ketchup?" she retorts quizzically, before holding out the bottle to me. "Want some?"

"No, thanks," I say, smiling to myself. "I tend to have ketchup with food."

"I've told you before, it's perfectly delicious on its own as a starter, main course and dessert," Sharptooth tells me, screwing the lid back on the bottle. "Right, shall we try this seek-and-hide game again? I'll concentrate on the rules this time, promise. Do they have a league of seek-and-hide teams like they do with ankle ball?"

"It's hide-and-seek, not seek-and-hide," I correct her, giggling. "And no, they don't have a league like in *football*. Hide-and-seek is more of a kids' game than a sport. The woods is a good place to learn it."

"Because there's lots of good places to hide, like behind this tree where I was."

"Exactly."

"If I hadn't jumped out and shouted 'VAMPIRE ATTACK', would you have found me?"

"Well, technically, as a Helsby I can sense when a vampire is near," I remind her. "So it's kind of cheating, me playing with you. BUT a normal person might not have found you."

"And then would I have won?"

"Yes."

"Hmmm, I see." Sharptooth hesitates before mumbling, "I still think my way is more fun."

"You know what? I agree," I confess, watching Bat-Ears as he begins to fall asleep on Sharptooth's shoulder, eventually toppling forwards and hanging by his little claws from her sleeve, snoring soundly. I check my watch. "Hey, Ari and Miles will be on their way, we should go meet them."

"I can teach them seek-and-hide," Sharptooth

announces excitedly, "but the fun vampire version!"

"Great idea. Miles in particular would love it," I say encouragingly, knowing full well that he'd likely keel over if a vampire jumped out of nowhere at him. Despite his knowing several vampires these days, he still gets goosebumps at the thought of anything spooky.

I grab my backpack from Sharptooth and insist she holds on to the ketchup bottle, just in case she wants a snack on the way. We set off towards a field at the edge of the woods, our usual evening meeting spot – it's outside of the enchantments so Ari and Miles can join in and we meet in the evenings so Sharptooth doesn't have to worry about turning to dust in the sunlight.

A lot of thought has to go into humans and vampires hanging out together.

Sharptooth is in the middle of telling me about how, since Christmas, Count Bloodthirst is completely fascinated by baubles, when I get a strange feeling.

I stop in my tracks.

"What's wrong?" Sharptooth asks, examining my expression.

"I … I don't know."

I glance around at our surroundings.

Everything is quiet, peaceful and still. There's no

movement, nothing notably wrong.

"Something feels different about the woods," I say, biting my lip. "I feel as though … as though we should be careful."

Sharptooth raises her eyebrows in surprise. "Maggie, I'm a vampire, remember? I can hear everything nearby. The other day, all of us could hear some kind of dog creep right up to the edge of the trees, even though we were in the castle listening to a very boring lecture from Count Bloodthirst about the history of pumpkins. I can even hear Miles and Ari cycling along on their bikes towards us now."

"I can't hear anyone; it's more a feeling. Something isn't right."

She blinks at me. "Huh?"

"Never mind. It's probably nothing. Let's carry on."

She continues with her story about Christmas baubles and I walk alongside her, attempting to listen and nod along in all the right places. But every now and then, I glance back over my shoulder, trying to work out what is different about Skeleton Woods.

Whatever it is, it makes the hairs on my arms stand on end.

CHAPTER

TWO

Ari throws her bag down on the grass and sits down in a strop.

"You'll never believe this, Maggie," she begins crossly. "But I've been given detention. AGAIN!"

Miles and I share a look. I actually *can* very much believe that Ari has landed herself in another detention. She has a knack for getting into trouble, something I deeply admire about her.

"I thought you were at art class after school today," I remark, sitting down cross-legged beside her, while Miles passes a football to Sharptooth and she begins dribbling it away from us, disappearing in a blur.

In the few seconds it takes Ari to reply, Sharptooth

has already done three laps round the field. Miles has seen Sharptooth do this dozens of times, but he still watches her in disbelief, dreaming of the day when vampires will be allowed to join the school football team so they can win every match without fail.

"I *was* in art class today," Ari confirms, "but now I have detention tomorrow! And all because, just before I went to art, Miss Woods caught me sneaking into Mr Kelvin's classroom. Is entering a classroom now against the rules?"

"You were rooting around in his desk drawers," Miles clarifies. "That is *definitely* against the rules."

"I needed something he had," Ari huffs, narrowing her eyes at him. "It wasn't a big deal."

"You were stealing back a confiscated item."

"I was retrieving my own property!"

Ari glares at Miles, and I try to stifle a laugh at her surly expression.

Having grown up next door to each other, they are such good friends they're practically brother and sister, but they couldn't be more different. Clashes like this one are a common occurrence.

Ari is outgoing, loud and messy. Her school shirt is always untucked, her dark hair rarely brushed, and her room a complete tip. Miles, on the other hand, is shy and quiet, and takes great pride in being neat. His uniform is never out of place and he reads books in such an awkward way because he refuses to bend the spine. He likes things ordered and he's really smart, the top of the class in everything – except art, where Ari takes the crown.

I'm not really the best at anything when it comes to school, but I'd much prefer to stay under the radar and, anyway, I'm happiest in the library, where I can take out the latest horror book that Mr Frank has ordered in for me.

Mr Frank is the school librarian and by far my favourite teacher. He's great at recommending books, and he likes reading about Goreway's heritage too, so has been super helpful when I've needed to find out historical stuff about Skeleton Woods. Mr Frank is very enthusiastic about all the cool, spooky legends surrounding the place.

I wonder how he'd react if I told him that my family were real vampire slayers.

His brain might explode with excitement.

"You know, Ari, if you didn't doodle during Mr Kelvin's lesson, he wouldn't confiscate your art pad and pencils in the first place," Miles says pompously.

"Whose side are you on, Miles?" Ari asks, crossing her arms. "And I wasn't *doodling*. I was creating art, which was a lot more interesting than his boring lesson. How am I supposed to go to my after-school art class without my pencils and pad? Huh? And how exactly do they—"

POP!

Startled by the bang, the three of us turn to look at where it came from. Sharptooth is standing in the middle of the field looking extremely guilty, the football now hanging from her fangs, slowly deflating.

"Not again," Miles groans. "Sharptooth, I've told you that you're not allowed to use your teeth in football!"

"Whoops," she says, appearing next to us and shaking the ball off her fangs so it drops to the ground. "Uh-oh, I woke up Bat-Ears, too."

Bat-Ears stretches out his wings and flies up into the air, looking FURIOUS at being awakened from his slumber in such a loud fashion. He begins screeching loudly at her.

"Uh … it wasn't me," she quickly claims. "It was … Miles!"

A cantankerous Bat-Ears responds by swooping

straight at Miles, soaring around his head and flapping his wings in a frenzy.

"Sharptooth!" Miles cries out, shielding his face with his arms. "Tell the truth!"

"Okay, fine," she says, holding up her hands. "It was me, Bat-Ears. I popped the football. It wasn't my fault, though. They should make them less breakable."

Bat-Ears chooses not to hear Sharptooth's confession, continuing to bother Miles.

"I don't think football manufacturers aim to make them vampire-proof." Ari grins, her mood instantly lifted by this comical mishap, as Miles attempts to shoo Bat-Ears away. "How many have you popped now, Sharptooth?"

"One or two," she says innocently.

"Five," I inform her.

"SIX!" Miles corrects through gritted teeth, as Bat-Ears finally gives up and flies back to land on the top of Sharptooth's head.

Sharptooth shrugs, sitting down opposite Ari. "Hey, did you draw us again in art class today?"

"Yes, I did," Ari says brightly, reaching into her bag. "You want to see the next strip of your story?"

"Yes, please!" Sharptooth flashes me a wide grin.

"It's so cool, isn't it, Maggie? I still can't believe that me and Bat-Ears are going to be the stars of a human fiction book!"

Since our underdog victory over Mayor Collyfleur's dramatic bid to destroy Skeleton Woods, Ari's been working on an amazing graphic novel about Sharptooth and her friendly-vampire adventures, with Sharptooth's approval of course.

Ari flips through her art pad to get to the correct page. "Hope you like it."

Sharptooth peers over at the sketches, her red eyes glistening. "*Wow,*" she whispers. "These are incredible. What do you think, Bat-Ears?"

He swoops down to land on the art pad, squinting his eyes at the latest comic strip, before hopping up and down on the paper, emitting a series of high-pitched squeaks.

"He loves it," Sharptooth tells Ari. "He especially likes how terrifying you've made him look. You've really captured his vicious side."

Bat-Ears proudly stretches out his wings so Sharptooth can tickle his little fluffy belly.

"Yeah, he's vicious all right," Ari says, winking at me.

"How was football practice, Miles?" I ask as

Sharptooth pores over Ari's sketches, eagerly examining each tiny detail.

"Tiring," he admits, sitting down and shoving the burst football into his bag with a disapproving glance at Sharptooth. "I think my coach is still cross with me for missing so much last term. I have to prove he can trust me again and then I can get back on the team."

I wince, feeling partly responsible for Miles losing his place on the school football team, even though he's by far the best player. After I introduced Sharptooth to him and Ari, he became so wrapped up in our friendship with her that he kept making excuses to miss practice. It occurred so frequently that he began forgetting to bother with excuses at all, and then the coach became concerned about his star player, who had seemingly lost all enthusiasm for the game.

That's how Miles's parents found out about Sharptooth, when they came looking for him and discovered him here playing Frisbee with a vampire. They were freaked out at first, but they helped us to save the vampires of Skeleton Woods, and now they've accepted Sharptooth, just as my mum and dad have. Ari's parents, who never saw a vampire with their own eyes, think that it's all a big joke and Miles's family are in on it.

"You'll get back on the team, I know it," I assure him. "You might make captain."

"I hope so," he says, smiling gratefully at me.

"You know what would really help my comic about you, Sharptooth?" Ari says, watching Sharptooth flick through her art pad.

Sharptooth attempts a guess. "Ketchup?"

"No. I was thinking it would be really cool to be able to draw the castle properly. You see, in these scenes here" – Ari reaches over to turn to a specific page – "I've drawn you and Bat-Ears in the castle, enjoying your lessons with Count Bloodthirst."

"Oh yes." Sharptooth nods. "I'm not sure how accurate this is."

"That's because I've only been to the castle once," Ari points out, "for the party to celebrate saving Skeleton Woods. I was having so much fun, I didn't really get a proper look around the place."

A few days after Mayor Collyfleur scarpered, Count Bloodthirst invited us to the castle for a big party to thank us for our help. He asked an old witch friend to lower the enchantments around the woods just for the evening, so that Ari, Miles and my parents were able to come. It was a great celebration, albeit a strange one.

Watching vampires take turns to do the limbo is definitely a memorable experience.

After that night, the enchantments went back up, so Ari and Miles haven't been invited back to the castle since.

"I wasn't talking about the accuracy of the castle, Ari," Sharptooth says, pointing at a sketch of Count Bloodthirst smiling. "I was talking about his expression during a lesson. Vampires aren't really supposed to smile. I only learnt to do that thanks to Maggie!"

"I remember," I say, chuckling as I recall the first time the corners of her mouth curled up into a wonky smile, her eyes wide open with panic at what was happening.

"I think if Count Bloodthirst does anything near a smile, it's more like a smirk," Sharptooth explains brightly, "probably because he's plotting an evil vampire plan."

"Sure." Miles gulps. "That makes sense."

"And Count Bloodthirst is not exactly *happy* when he's teaching me," Sharptooth continues, before letting out a sigh. "I'm not his best student."

"Hey, you're the Chosen Leader," I say, reminding her of her destiny.

Every hundred years, the Chosen Leader of the

vampires reads a prophecy that directs them to the human who will succeed them. The Chosen Leader has to then turn that human into a vampire and train them up.

Count Bloodthirst is the current one and, as he was supposed to, he read the prophecy that instructed him the next leader was a little girl at an orphanage. When he arrived there, he found the girl and was about to turn her into a vampire, but another girl stood in his way, refusing to let him harm her friend. He was so astounded by her bravery that he decided to take matters into his own hands and made her the next Chosen Leader instead.

That strong, courageous girl was Sharptooth.

Her choice to be vegetarian wasn't exactly a hit at first with the vampire community, but now they're all on board with it. They go on night-time trips in disguise to supermarkets, lugging back crates of ketchup and beetroots to the castle.

My parents and I bought them a juicer for Christmas to make it easier to produce beetroot juice and they *literally* jumped for joy, and vampires can jump several metres in the air. It was the best present opening ever, much better than anything I've seen on YouTube.

"Being the Chosen Leader does not mean I'm the best at vampire school," Sharptooth says regretfully. "You should see how good Dreadclaw is at swooping from great heights! He does it so smoothly. In my last class, I landed, did a roly-poly and got tangled in my cloak. Count Bloodthirst was NOT impressed."

Miles shudders. "I can picture his scowl."

"Okay, I'll make some changes to the Count Bloodthirst sketches," Ari says. "But seriously, Sharptooth, do you think he might let us come to the castle again? It would be great to look around to draw it properly. I want to make sure I capture all the details."

Sharptooth considers Ari's request. "I don't know. He'd have to get the witch in to lower the enchantments temporarily again, and you know how much he dislikes asking witches for a favour."

"You'd think that witches and vampires would get on," Miles considers.

Sharptooth recoils and Bat-Ears lets out an insulted squeak. "Why would you think that?"

"Because you're both … uh … well" – Miles searches for the word – "non-human."

"That doesn't mean we get on," Sharptooth informs him with an appalled expression. "There is a huge variety of us 'non-humans' and it's very rare that we see eye to eye. For example, vampires are *vastly* superior to witches."

She puffs her chest out proudly. "We don't need spells to be awesome."

"That's true. You're already super strong and fast," Ari agrees. "But it would be quite cool to be able to create magic."

"Vampires can create magic," Sharptooth says defensively.

I turn to her in surprise. "You can?"

"Well, sort of." She shifts uncomfortably. "There's such a thing as *vampire magic*, but it's rare. That's because it's so special, though."

Ari and I share a smile. "What exactly is vampire magic?" I ask.

"I don't know much about it, but it's REALLY powerful. Much more powerful than stinky witch magic. I think you need to have certain objects to create it."

"Like spell books?" Miles asks curiously.

Sharptooth shrugs. "You'll have to ask Count Bloodthirst."

"Maybe we can ask him when we visit the castle," Ari prompts, flashing Sharptooth a winning grin. "You reckon you can speak to him about us coming again?"

"Sure!" Sharptooth nods. "I'll ask him and see what he says."

"Brilliant!" Ari beams at her. "I really hope he says yes."

"Hey, Sharptooth," Miles begins, his brow furrowed quizzically, "you know when you said there was a HUGE variety of you non-humans … uh, what did you mean by that?"

She blinks at him. "Exactly what I said. There are lots of non-humans."

"As in … vampires. And we know there are witches, too. But there's no other non-humans that live amongst us, right? No one else to be worried about," he says hopefully.

"None at all!" she replies with a wave of her hand. "Unless you worry about monsters, ghosts, werewolves, zombies, mummies and those sorts."

"Z-*zombies*," Miles repeats in a whisper. "*M-m-monsters?*"

"Anyone fancy a snack?" Sharptooth asks, oblivious to Miles's horrified reaction. "I'm so hungry, I could eat a human!"

Miles lets out a yelp and promptly faints.

"Oops!" Sharptooth claps a hand round her mouth. "Vampire turn of phrase."

CHAPTER

THREE

"How is Sharptooth getting on with her new toothbrush?" Dad asks, as we pull up to the school and park.

I undo my seat belt in the back. "She needs a new one."

"You're joking," Mum says from the front seat. "She broke another?"

"She chomped right through it. Accidentally, apparently."

"All right, we'll get her one from the practice today." Dad chuckles. "She just needs to get used to it, that's all."

Mum and Dad are dentists, and when we moved here, the old dentist retired so they were able to take over the local Goreway practice straight away. They now offer free dental care to the vampires of Skeleton Castle and do evening check-ups on the outskirts of the woods every now and then.

They've introduced toothbrushes and toothpaste to the vampires, who aren't exactly taking to them as smoothly as my parents might have hoped. They bit the first batch of toothbrushes into tiny pieces and spat them out, not really understanding what else you were supposed to do with them. The toothpaste didn't go down too well, either.

"UGH, BLEUGH, GAH!" Sharptooth cried when she'd applied the TINIEST blob to one of her fangs and tasted it. "What is that taste?! It's GROSS!"

"It's mint!" Dad said, stunned by her disgusted reaction. "It's a fresh taste."

"It's HORRID!" Sharptooth declared, her eyes watering as she scrubbed her tongue with the end of her cloak. "You use that stuff every day?"

"Twice a day at least."

"Humans are DISGUSTING!" she announced, wrinkling her nose.

"You drink ketchup in gallons, but we're the disgusting ones?" Mum said, amused.

"Can't we brush our teeth with ketchup?" Sharptooth asked.

"Absolutely not," Mum replied firmly. "It has to be toothpaste."

Meanwhile, another vampire, Maggothead, had figured out that the toothpaste squirts out the tube if you press it hard enough, which seemed a lot more fun than smothering his fangs in the stuff.

He excitedly slapped his hand down on the tube and Nightmare got a splat of toothpaste right in the face. Maggothead cackled so hard, he had to lie on his back and kick his feet in the air. Nightmare retaliated by covering Maggothead's hair in toothpaste, which was NOT so funny. Maggothead then tried to get Nightmare with toothpaste again, only Nightmare ducked and Dreadclaw's cloak got hit. Dreadclaw snarled and, waving another tube of toothpaste around, cried out, "I'LL GET YOU, MAGGOTHEAD!" but got Fangly instead. A huge toothpaste fight broke out and it took Count Bloodthirst a long time to get things under control, by which time we'd run out of toothpaste.

My parents are determined to get the vampires taking good care of their fangs, so are patiently continuing to provide toothbrushes, even though their new patients aren't exactly making it easy.

"Have a good day at school, Maggie," Mum says, swivelling around in her seat to smile at me.

"Thanks. Oh, I forgot to tell you, Ari asked Sharptooth if Count Bloodthirst would lower the enchantments again so they could come to the castle one day and have a proper look around. You could come too, if you like?"

"That would be great!" Dad exclaims, Mum nodding along in agreement. "Only if Count Bloodthirst is happy for us to join, of course."

"Cool. See you after school!"

Slinging my backpack over my shoulder, I hop out of the car, shut the door behind me and wave them off, before joining the trickle of students heading through the school gates. I see a boy lingering by the steps with a man I assume to be his dad – they have the exact same thick, dark, scruffy hair and bold eyebrows.

The boy is tugging on his school uniform, as though it's uncomfortable and scratchy, and I recognize his apprehensive expression, because it wasn't so long ago that I wore the same one. It's obvious he's new here. This must be his first day. His eyes flicker uncertainly towards the grey stone of the walls. Goreway School is a grand and imposing building of Gothic architecture with tall, wide windows and heavy wooden doors. With its dark stone structure and ornate stacked chimneys, it wouldn't look out of place in a horror movie, so of course

I love it, but I can understand why it might not appear as particularly warm and welcoming on first glance.

His dad is speaking to him in a low growl, and I assume he's wishing him good luck on his first day.

I immediately sense something strange about both of them. I can't put my finger on it, but I feel oddly aware of their presence. Like I'm *supposed* to notice them. As I approach, the dad straightens and turns to face me with a curious expression before I reach them. He must have heard me coming.

"Hi!" I say cheerily, deciding to make the effort to welcome the boy, since I know exactly how it feels to be the new student.

The boy starts at my greeting, looking me up and down suspiciously, wearing a serious, guarded expression.

"Hello," the dad says.

Now that I'm closer to them, I notice that they also have the same piercing ice-blue eyes. The dad is watching me intently, his brow furrowed in concentration, like he's trying to work something out.

"I'm Maggie," I say. "Are you new here?"

The boy nods.

"This is Marrok," his dad says for him. "We've just moved here."

"I was new last term and was nervous, too, but trust me, you'll love it. It's a great school."

I notice Marrok's dad is holding a book and instantly recognize the cover. It's one that I loaned from the school library when I first arrived.

"I read a lot about Goreway when I first moved here, too," I inform him, gesturing to the book in his hands. "I've read that one and actually, if you want to learn more about Goreway and Skeleton Woods, I would recommend a few others instead."

The dad raises his eyebrows, bemused. "Is that so? Why?"

"That book only has one chapter on Skeleton Woods and the author wastes it by going on and on about the completely unproven and random theory that there may be hidden treasure in Skeleton Castle."

"You don't believe it?" he replies, while his son listens to our exchange. "It seems to make perfect sense to me – Skeleton Woods and its castle must hide many secrets."

"If the castle exists," I say breezily. "It's just ghost stories and spooky legends designed to interest tourists."

"You don't believe in the vampires, then."

"Vampires. No way." I force a laugh. "Do you?"

"As you say, I'm sure it's simply ghost stories and spooky legends," he replies.

The way he says it makes me nervous, as though this conversation is both amusing and fascinating to him. We stand in silence as I start to wonder if this man knows something he shouldn't…

"Anyway," I say eventually, unnerved. "Marrok, do you want me to show you to the head teacher's office?"

"Okay," he says, still looking a bit wary.

"Goodbye, Marrok," his dad growls, giving him an encouraging nod. "Have a good first day. And nice to meet you, Maggie. It's been … enlightening."

I lead the way up the steps into school, Marrok trailing behind. He doesn't say anything as we head down the corridor to Miss Woods's office, where we find her door open.

She's standing by her desk, reading a file, and looks up when I rap my knuckles on the door to alert her to our arrival.

"Ah, hello, Maggie. And you must be Marrok Grey, welcome!" She smiles and gestures for him to come in. "Thank you, Maggie. You can go to your classroom now."

"Good luck," I say to Marrok.

He watches me curiously as I go, his stern eyebrows knitted together.

There's something different about that family, that's for sure.

I shake my hands out as I make my way to my classroom, because I'm still getting a strange feeling. I know from experience and from studying *How to Be a Vampire Slayer* that slayers are uniquely attuned to certain atmospheres, sensing danger before it appears. It's almost as if that's happening to me now. As if I should be cautious.

It feels like a warning.

"Maggie!" Ari appears at my side, jolting me from my thoughts. "What are you doing?"

I realize I've been standing still at the door to our classroom.

"I was just … uh … I was in a daydream."

"Yeah, I can tell. You're just hovering here, blocking the way. What were you thinking about?"

"I was … I was thinking about … the school trip," I say quickly, walking over to our desks, which are next to each other.

Her eyes light up. "Oh YES!"

Since we got back from the Christmas break, all anyone

can talk about is the school trip to Rome that Mr Frank has organized for our year and the one above. We're going in just a few weeks and it's billed as "an educational long weekend filled with cultural and culinary delights", which Ari translates as a glorious opportunity to eat as much pasta and pizza as possible, with the added bonus of missing at least one day of school.

"The trip is going to be amazing," she assures me for the hundredth time. "I am going to eat my weight in ice cream, it's meant to be so good in Italy."

"It's called *gelato*," Miles pipes up from where he's sitting at his desk already, reading what looks like a very hefty guidebook on Rome.

"Right, gelato." Ari shoves her bag down and plonks into her seat. "I'm going to eat tonnes of the stuff. You reckon Mr Frank will let us have some time to ourselves while we're there?"

"Highly unlikely," Miles answers, finally looking up from his page. "Have you seen the itinerary? We have a lot to see in very little time."

"We're there for three full days," Ari says. "We can't spend that whole time looking around boring museums and stuff. I want to do cool things, like ride about the city on a scooter."

"Right, because I'm sure an eleven-year-old will be able to rent a scooter," Miles says sarcastically. "Have you read *anything* about Rome? The museums are hardly boring and there are so many other things to see, too, like all the incredible art in the churches and galleries. You won't want to miss out on those, being an artist yourself."

"Please tell me the itinerary has more stuff on it than traipsing around museums and churches," Ari groans. "Otherwise I'm going to have to speak to Mr Frank and tell him that, unless he wants to be known as a VERY BORING teacher, it's important that he adds a scooter trip to the list ASAP. Or at least a visit to a water park."

"I'm glad it's Mr Frank who's in charge," I say, laughing at Miles looking so aghast by the water park idea. "I'm sure he'll make it fun and interesting."

"You just want him to teach us about Rome's spooky stories," Ari correctly guesses.

"Are there any?" I ask innocently.

"Oh, yes," Miles says. "You ever heard of *La Sedia del Diavolo*? Otherwise known as the 'Devil's Chair'?"

Ari and I shake our heads.

"It's the ancient ruins of a mausoleum," he says.

"What's that?" Ari asks.

"A tomb."

"*Cool*," Ari and I chorus, eagerly leaning in for him to tell us more.

"It's got lots of legends surrounding it. Stuff like, if you find an old inscription on it, you'll gain magical powers that will enable you to change the course of your fate."

"Awesome," Ari says, turning to look at me. "We HAVE to go there and find that inscription. It would be really handy to change having to do any tests at the end of term."

"That's your first thought if you got magical powers? You would get out of school tests?" Miles says, unimpressed. Ari sticks her tongue out at him.

"Is the Devil's Chair on the itinerary?" I ask Miles hopefully.

"Not that I saw, but I'm sure you can persuade Mr Frank to add it. You are his favourite student, after all," Miles points out, with a hint of jealousy to his tone.

Miles has tried to be enthusiastic about scary stories and he has read books I've recommended, like Neil Gaiman and the Goosebumps series, but he just doesn't *love* the genre like I do. Not that it matters, but, as a dedicated bookworm, I think he gets envious at the excited conversations Mr Frank and I have about the characters and scenes we love.

Mr Kelvin sticks his head round our classroom door. "There's assembly today, people! Everyone make your way into the hall. And try to do so QUIETLY."

"Assemblies are so boring," Ari grumbles, pushing her chair out and standing up.

"I heard that, Ari," Mr Kelvin says tiredly. "I hope you're not looking for another detention!"

"Not me, Mr Kelvin," Ari replies through gritted teeth, plastering on a smile. "The one I've got today is more than enough for the week."

"Very good," he says, disappearing down the corridor towards the hall.

"I swear he has it in for me," Ari mutters crossly, as we join the rest of the class in filing out of the room. "He can tell I'm not one to be oppressed by his stupid rules and he's trying to stifle my creativity."

"Yes, it could be that," Miles begins, falling into step with her, "or maybe it's because you changed the ringtone on his phone to a fart noise and he couldn't change it for days."

Ari smiles proudly. "That was funny, wasn't it?"

Miles and Ari discuss her best pranks as we make our way down the corridor, but that strange feeling of danger begins to creep through me once again, my blood running cold, my senses sharpening as I feel suddenly alert and on edge.

That's when I notice him watching me.

He's standing by the door of the school hall, his eyes meeting mine over the heads of the mass of students going into assembly.

"That's the new boy," Ari whispers, spotting him. "His family just moved to Goreway, apparently. Think his name is Marvin or something."

"Marrok," I correct her, distracted.

"That's it. Strange name, isn't it?" Ari considers.

It being a clear, crisp January morning, beams of sunlight are streaming in through the windows, so it's clear that he's not a vampire. He *can't* be a vampire.

But there's one thing I know for certain.

Marrok Grey isn't human.

CHAPTER

FOUR

A few days later I'm in the shower, belting out one of my favourite songs, when I notice that I'm not the only one in the room singing. Someone – or some*thing* – is screeching along with me.

Steeling myself, I peer around the shower curtain.

A small bat is sitting on the heated towel rail, throwing his head back while ecstatically squealing the melody of Tina Turner's "Simply the Best".

I clear my throat. The bat abruptly stops and blinks at me.

"May I help you?" I ask.

He squeaks at me indignantly and nods towards a scrap of parchment that has dropped on to the bath mat.

"Ah," I say, understanding immediately. "I'll read Count Bloodthirst's invitation once I'm out of the shower. Thank you for delivering it."

The bat proudly puffs out his fluffy chest. He doesn't move, though.

"You can go now," I prompt.

Instead of flying back out the bathroom window, he pointedly hops up and down on the towel rail before letting out a contented sigh.

"Oh, I see. You're warming your toes. All right, you carry on."

I finish getting the conditioner out of my hair and then turn the shower off, reaching for my towel that's hanging a few rungs below the bat. Stepping out, I pick up the scrap of parchment and read the elegant calligraphy written across it:

His Excellency Count Bloodthirst
is pleased to invite

the Helsby family

to Skeleton Castle this coming Saturday

Please RSVP at your
convenience by return bat

I smile in the knowledge that Ari and Miles will be receiving a similar invitation by bat at this moment also. I place the parchment down at the edge of the sink and address the bat waiting on the towel rail.

"Please thank Count Bloodthirst for his invitation and let him know that we will be there. We're really looking forward to it."

The bat listens to my instructions, but doesn't move a muscle.

"Okay, well, you can let him know when you're ready," I say, exiting the bathroom to plod across the landing into my bedroom.

As I get dressed, I hear a swishing sound behind me, and spin round to find the bat has followed me into my room. He lands on my pillow and looks startled at how soft the landing is, before he starts happily bouncing up and down, as though it's a trampoline.

"Guess they don't have pillows in Skeleton Castle," I ponder, remembering the coffin I found in Count Bloodthirst's office the first time I visited.

I pick up my hairdryer and turn it on. The bat stops bouncing and stares at it in wide-eyed wonder.

"It blows out hot air," I explain to him over the noise. "It's to dry my hair, see?"

He watches as I do so, before spreading his little wings and flying straight towards my head to give it a closer inspection. I put the hairdryer on a low setting and point it at him. He gasps in excitement, enjoying the warmth. I then turn it up to the highest setting, laughing as he hovers in the blustering hot air stream.

"What are you doing?" Dad asks, suddenly appearing in the doorway, surprised to find a bat in my bedroom.

"We got an invitation from Count Bloodthirst to go to the castle this weekend," I explain, turning off the hairdryer, much to the bat's disappointment. "This little guy seems to want to hang around for a bit."

As though to prove my point, the bat comes to land on my head.

"Lovely. Dinner will be ready soon," Dad says, unfazed by the vampire postal service.

The last time Count Bloodthirst invited my parents to the castle, a bat dived down our chimney when we were in the middle of watching a nature documentary about beetles. It dropped a scrap of parchment in Mum's hands and landed on Dad's lap, using his jeans to wipe away the soot on its feet, before flying off again back up through the chimney.

I expect today's bat to swoop off soon enough to return

to Count Bloodthirst, but, instead, he makes himself right at home, refusing to leave my side. When Mum comes into my bedroom later on, she finds me reading a book, with the bat asleep, comfortably nested in my hair.

"Um, Maggie?" she begins, raising her eyebrows.

"Yes?"

"There's a bat on your head."

"I know."

Mum hesitates. "Okay then. Well, dinner's ready."

The bat jerks his head up at that announcement and gives a squeak of excitement, stretching his wings and circling round my head before following me down the stairs.

"Can you set the table?" Dad asks me, stirring a pot and glancing up to see the bat land on my shoulder. "Is our guest joining us for dinner?"

"Looks like it," I reply with a shrug.

"Does he like homemade vegetable soup?"

"No idea," I say, getting the cutlery out the drawer.

The bat squeaks and hops up and down.

"I think that means 'yes' actually," I inform them.

"Oh, good."

Using the oven gloves, Dad slides the pot on to a mat in the middle of the table and goes to get the ladle, while

Mum slices up some sourdough bread and I set out the spoons. As Dad begins to scoop the soup out into bowls, I take my seat and the bat slides down my arm, landing neatly on the tablecloth.

Dad puts dinner in front of me and the bat leans forward to give it a big sniff. He squeaks in delight.

"Maybe I'll get him his own bowl," Dad considers.

Mum nods, passing me a slice of bread. "I think you should."

Going to a cupboard in the corner of the kitchen, Dad retrieves an egg cup. He pours some of the soup in and places the egg cup next to my place setting.

"Bon appétit," Dad declares.

The bat squeaks at him in thanks, before jumping up to perch on the edge of the egg cup and dipping his head forwards. He begins to slurp the soup, gleefully smacking his lips.

"I think he likes it," Dad says proudly, as we all dig in. "Won't Count Bloodthirst be wondering where he is?"

"Maybe. I don't think this is his main bat companion, though," I say. "Count Bloodthirst is sort of the leader of all bats too, so he can use any of them to deliver his messages. The bat that's stuck to his side is a lot bigger and scarier than this one."

At that, the bat stops eating his soup and looks offended. He turns to me, narrows his eyes and bares his sharp little fangs.

"Oh, uh, sorry, you're very scary too," I say quickly.

He covers his teeth again, content with my correction, and returns to enjoying his soup. He still doesn't leave after dinner, curling up on my lap to enjoy some old episodes of one of my dad's favourite sitcoms. When I say goodnight to my parents and head up to bed, he joins me, swooping up ahead on the stairs and perching on my shoulder while I brush my teeth. I climb into bed, pulling up the duvet, and, with a loud yawn, he settles next to my head on the pillow.

"'Night," I whisper to him, turning out the lamp on my bedside table, but he doesn't squeak a reply.

He's already snoring.

"Wait a minute," Ari says, putting her hands on her hips. "Are you saying you have a bat now?"

I throw my hands up in the air. "Sort of."

"A *pet* bat?"

"He delivered Count Bloodthirst's message and then … stayed."

Miles glances to Ari before whispering, "And now you've brought him to school?"

"Not on purpose," I reply, glancing around to make sure no one's listening. "He won't leave my side. I tried to tell him to stay around the house, but he refused. Do you think it's obvious that I have a bat with me?"

They stare at the bat, whose head is sticking out from the zip of my backpack.

"Kind of," Ari says. "I mean … it's a BAT."

"Yeah, but he's only small," I insist, giving his head a little tickle. He lowers his ears contentedly as I rub his head with my finger. "And he'll sleep in my bag all day, out of sight. I've already had a word with him."

"You've had a word with him," Miles repeats slowly. "You've had a word *with the bat*."

"That's right. He's very clever. I think he can understand me. This morning, I told him I was going to put my hair in a ponytail and he went off and returned with my hair tie. How cool is that?" I smile down at the bat in my bag. "You're very handy to have around the house."

Miles leans in to Ari. "Is it just me, or has she lost her mind?"

"She's lost her mind," Ari confirms.

I roll my eyes. "It's not that big of a deal."

"You've brought a *bat* to *school*."

"Yeah, well, we're also friends with a vampire," I point out, turning to walk towards our classroom. "Compared to that, this isn't that weird."

With a loud sigh, Miles follows behind. "She's got a point."

By Saturday, the bat has settled nicely into my routine.

There were a few hiccups at school, but nothing too major. Most of the time, he slept in my bag, hanging upside down from the top of it, happily zipped away in the darkness. We did have a bit of a moment during lunch, when someone sitting nearby accidentally dropped a green bean on the floor. Before I could stop him, the bat poked his head out of my bag that I'd carefully placed in between my feet on the floor, spotted the bean, pushed open the zip and flew out to investigate.

"RAT!" someone shrieked at the top of their lungs, pointing underneath the table. "RAT! There's a RAT!"

All the students began screaming and jumping up on their seats, and as the canteen erupted into a chaotic scramble, Ari and Miles looked at me in a panic. I quickly ducked my head under the table.

"*Psst!*" I hissed at the bat, who cautiously nibbled at

the bean before making a disgusted face. I pointed to my backpack. "Get back in here!"

He willingly returned to his makeshift cave, digging his claws into the top curve of the bag and draping his wings around him to go back to sleep. I did up the zip, leaving a little gap open, and then stood up from my chair.

"I can't see anything!" I announced to the few who were still in the room, all of whom were watching me with great admiration, clearly impressed that I had gone looking for the rat instead of running away. "Not a rat in sight! No need to panic!"

It was a bit late, though, considering everyone had already panicked BIG TIME and left the canteen almost deserted. Miss Woods had to call in a professional exterminator to check that there were no rats in the vicinity.

The only other time the bat caused an issue was during my PE lesson, when he decided that he didn't want to stay in my bag in the changing rooms where he couldn't see me. He escaped through a window and, spotting me doing a lap of the sports field, he let out a triumphant screech and then came soaring through the air to circle my head.

"You're supposed to be *hiding*!" I reminded him through wheezes, stopping to catch my breath.

Luckily, most people were either too focused or exhausted to notice a bat hanging around my head, and our teacher was busy telling Ari off for cutting a corner and instructing she complete the lap again. The only person who might have noticed something unusual was Marrok. By far the fastest runner, he'd already finished the mandatory lap and was standing with his arms crossed, watching me curiously from the other side of the field. I pretended to have a stitch. I had to wait until Marrok looked away to pay any attention to the bat.

"You need to go back to my bag," I told him, but he looked distraught and came to land on my shoulder, giving me big puppy-dog eyes. It was impossible for me to send him away. "All right, you can stick with me. But no one else can see you."

He acknowledged my instruction with a squeak and decided the best course of action would be to crawl up my leg and hang upside down on the inner lining of my gym shorts. It was not particularly comfortable to have a bat knocking against my leg at every stride, but it was better than leaving him behind in the changing rooms.

Other than that, he behaved impeccably throughout the week and I've got used to having him around.

I'm feeling forlorn at the idea of him returning to Skeleton Castle, but I guess he has to go back. Count Bloodthirst must be confused as to why the bat he sent to deliver a simple message has camped out with us for a week. Luckily, he won't think we're rude not replying thanks to Sharptooth, who passed him a message from me that we were unable to RSVP by return bat as requested, but that we had accepted his invitation to go to the castle today.

Miles and Ari arrive at our house first before we set off towards the woods together with my parents, the bat swooping along just ahead of me, occasionally circling back to make sure I'm following.

"Do you think I'll be allowed to take photos?" Ari says as we get nearer.

"Not sure," I reply, shoving my hands in my pockets. "They might not want any evidence of the castle's existence out in the world."

"You can't take pictures of vampires," Miles says.

"I know that," Ari huffs. "It's the castle I want to photograph, so I can draw it better in my comic."

"You may have to take notes instead," Dad suggests.

"I'm sure Count Bloodthirst won't mind you jotting down some of the details you want to remember."

"Have you almost finished the graphic novel, Ari?" Mum asks. "I'm looking forward to seeing it."

"It needs a bit of work," Ari tells her. "I have to come up with a good ending."

Mum offers her an encouraging smile. "You'll think of something."

Count Bloodthirst appears at the edge of the woods with a woman I don't know, and she's speaking to him in a low voice with some urgency. She's my parents' age, with dark, curly hair and large brown eyes. As we approach, she stops talking and turns to look straight at me, tilting her head slightly in surprise. A small smile creeps across her lips.

"You must be Maggie," she says, watching me closely.

The bat comes to land on my shoulder.

"Yes, hi," I say, giving an awkward wave.

The woman turns back to Count Bloodthirst. "You can certainly sense it."

He nods. "Indeed."

"Sense what?" Ari asks.

"That you, Maggie Helsby, are not what you seem," the woman answers calmly, her soft voice weirdly soothing. "One magical creature can usually recognize another."

"I'm not magical," I tell her quickly, my cheeks burning.

"You're a Helsby Vampire Slayer," she points out.

"Yeah, but that doesn't make me magical. And I'm not really a slayer, anyway. The vampires are my friends."

"Yes, I can see that." Her eyes shift to the bat. "When did your bat find you?"

"He's not mine," I explain, trying not to sound too sad about the fact. "He belongs to Count Bloodthirst. He's just stayed with me for the week."

"I wondered where he'd got to," Count Bloodthirst says, looking at the bat with disapproval. "Nice to see you again, Bat-Head."

The bat squeaks in reply.

"Sorry." I hold my hand up. "This bat's name is … *Bat-Head*?"

"That's correct," Count Bloodthirst says.

"Bat-Head," I repeat, as Ari and Miles stifle their laughter behind me.

"So, Sharptooth has a bat called Bat-Ears, and this bat is named Bat-Head."

"They're good friends, I believe," Count Bloodthirst

explains. "Of course, Bat-Foot is close to Bat-Ears, too, and I think Bat-Toe enjoys their company also."

"Are all bats named Bat-something?" I ask in disbelief.

He shakes his head. "No, no. There's only one Bat-Something and I think he resides in Derbyshire these days."

Ari and Miles burst into giggles. Count Bloodthirst shoots them a stern look and they both shut up immediately.

He gestures to the woman beside him. "This is Diana Dazzle. She's a witch and an … acquaintance of mine. I suppose."

"No need to sound so appalled by our truce, Count Bloodthirst," she huffs. "Frankly, you're lucky to have me as an *acquaintance*. I've granted you a lot of favours over the years. Most witches wouldn't give you the time of day."

"That's because they have an unreasonable dislike of vampires."

"Difficult to trust creatures who lurk in the shadows."

"Vampires aren't all like that," I jump in, angrily defending my friends. "And they have to stick to the shadows considering they'd turn into dust in the light. I'd say that's fairly understandable."

She looks at me with great interest. "She really is an ally, Count. I'm shocked."

"Do witches have a spell that would mean vampires could walk about in the sunshine?" Ari asks. Miles nudges her with his elbow, but she shrugs. "What? They might have one!"

The corner of Diana's mouth twitches as she tries not to smile. "There is a spell that will allow a vampire to step into light, but it's only temporary and quite difficult, plus you need to ask warlocks for a potion to top the spell up every few hours. Most witches don't think vampires are worth the hassle."

"We're perfectly happy living in the dark, thank you," Count Bloodthirst interjects.

"I prefer the dark, too," says a voice that seems to come somewhere from Diana, but she hasn't opened her mouth.

She pulls her shirt collar to the side to reveal a large spider sitting on her neck.

"This is my familiar, Oz," Diana introduces us. "All witches have a familiar – they're our spirit guides. A bit like how all vampires have a bat."

"Please refrain from comparing a witch's wise and insightful familiar to a vampire's bat," Oz spits, furious. "They're more like pets."

Bat-Ears and Bat-Head curl their lips back to bare their fangs at Oz, who doesn't flinch. Count Bloodthirst's bat does not deign to respond.

"Charming, as ever, Oz," Count Bloodthirst says drily. "Shall we all make our way to the castle?"

"The enchantments are down?" Dad checks.

"Yes," Diana says, lines forming on her forehead as she looks to Count Bloodthirst in concern. "But as I was telling the count before you arrived, it was too … easy."

"What do you mean?" I ask.

"The spell to lower the enchantments around Skeleton Woods to permit you all to enter should be difficult," she explains, gesturing to the trees. "It's a very intricate bit of magic. The enchantments were formed in harmony with the trees, to protect them as much as those who live amongst them. When I lowered these enchantments temporarily for your party last time, it took me a long time. I had to be extremely precise and focused. This time, it was as though…"

She trails off.

"As though what?"

"As though they were already weakened," she finishes. "But that can't be the case."

"Of course it's not," Count Bloodthirst states

confidently. "I'm sure it's just because you did the spell recently, Diana. It must have come easier to you this time. Now, let's get to the castle. Time is ticking and I have badminton practice to get to later this evening. You humans take for ever to get anywhere. I will lead at a snail's pace for you."

Under his breath, he drily adds, "Perhaps we'll make it to the castle before dawn."

With a dramatic swish of his cloak, he turns on his heel and glides through the trees. My parents, Ari and Miles quickly follow him, twigs and leaves crunching under their feet as they try their best to keep up. Diana hangs back to fall into step with me.

"You were wrong before," she says.

"About what?"

"The bat. When you said he didn't belong to you."

We watch Bat-Head as he flutters just ahead of me.

"Bats are supposed to choose a vampire, but this one hasn't," Diana says with a quizzical expression. "This bat has chosen you."

CHAPTER

FIVE

It's not surprising that there are so many spooky legends surrounding Skeleton Castle. Just one glance at the mysterious ancient fortress with its jagged tower, great arches and old wooden door – not to mention the colony of bats that tends to linger around it – is enough for anyone to understand these dark stone walls are brimming with spooky history.

Count Bloodthirst turns the heavy wrought-iron doorknob and stands aside to let us step into the hall. Everyone naturally huddles together, a cold draught sweeping in. As the door loudly creaks shut behind us, the chain of the black iron chandelier hanging above our heads rattles, the flames of its lit candles flickering in the gust of wind.

"Not sure if I mentioned this last time we were here, but I love what you've done with the place," Ari comments, her voice echoing off the high walls and ceiling. "It's so" – she glances at the angry gargoyle statue in the corner – "homely."

"I've always had a flair for interior design," Count Bloodthirst informs us proudly. "It was me who added the spikes to the door of the ballroom."

"Oh, lovely!" Mum says brightly. "What a unique addition!"

Dad nods. "Yes, very original."

Count Bloodthirst pauses, narrowing his eyes at Diana. "I didn't think you'd be joining us for the tour of the castle."

"I thought I'd take another look about the place," she says. "It's been a few decades since I've stepped foot in here."

"Spying, I presume," he says cynically.

"Yes, because the witch community is just DYING to know all about your fabulous decorating." She rolls her eyes as Oz cackles at the notion from under her collar. "Don't be so sceptical. I'm curious, that's all."

His jaw clenches, but he must accept her explanation as he eventually clears his throat and returns his attention to the rest of us.

"Follow me, please," he instructs, leading us down the corridor, past the winding staircase to the left. "I thought I'd start the tour with my office. It is where I spend most of my time, when I'm not teaching. It is there where I make important decisions for the vampire community, write philosophical essays, and occasionally take the time to practise one of my many hobbies. It's also where I rest, lying in an elaborate bespoke coffin that was painstakingly carved decades ago with ancient vampire symbols."

Diana leans down to whisper in my ear. "Does he know this is a tour about the castle, not a reality TV show about his life?"

"I heard that," Count Bloodthirst snaps.

I attempt to stifle my laugh. He gestures for us to enter his office. Leading the group, I take one step into the room and then stop, causing everyone else to halt abruptly behind.

His study is just as I remember, a room that seems to be stuck in the past. Straight ahead of me is the striking antique oak desk with a high-backed, dark red armchair behind it and, on top of the desk, a pile of parchment, a feathery quill and an inkpot. At the back of the room is a purple velvet curtain and I know that if I were to walk over and pull it back, I'd find the coffin in which Count Bloodthirst rests. I know that because the first time I found the castle, I hid in it.

The room is deathly silent. Everything is still.

"What's wrong?" Miles whispers anxiously.

I stare at the curtain and say, "Hello Sharptooth", just as she leaps out from behind it.

"VAMPIRE ATTA—" Her face drops. "Oh. How did you know I was here?"

I tap the side of my head. "Heightened senses, remember?"

"I was going to demonstrate my version of seek-and-hide for everyone," Sharptooth explains. "Ari and Miles, don't you think it would be fun if I jumped out at you suddenly and pretended it was a vampire attack?"

"Sure." Ari nods, while Miles looks horrified. "That sounds great fun."

"I'll have to try it again when Maggie's not with you." She beams at Miles. "Then you won't have any warning!"

"From now on, Maggie, you're coming *everywhere* with me," he mutters.

"What a beautiful study!" Mum opines, looking in wonder at the parchment and quill. "It's like stepping into a different age."

"Yes," Dad agrees. "It's very calm in here. A place where you can sit in peace and have a proper think about—"

He's rudely interrupted by a high-pitched squeak from my shoulder. Bat-Head, who has been sitting very quietly up until this point, launches himself straight at a snoozing Bat-Ears, who is hanging upside down from Sharptooth's sleeve. Bat-Ears doesn't wake up straight away, but after another resounding screech from Bat-Head, he suddenly unfurls his wings and his eyes widen with joy at the sight of Bat-Head hovering next to him.

Emitting a chorus of shrill squeaks, the two of them fly up in the air in an excitable spiral, a tornado of fluttering wings.

"Not so peaceful any more," Ari remarks to Dad.

Count Bloodthirst sighs. "As long as they don't dip their bat feet into my inkpot. These two have a habit of causing as much mess as possible."

Listening to the bats, Sharptooth's expression brightens and she turns to me, having understood their conversation.

"Bat-Head is your bat now?" She gasps, turning to Count Bloodthirst. "How is that possible? Do humans get bats, too?"

"They certainly do not," he replies with a grimace, as though insulted by the idea.

"Bat-Head is filling Bat-Ears in on everything, and he's pretty certain that he's landed on Maggie for life," Sharptooth explains.

"That bat will be with Maggie for *life*?" Mum winces before addressing Count Bloodthirst. "Did you mean it when you said he likes to cause as much mess as possible?"

"You're in for a treat," Count Bloodthirst drily replies, as Bat-Head zooms around the room, forcing us all to duck as he narrowly avoids crashing into our heads.

"I was informing Maggie of Bat-Head's choice to remain with her on our way to the castle," Diana says. "A very strange occurrence, don't you think?"

Sharptooth stiffens, only just noticing Diana's presence. Her eyes dart nervously to Count Bloodthirst.

"Oh, hi, Diana. I didn't realize you'd be joining the tour. How's everything in the witch community? Did you get that whole troll thing under control?"

"Of course," Diana replies breezily. "They've made their way safely back to Iceland."

"Not before they scared away the starlings," Count Bloodthirst mutters. "I had only just seen them making themselves at home here in the woods and made a note of them in my birdwatching log book. Beautiful little birds. Of course, it's very unlikely they'll return thanks to those trolls and the racket they made."

"Excuse me." Ari lifts up her hand to pose a question. "What exactly are you talking about?"

"We had a few unwelcome guests near the woodland recently," Count Bloodthirst informs us. "A family of trolls, who trampled right up to the edge of the trees and scared away some of the wildlife in the area. I don't know why they were here."

"They said they wanted to visit Skeleton Castle, as you well know," Diana reminds him, but he looks unfazed. "They were on holiday. Luckily, the witches managed to persuade them to steer clear of the area. They're very pleasant, trolls. But I doubt the vampire community would have had much time for them."

"Yes, well, considering the one I met in Norway twenty years ago attempted to bite off my head, I'm not a huge fan," Count Bloodthirst says drily.

Diana snorts. "A vampire scared of a little bite."

"I wasn't *scared*," Count Bloodthirst hisses.

"I've never met a troll," Sharptooth chimes in. "But they sound fun!"

"Why would they suddenly be interested in coming here to Goreway?" I ask curiously.

"Um, HELLO!" Miles looks baffled. "THAT'S what you think is weird? That they happened to stroll into Goreway? I'd say the weird part to focus on is the fact that everyone is casually talking about TROLLS in the first place! Trolls exist? As in, TROLLS?!"

There's a pause in the conversation as he waits for someone else to join in his horror. Mum and Dad glance at one another, looking unsure about what to say. Ari seems more intrigued than scared, while Sharptooth, Diana and Count Bloodthirst appear fascinated by his outburst.

Bat-Ears and Bat-Head have now finished their screechy catch-up and are busy taking turns to dip their feet into the pot of ink on Count Bloodthirst's desk and dance around all his parchment, leaving tiny footprints everywhere, a task that they find absolutely hilarious judging by their mischievous squeals. Count Bloodthirst doesn't seem to have noticed yet, and I'm not going to be the one to alert him to it.

Diana is the first to reply to Miles. "Yes, trolls really

exist. I thought you would have known that, being friends with a vampire."

"I told you this the other day, Miles. Remember our conversation about the non-humans?" Sharptooth says helpfully. "Zombies, ghosts, mummies – that sort of thing. They're all around somewhere. Ooh" – she suddenly straightens as though a light bulb has just gone off in her head – "I know what I meant to ask you. What exactly is hummus?"

Miles blinks at her, too stunned to speak.

"Maggothead went to the supermarket yesterday and he came back with this beetroot hummus," Sharptooth continues, oblivious to Miles's silent freaking out. "It has the weirdest texture, so we thought it CAN'T be something humans eat. Do you bathe in it? Or is it some form of hair product? Maggothead's been wearing it combed through his hair all day, but it looks a bit weird to be honest."

"Honestly," Diana sighs. "*Vampires.*"

Count Bloodthirst opens his mouth to speak but I jump in before he can start bickering with her.

"When I was with Sharptooth in the woods recently, I could sense that something was wrong," I tell them hurriedly. "Do you think that's because the trolls were nearby?"

Diana frowns. "Maybe. What do you mean by 'wrong'?"

"Honestly, I don't know. Like I should be ... prepared for something. And there's this new boy at school. He's..."

I trail off, unsure if I should voice my concerns about Marrok. It doesn't seem fair to draw attention to him before I know anything about him. What if he's like me? Someone different, who's simply trying to fit in.

"Yes?" Count Bloodthirst prompts.

"Never mind. The important thing I'm trying to say is, don't you think it's strange that trolls were trying to find Skeleton Castle and, at the same time, I'm sensing something off about the woodland? Have you ever had trolls approach the woodland before?"

"No," Count Bloodthirst confirms.

"Would the enchantments have worked on the trolls if they'd tried to come into the woods?" Ari asks, trying not to be distracted by Bat-Head and Bat-Ears, who are now dipping their bottoms in the inkpot before taking it in turns to sit down on the parchment.

"Yes, they were made to keep everything out," Diana says gravely. "But perhaps they're not as strong as they should be. The trolls might have sensed that."

"I can't believe there were trolls in Goreway," Miles

says, leaning on Count Bloodthirst's desk and accidentally knocking over the inkpot with his hand, much to Bat-Ears and Bat-Head's joy. They start rolling around in the black ink pooling on the desk before pointing their wings at each other and screeching with delight at the sight of the other one.

"It's hardly surprising that they would hope to see Skeleton Castle on their holiday," Count Bloodthirst remarks, unperturbed. "It's a magnificent architectural feat and a legendary landmark."

"Yeah, but crazy that they would risk disturbing a bunch of vampires just to see a castle," Ari comments. "Even if they're trolls, they've got to be afraid of you, right?"

Count Bloodthirst lifts his chin and in a low, spine-chilling growl, proudly declares, "*Everyone* is afraid of us."

Sharptooth rolls her eyes at me.

"Who knew that trolls were so interested in architecture?" Dad muses.

"Maybe they were more interested in the treasure that's supposedly here," I suggest.

All the heads in the room spin towards me.

"*What?*" Ari's jaw drops to the floor. "There is TREASURE here? How come this is the first time I'm hearing about it?"

"How did you know about those rumours?" Count Bloodthirst asks me.

"I read it in a book ages ago," I tell him. "I saw a parent at school reading the same one recently and it reminded me of the theory that there's treasure hidden away in the castle."

"Can we see the treasure?" Ari asks eagerly.

Mum shoots her a disapproving look.

"What?" she says with a shrug. "Who wouldn't want to see treasure?"

"There is no treasure," Count Bloodthirst states firmly. "It's a baseless rumour. A completely made-up story told through the generations."

"Yeah, I didn't think it sounded right," I say, nodding. "Others may believe it, though."

Ari looks disappointed. "So, there's no treasure?"

"None," Count Bloodthirst confirms. "I've searched the castle just to be sure and found nothing. What would vampires want with treasure anyway? What would we do with it? It's not like we can go on a spending spree, is it? We can't eat out at top restaurants or buy mansions in Hollywood."

"Or an island in the Caribbean," Ari says wistfully.

"Quite," he concurs. "Unless we're happy to disappear into a pile of dust before we get there."

"I think we need to leave," Diana says suddenly, her forehead lined, her eyebrows knit together. "Maggie's right. It is odd that the trolls were sniffing around AND that she felt strangely about the woodland. I think I need to put the enchantments back up straight away. Maybe last time I didn't return them to their full strength. I'm only thinking of your community, Count Bloodthirst, and the people of Goreway."

"We're vegetarians now," Sharptooth announces proudly. "No one here would harm a human should they come into the woods by accident."

"Still, I wouldn't like to test that theory," Diana says.

"Good idea." Miles nods vigorously. "I think we should leave and get those enchantments back up and running."

"But we only just got here!" Ari moans. "I've hardly taken any notes for my graphic novel."

"You have enough inspiration," Diana says in such an end-of-discussion tone that not even Ari pushes back. "Sharptooth, if you wouldn't mind accompanying them to the edge of the woods and letting me know when they're gone. I'll start preparing the spell to get the woodland enchantments returned to normal."

Sharptooth nods. "You can all tell me about hummus on the way!"

Promising Sharptooth we'll give her as much information on hummus as possible, we thank Count Bloodthirst for the brief but interesting tour.

"You're welcome, and before you go with your bats" – his eyes flicker to the inky mess on his desk – "if you wouldn't mind, Diana."

With a wry smile, Diana clicks her fingers. The ink instantly disappears from everywhere, the parchments, the desk, and Bat-Ears and Bat-Head, who are returned to their normal colour. The inkpot flips up from its side and, once safely upright, fills with ink. We stand frozen to the spot, watching the magic, completely mesmerized.

"*Whoa,*" Ari breathes. "That is amazing."

"Yeah, whatever," Sharptooth mutters. "Vampire magic is better."

With a final goodbye, we traipse out of Count Bloodthirst's office and exit the castle. Sharptooth and I lead the way through the woods, the others following behind, chatting animatedly about the magic, Bat-Ears and Bat-Head fluttering around us.

"It's strange," Sharptooth says quietly to me. "That dog is back again."

"Really?"

"Yeah. It's at the edge of the woods somewhere. I can hear it panting. It must have run here."

"Are you sure it's a dog?" I ask, keeping my voice low so the others don't panic. "You wouldn't get it mixed up with a ... uh ... troll, right?"

"Trust me, Maggie, even your useless human ears would hear a troll coming. They are very boisterous. No, this is definitely a dog. It's getting closer to the woods. I hope it gets out before the enchantments go up again."

She frowns in concentration, listening carefully, before adding, "It's not alone this time. Another one has just joined them."

"Two dogs?"

"I'm not sure. I think so. But it sounds more like voices than barks. It's very muffled. Hard to hear what's going on." She hesitates. "That's weird."

"What?"

"They've turned away. They came right up to the edge of the woods and then it's as though the second one persuaded the other one to leave."

I bite my lip. "How can a dog persuade another dog?"

"Maybe my hearing is off," Sharptooth reasons, sticking a finger in her ear and wiggling it around.

"Fangly did practise her evil cackle very loudly next to me this morning."

"I don't think it's your hearing, Sharptooth. I think something is wrong," I say, a shudder running down my spine, "and I need to find out what it is before anyone gets hurt."

CHAPTER

SIX

Strange things are happening in Goreway.

The week after our visit to Skeleton Castle, a rumour started to spread through the school about Jenny Tan's grandmother: she'd been on her way home from her ballroom dancing class when she'd noticed an odd-looking group of people playing on the swings in her local playground. On closer inspection, she realized with some surprise that they were, in fact, zombies.

"Z-zombies," Miles repeated, when we first heard the rumour from our classmate Priya. "You're not serious."

Priya nodded. "Yep. That's what she's saying. Obviously Jenny's family thinks she's messing with everyone, but she swears she's being completely serious.

Says she saw five of them taking turns on the swings."

"What did she say they look like?" Ari asked, fascinated.

"Their skin was all grey, their yellow eyes sunk into their heads, their lips pale with death!" Priya described dramatically, before bursting out laughing. "Clearly great make-up."

"And they were … playing on the swings?" I checked.

"Ask Jenny," Priya recommended. "She'll tell you."

We spotted Jenny by her locker later that afternoon and sidled up to her, asking for a quick word.

"Let me guess," she said, sounding bored as she shut her locker door, "you want to ask me about the zombies. Look, as I've said to everyone else, Nan swears she saw them and no matter how much we tell her that they weren't REAL zombies, she keeps saying we're wrong. I've tried to tell her that it must have been people in dress-up or something, but she's convinced they were real. I wish she hadn't told EVERYONE she knows. Then people wouldn't be laughing at her."

"We're not laughing at her," Ari assured her.

"Did your nan say anything else about the zombies?" I asked. "Any other details? Like, did she hear them saying anything? Maybe talking about why they were in Goreway?"

"No, she ran away screaming, obviously," Jenny said, looking at me like I was an idiot. "She thought they were *real* zombies."

I felt a bit sorry for Jenny's grandmother, because – knowing Goreway and its spooky secrets – chances were she was absolutely right, and had seen genuine zombies, but no one was going to believe her. The question wasn't *if* they were zombies, but *why* they were here in the first place. Ari, Miles and I agreed that we'd keep an ear to the ground for any other abnormal goings-on, but we didn't have to wait very long.

Despite no warnings of any storms, several residents on one particular road of the town woke up one morning to find all their fences and garden sheds blown over. The local weather reporter, who descended on the scene at once with a camera crew in tow, declared it to be a most peculiar phenomenon – no satellites had picked up this strange, rapid and remarkably strong gust of wind that blew across this row of houses in a matter of seconds and then subsided.

But one person in Goreway had an explanation, and she interrupted the live report to offer it: Mrs Hollyhogg, who works at the post office, claimed that she happened to be out that night walking her Pomeranian when she saw an ogre standing on that very road.

"Excuse me." The weather reporter looked baffled. "Did you say … an *ogre*?"

"Yes, an ogre," Mrs Hollyhogg repeated clearly into the microphone, holding her dog in her arms. "You see, Twiglet here has taken to waking me up late at night to go outside for a wee. His bladder isn't what it was, now that he's getting on in years."

Twiglet emitted an impatient whine. With a fixed smile, the reporter glanced nervously to someone off camera, looking worried about where this was going.

"So I took him for his late-night walk," she continued, "and that's when I saw the ogre, standing right there at the end of the road. Then he did a big sneeze."

The reporter looked lost for words.

"And the ogre's sneeze blew down all those fences and sheds," Mrs Hollyhogg explained matter-of-factly. "I've never seen anything like it. I was completely frozen in shock. It's lucky Twiglet and I were far away enough not to be blown across town ourselves! Good thing he was out and about at night, too. It's a miracle no one was hurt. I didn't get a wink of sleep. I ran home, woke up Mr Hollyhogg and off he went straight away, armed with his golf club, to see if the ogre was still there. By that point, of course, he'd disappeared."

The reporter stared at her before slowly turning to the camera and managing to splutter, "Now back to you in the studio."

The clip went viral.

That wasn't even the weirdest occurrence of the week. The very next day, two people reported to the police that they had been chased down the road, scared out of their wits, by a monster with long pink hair, yellow spikes down its back and just one giant eye in the middle of its face. During both incidents, it had caught up with the person it was chasing, reached out with its razor-sharp claws and only managed to swipe the hat off their head, before thankfully retreating. The police came to the conclusion that a thief was dressing up as a monster to conceal their identity.

"Lucky they were both wearing hats!" Miles commented, reading the online report out loud to us. "Imagine if the monster had managed to reach just that bit further and … I don't want to think about it.

"This is getting *bad*," Ari remarked, with a worried expression.

"Soon, someone might get hurt," Miles agreed.

A few days later, there is another incident, this one involving Toby Flynn, who is in our class, so we are the first people to hear about it.

"Toby!" Mr Kelvin exclaims, as Toby drifts into our classroom on Friday morning before registration. "What's wrong?"

I glance up from reading about the history of zombies, a new library book I've borrowed, to see Toby looking pale and shaken. I reach over to prod Ari, who's busily sketching Bat-Head on my request. She, in turn, alerts Miles to Toby's rattled state.

"N-nothing," Toby replies.

"Are you sure?" Mr Kelvin asks, extremely concerned.

"I don't know. I mean, it can't have been. Can it?" Toby says, shaking his head in disbelief. "It can't be right. I'm seeing things."

"What are you talking about? Sit down, Toby, let's get you some water." Mr Kelvin guides him to his seat. "Ari, would you mind getting some water for Toby?"

"No way!" Ari replies. "I'm not leaving, I want to hear about what happened!"

"*Ari*," Mr Kelvin seethes.

"I saw … I saw" – Toby's eyes glaze over as he tries to make sense of whatever's just happened – "a m-monster!"

"What?" I squeak.

"A green, slimy monster. It was in the bin."

Mr Kelvin clears his throat. "Toby, I think—"

"I'm not making this up," Toby insists, sounding surer now. "Dad asked me to take the bins out as I left for school. I opened the lid of the recycling bin outside and there it was … sitting in there…"

"Are you sure?" Miles asks, leaning forwards across his desk.

"He's not going to mistake seeing a monster, Miles," Ari points out. "It's not the kind of thing you get mixed up with a bin bag."

"It was covered in slime and it had ten eyes," Toby continues. "It looked right at me – as in, with all of its ten eyes – and then … and then it—"

"All right, enough of this," Mr Kelvin interjects grumpily. "I don't know what kind of joke you think—"

"I'm telling the truth!" Toby declares stubbornly. "There's a monster in our recycling bin!"

"What happened after you lifted the lid?" I push.

Toby turns to me. "I was so scared, I couldn't move at first. It said something in gobbledygook. I … well …

I slammed the lid down and ran straight here to school. I can't go back home. Not until that … that *thing* is gone."

Mr Kelvin raises his eyes to the ceiling, muttering something inaudible under his breath.

"So, the monster could still be in your bin?" I check.

Toby shudders. "I hope not."

Ari looks at me, her lips pursed. An unspoken agreement formed between us, we both turn to Miles.

He takes one glance at our expressions and groans, before nodding reluctantly. "Oh, all *right*."

I pick up my backpack. Mr Kelvin suddenly works out what's going on and holds up his hands with a VERY stern expression.

"Don't you dare—" he begins.

But we're already scraping our chairs back and leaping to our feet, rushing out the classroom with Mr Kelvin calling out for us to stop and get back to our desks immediately. We obviously ignore him, pelting full speed down the corridor and out the school. Like most of the students that go to school here, Toby lives a short walk away, and we know where his house is from his birthday party just before Christmas.

As I run, I open my backpack, letting Bat-Head out so he can fly along with us.

"What exactly are we going to do when we see the monster?" Miles cries out, slowing down slightly to run next to me.

"No idea," I reply. "We'll have to wing it!"

"Oh good, a firm plan, then," Miles says, slowing down once Toby's driveway is in sight. "Remember when we had a normal life? You know, before the vampires and the trolls and the monsters? My biggest worry used to be getting homework in on time."

Stopping at Toby's house, we take a moment to catch our breath, cautiously approaching the line of bins. I slowly reach out for the handle of the recycling lid. With an encouraging nod from Ari, and Bat-Head coming to land on my shoulder for comfort, I take a deep breath and throw the lid open.

Instinctively, we all jump backwards.

Nothing happens.

I lean forwards to peer down into the bin.

"It's empty," I declare, disappointed.

"Maybe it's moved bin," Ari suggests, pointing to the general waste.

We check that one too, but there's nothing. There's

no point inspecting the small food bin, but I do anyway, in case it's the kind of monster that can squeeze into tiny spaces.

"Where do you think it went?" I ask, glancing around at our surroundings. "Bat-Head, can you see anything from up there?"

Bat-Head soars upwards and takes a good look into the distance, but returns to my shoulder with a nonchalant squeak, which I take to mean he didn't spot any monsters hanging out anywhere in sight.

"This is getting out of hand," Ari declares, folding her arms. "First there are trolls near the woods, then zombies in the playground, and now ogres and monsters lurking around town. What is going on?"

"I don't know," I say, "but we need to make sure the town doesn't start panicking about all these weird incidents."

"That won't be much of a problem," Ari assures me. "Nobody believes anything strange that happens. They'll keep thinking it's attention-seekers making it up."

"Which, for now, is a good thing."

"What do we do, Maggie?" Miles asks.

"We do the first thing anyone can do in these situations," I say determinedly. "We go to the library."

"Monsters in the bin!" Mr Frank, the librarian, laughs a little too hard. "How RIDICULOUS! I didn't know Toby had such a silly sense of humour."

"You don't believe him?" I say, watching him carefully as he continues to place books from the returns trolley on to the shelves.

"Of course not. Who would?"

I shrug. "Goreway is a spooky place. There have been lots of odd happenings recently."

Mr Frank hesitates. His eyes betray a flash of panic.

I get the feeling that Mr Frank is hiding something. Ever since the Christmas break, he's been distracted. I didn't think much of it at first, but now that these rumours are flying around, he seems a little more on edge than normal.

As someone who's as fascinated in Goreway's myths and legends as I am, I sometimes wonder if Mr Frank can't help but believe there's some truth to them.

"Mr Frank, do you believe in any of the—"

"There is nothing spooky about Goreway," he snaps. "Just fairy tales and nonsense."

I'm thrown by his outburst. He quickly collects himself, plastering on a smile.

"Hey, are you excited about the Rome trip?" he says, changing the subject. "It's going to be a great weekend!"

"Sure." I clutch the book I've just retrieved from the shelf. It's the book with the chapter on Skeleton Castle that I mentioned to Count Bloodthirst, the one that talks about the rumoured treasure. "We're really looking forward to it."

"Good. Well, if there's any other books I can help you to find…"

He trails off, clearly wanting to bring our conversation to an end.

"No, this is it. Thanks."

I stroll over to the table where Ari and Miles are examining various monster books. I slide into the chair next to Ari.

"Any luck?"

She shakes her head. "Not really. Although, to be honest, I'm not really sure what we're looking for."

"Anything that mentions a green, slimy, ten-eyed monster, I guess. Or one with pink hair and yellow spikes."

"The word 'monster' covers a number of things," Miles insists, flicking back to the first page of the book he's studying and reading out the beginning of the introduction: *"The dictionary defines monster as 'any imaginary frightening creature, especially one that is large and strange'."* He sighs heavily. "We have no idea what exactly Toby saw."

"And even if we find a reference to a similar-looking monster, that still doesn't explain what it's doing in Goreway," Ari points out. "We won't know why it's appeared at the same time as all these other non-human creatures. Are you sure we'll find any answers in these books, Maggie?"

"No, I'm not sure," I admit dejectedly, before placing the history book on the table. "But maybe we'll find an instance when this has happened before in Goreway, and that might help."

"What is it with Goreway and non-human creatures?" Miles huffs.

"Well, for a start—"

A growling voice interrupts my conversation: "What's that about non-human creatures?"

We look up to see Marrok Grey towering over our table.

"Nothing," Ari says quickly. "We were talking about … uh…"

"Monsters." Marrok gestures to the books scattered in front of us. "You think Toby is telling the truth, then."

"You heard about that?" I ask, although I shouldn't be surprised that it's all over school by lunch break.

"Looks like I came here for the same reason you did," he reveals.

Miles is stunned. "*You* came to the library on your lunch break to research monsters?"

Marrok frowns. "Is that so weird?"

"No, no, course not. I didn't know you were interested in the supernatural," Miles reasons. "Guess we don't talk about stuff like that during football practice."

"Not the sort of thing that naturally comes up during a game," Marrok says, before adding with a teasing smile, "especially when you're losing by so many goals."

"Miles losing football? Not likely," Ari comments.

"Actually, in practice I was in the team against Marrok and we lost by a long shot," Miles admits. "You sure you've never played professionally?"

Marrok laughs. It's a strange laugh. More like a bark.

"I promise," he says, holding up his hands. "It's the first time I've ever really played on a team. My last school didn't ... well, let's just say I wasn't welcomed on to the pitch."

"Are you kidding? The people at your last school must have been nuts," Miles claims, causing Marrok to look down at his feet modestly. "You're the best player here."

"Thanks."

Marrok's entire demeanour has changed throughout the conversation. His shoulders have dropped and his expression, usually taut and brooding, has eased into a warm smile.

He gestures to the chair opposite me. "Can I join you?"

I nod. "Sure."

He asks Miles if he can borrow one of the monster books from the pile and then turns to the page listing the chapter headings. It's slightly annoying that he's joined our group, only because we can't talk freely about everything we know in front of him, but he seems genuinely interested, so it would be unfair to turn him away.

Noticing the book his dad was reading amidst the many books scattered on the table, he frowns at it.

"Do you think there is hidden treasure in Skeleton Woods?" he asks, looking to me for the answer. "My dad is convinced of it."

"Like I told him the day we met, no, I don't," I insist.

"The day we met you also said that all the spooky rumours about Goreway were merely ghost stories designed to interest tourists," he recalls, before gesturing to all the monster books. "Looks like you've had a change of heart."

I don't say anything.

He goes back to reading the pages open in front of him and I try my best to concentrate on mine, every now and then stealing a glance across the table. I still can't work out Marrok Grey. I knew from the day he arrived here that he's different, potentially non-human. But, since nothing bad has happened to anyone at school, I've let myself get distracted by everything else going on.

I think about it for the rest of the afternoon, hardly concentrating throughout all of my lessons. I consider talking about him to Miles and Ari, but as we leave school together at the end of the day, Miles starts saying how Marrok is coming out of his shell during football practice and he seems like a really nice person, and Ari agrees. I don't want to be negative about him before I know anything, so I nod along, too.

But at home, while Bat-Head is busy balancing on top of a roll of toilet paper and running it across my bedroom floor, letting it unravel everywhere, I type the name "Marrok" into a search engine.

I inhale sharply as the results flash up on my screen.

<u>MARROK</u>
In Arthurian legend, the meaning of the name Marrok is a knight thought to be a werewolf.

SEVEN

Marrok Grey is a werewolf.

It all makes sense. No wonder I could sense danger! And *of course* he's good at sports and runs like the wind – he's a WOLF. There is no chance that any human shampoo and conditioner are the cause behind that thick, luscious hair of his. That has to be natural fur. It's all coming together.

"GROSS!" Sharptooth wrinkles her nose and makes a "bleugh" sound when I tell her my hunch that weekend. "You have to go to school with him? How do you stand the STINK?"

"He doesn't stink."

"Count yourself lucky you have a human nose," Sharptooth says, sitting back against a tree and stretching out her legs. "Does he drool everywhere?"

"Not in human form. He seems nice. A bit serious, but I don't think he's dangerous."

"Pah!" Sharptooth sniggers. "Werewolves aren't dangerous. They're stinky fleabags who attack humans because apparently" – she uses her fingers to mime quotation marks – "the 'moon tells them to'. Honestly, they're harmless."

"Harmless?" I blink at her. "But you just said they attack humans."

She hesitates. "Oh yeah. Sometimes I forget you're a human, Maggie."

"I'll take that as a compliment." I pace back and forth in front of her, twigs cracking under my feet.

Bat-Head and Bat-Ears are both fast asleep, hanging from the branch above where Sharptooth is sitting. They were so excited to see each other when I met Sharptooth here that they flew round and round in circles until they were completely exhausted.

Sharptooth watches me walking up and down for a bit and then says, "You have the same look on your face that Maggothead gets when Count Bloodthirst announces a surprise test on stake dodging. Worried and scared at the same time."

"That's because I *am* worried and scared," I confess.

"If the werewolf was going to hurt you, he probably would have done so by now."

"I'm not worried about Marrok hurting me. I'm worried about everything else that's going on around us and we're not doing anything about."

She tilts her head. "Like what?"

"Trolls, zombies, werewolves, monsters," I list, throwing my hands up in exasperation. "Why are they *here*? And how do I get rid of them?"

"Why is it down to *you* to get rid of them?" Sharptooth asks, confused.

"Because I'm meant to protect everyone! That's my destiny, remember?"

"Technically, your destiny is to slay vampires," Sharptooth says matter-of-factly. "Not that I'm encouraging that behaviour."

"Sharptooth, help me," I plead, coming to sit down. "I don't know what to do."

Pondering her answer for a moment, she suddenly clicks her fingers. "I'll talk to Count Bloodthirst. He'll know what to do."

"He didn't seem too bothered about the trolls," I remind her. "What if he brushes you off?"

"Then maybe there's nothing to worry about," she suggests. "Think about it, Maggie, he has been here a LONG time. He pretends to be younger than he is, but he talks about the nineteenth century like it was yesterday. No one knows Skeleton Woods better than he does. If he thinks a few trolls and dogs appearing isn't a problem, then chances are, everything's just fine."

"Don't forget to tell him about the zombies and the monster."

"I won't," she promises.

"Hey, you know how you just referred to a werewolf as a 'dog'?" I say, an idea dawning on me. "When you heard dogs approaching the woods today, you don't think—"

"It was Marrok!" Sharptooth grins at me, her fangs on full show. "They did sound like large dogs. That makes a lot of sense now."

"Marrok is interested in Skeleton Woods, then," I say, recalling his disapproving reaction to the book on Goreway in the library. "And there was definitely more than one dog that you heard?"

"Oh yes. There were two."

"One of them persuaded the other one to leave," I remember aloud.

"Lucky, too. They could have got into the woods if they'd wanted, because Diana hadn't put the enchantments back up at that point."

"Right." I check the time on my phone. "I better get going. Mum and Dad want to go to the garden centre this afternoon and they're forcing me to go with them."

"What's a garden centre?" Sharptooth asks curiously.

"A place where you can buy flowers and plants."

"To eat?"

I laugh at this assumption from Sharptooth, and immediately feel a little bit better about all these worrying things. One of my favourite things about being best friends with a vampire is that she never fails to make me laugh, even on a bad day.

"No, not to eat. Humans use them to make their house and gardens look nice."

"Are Miles and Ari going to the garden castle with you?"

I don't bother to correct her, deciding that garden castle sounds better than garden centre anyway. "No, Ari's at the cinema with her family and Miles has a football match today against another school."

"That reminds me!" Sharptooth cries, gasping. "Nightmare and Dreadclaw would have thrown a garlic bulb at me if I'd forgotten."

"Forgotten what?"

She dramatically clears her throat, as though giving an important announcement. "That we would like to challenge you to a football match."

"*What?*"

"Come on, it will be so fun!" she insists, grabbing my hand and shaking it, her ice-cold fingers instantly making me shiver. "We PROMISE not to use vampire speed or strength. We will vow to play as slowly and badly as humans. That way it's fair."

"But why would you want to bother playing humans?"

"Because we have been practising and we think we know all the rules now," she declares proudly. "Nightmare thinks that even if we play at the same low level as humans and don't use any of our advantages, we'll still win."

"I see. And who exactly do you plan on playing?" I laugh. "I'm not sure I could rally enough players to take on a team of vampires."

"Nightmare says we could play" – she stops to think hard about the next bit, saying it as though she's learnt it off by heart and repeated it many times to get it right – "FIVE-A-SLIDE."

"Five-a-*side*," I correct her, giggling.

"Yes! Then your team could be Miles, Ari, you, and your mum and dad! We could play on the field by the woods after sunset, and set up lights around it. Maggothead is going to mark the lines of the pitch using a gooey white paste that he found in the supermarket called rice pudding!"

"That's a dessert," I inform her. "Tell him to try white paint instead."

"We even thought of a good forfeit for the losing team," she continues, sniggering behind her hand. "The losers have to … BRUSH THEIR TEETH!"

I watch, amused, as she hops up and down on the spot, scrunching up her face and going, "YUCK, YUCK, YUCK, MINT BREATH!" at the repulsive idea of brushing teeth.

"All right," I say. "I will ask the others and we'll pick a day to play this match. I have a feeling that Miles is going to be intrigued by this idea."

"Go Team Vampire! Go Team Vampire!" Sharptooth chants, awakening Bat-Ears and Bat-Head, as I prepare to go by picking up my backpack.

The bats stretch out their wings and come to land on our shoulders. I give Bat-Head a tickle behind his ears and he yawns contentedly. Bat-Ears squeaks goodbye to him.

"One quick question about the football match before you go," Sharptooth says, stopping me as I turn to leave. "Are you happy with a bat refereeing?"

"A bat refereeing a vampire football match." I nod thoughtfully. "That makes perfect sense."

Having left Sharptooth and the woods, I'm passing one of Great Uncle Bram's old "keep out" signs on the path that trails down the side of the field next to the woodland when I notice two figures in the distance approaching.

Squinting at them, I can see it's not Ari and Miles, and it's not my parents either. As they get closer, I realize it's two men, one much older than the other. I slow down as I realize that the older one is wearing an old-fashioned hooded cloak, but I come to a complete stop when I notice what is wrapped around his neck: a string of garlic bulbs.

"Bat-Head," I say quietly, spinning round so that my back is to the men and swinging my bag off my shoulder, "get in and stay hidden."

He does what he's told, dropping into his manmade portable bat cave. I turn round, pretending I had just been checking for something in my bag.

"Good afternoon," the man drawls as he gets nearer.

"Hi," I squeak in reply.

Wearing all black from head to toe, with heavy, silver-buckled black boots, he has dark eyes and a strong, square jaw, with long brown hair slicked back from his face using way too much gel. He's carrying a large brown shoulder bag and some kind of fishing net. As he stops right in front of me, I can see an emblem embroidered into the cloak, which looks like the silhouette of a monster with raised arms with a big red cross over it.

"Those woods are dangerous," he states, stopping in front of me, looking over my head, his beady eyes focused on the trees beyond. "You shouldn't be here. No one should."

"Then how come *you're* here?" I ask, glancing at his companion, who looks like he's just older than me.

Unlike the cloaked man, his outfit is not so eye-catching: a parka over a knitted jumper and jeans. He has dark red hair and a smattering of freckles across his nose and cheeks, visible underneath his dark-rimmed glasses. He's also carrying a net, but a smaller one which has "PRACTICE NET. NOT FOR USE ON REAL MONSTERS" labelled on the handle, and a large holdall that looks heavy and rattles as he moves.

The older man's mouth curls into a sneer at my question. "I'm here because I have to be. I'm *tracking*."

I blink at him. "Huh?"

The young boy gives a small "ahem" and steps forwards to gesture at the older man, who strikes a pose, lifting his chin in the air and putting a hand on his hip.

"This is the great Oscar Fowler," the boy announces, having clearly rehearsed this many times. "The famous and much revered monster hunter!"

There's a long silence.

"Sorry," I begin, "you're what?"

"The *monster hunter*," Oscar seethes, coming out of his pose and looking irritated. "Haven't you heard of me?"

"Do you have a TV show or something?"

"No, I do NOT have a TV show!" he thunders. "I'm a REAL monster hunter!"

"Oh, sorry, I've never heard of you. Or monster hunters in general, to be honest." I turn to the boy. "Are you his assistant?"

"I'm his son, Chase," he mutters haughtily.

I cross my arms. "The stories about Skeleton Woods

aren't real. They're silly myths to boost tourism. You do know that, right?"

Oscar sneers at me. "I'd stay away from Skeleton Woods if I were you. You might find some *unexpected* new arrivals."

That gets my attention.

"Who? What do you mean?"

He ignores my questions, stepping round me and saying to Chase, "They came this way."

"Who came this way?" I ask, but he continues to go towards the woods. "WHO?"

"You don't want to know," Chase whispers to me.

"Chase! Keep up!" Oscar bellows, striding on.

Chase scuttles along after him and I watch nervously as they get closer to the line of trees at the edge of the woodland. Oscar stops, crouches down and examines the ground, using his fingers to scrape up some soil from the path.

He holds the clump of dirt in the palm of his hand.

He sniffs it. Then he sticks his tongue out and licks it.

"*Eugh*," I comment.

Oscar suddenly spins round to face me again and comes marching back down the path. Even though there are enchantments, I'm relieved that he's turned away from the woodland and the vampires don't need to worry about him disturbing them. If he is a true monster hunter, I wonder whether the enchantments would have worked on him if he'd gone into the woods.

"Come along, Chase!" Oscar bellows. "They got there and then they turned back. We need to find out what they did next and why they left."

"Nice to meet you!" I call out as he stamps past, not bothering to acknowledge me this time round.

Hurrying to keep up with him, Chase stops in front of me to place the heavy bag down for a moment, beads of sweat forming on his forehead from lugging it around.

"Do you need any help with that?" I ask.

"No," Chase snaps, seemingly insulted that I'd think he might need a hand.

"All right. I was just asking."

I glance over at his dad in the distance, who is holding a compass aloft. He turns at the end of the path in, thankfully, the opposite direction to my house.

"There's nothing weird here in Goreway," I insist to Chase, as he wipes his forehead with the back of his hand. "Being a monster hunter sounds like a waste of time. Wouldn't you rather spend your afternoon having fun with friends than chasing around imaginary monsters with your dad?"

Scowling at me, he hoists the bag up on to his other shoulder.

"It's not that simple," he says, walking away. "Sometimes, you don't have a choice."

CHAPTER

EIGHT

Mr Frank flinches at my question.

He doesn't answer right away, his eyes glazing over as he disappears into his thoughts.

It's Monday morning and I asked Dad to get me to school early so that I could go to the library to find out more about the monster hunter. I tried searching on the internet, but so many results came up that it was difficult to make sense of it all. I pored over *How to Be a Vampire Slayer* to see if any of the past Helsby slayers mentioned a monster hunter in their exploits, but I couldn't find a reference to one anywhere. As usual, I've ended up in the library searching for answers.

"Mr Frank, did you hear me?" I prompt, before

repeating the question. "Do you know if any books about British myths and legends reference a monster hunter?"

He jolts out of his trance, eyeing me warily. "Why would you be interested in that?"

"No reason. He came up in something else I was reading and I thought it might be cool to know more about this mysterious person. Have you heard of him?"

"Of course not," he says sharply. "There's no such thing as monsters."

"Are you okay?" I ask, stunned by his defensive behaviour. "Usually you love talking about horror stuff."

"Yes, yes, I'm fine," he says impatiently. "Sorry, I've had a lot on my mind recently."

"With organizing the school trip?"

"What? Oh, that." He clears his throat. "Yes, that's it."

He's clearly lying, but I don't know whether I'm allowed to probe a teacher.

"It's going to be great," I assure him, before gesturing to the rows of shelves holding the mythological non-fiction. "Anyway, I'll go look—"

"Maggie," he interrupts, after a deep breath, "you don't have anything you want to tell me, do you? There's nothing ... odd that you need to share?"

"Odd how?"

He waves his hand about. "You know, anything strange about Goreway, for example. Since you arrived here, you've been fascinated in the town's history, in particular its supernatural associations ... and I heartily approve of that curiosity, but I wonder if there's a specific reason for it."

"No," I say. "Why? What specific reason would I have to be interested in it other than natural curiosity?"

"I don't know. Maybe a secret reason that has something to do with ... vampires?"

I blink at him. He stares back at me.

He couldn't possibly know.

Could he?

Before either of us can say anything more, a piercing scream echoes through the school. We both start, spinning to look at the door of the library, wondering what on earth has happened. The scream sounded like it was close.

"I think that came from the toilets opposite the library!" Mr Frank says, before pelting towards the door.

I follow hot on his heels and as we burst into the corridor, the door to the loos swings open and a boy comes quickly crawling out on his hands and knees, looking petrified.

"Jason!" Mr Frank exclaims, halting in front of him. "What's wrong? You look as though you've seen a ghost!"

"THAT'S BECAUSE I HAVE!" He scrambles to his feet and runs away as fast as he can down the corridor, screaming, "GHOST! GHOST IN THE LOO!"

Mr Frank and I share a look before boldly marching into the toilets to see what's going on. We're confronted with a bathroom of chaos. All the taps are on, water gushing from them into the bowls, already full and overflowing, the tiled floor fast becoming a slippery hazard. The mirrors over the row of sinks are all fogged up and the window is completely misted over. We can hear the toilets flushing constantly and what sounds like the lids being repeatedly opened and slammed shut again, accompanied by shrieks of impish laughter.

"Maggie," Mr Frank whispers, gulping audibly as he takes in the scene, "you need to get out of here. Leave now, please."

"No chance," I reply firmly, clenching my fists.

Our conversation is overheard. The toilet seats abruptly stop being played with and the cackling ceases.

A ghostly figure comes floating up, hovering above the cubicles. He's got a narrow face and long, wavy, wispy hair held back with a printed bandana wrapped round his head, and he's wearing distinctive round, circular sunglasses, a sleeveless shirt with baggy shorts and high-top trainers. If I had to guess, I'd say that before this guy was a ghost, he was a rock star.

Taking us in, a playful smile creeps across his lips.

"Hello, humans," he says, his voice hollow and eerie as it echoes off the bathroom walls above the splashing water.

I'm not afraid of him. Instead, the sight of him makes me instantly determined to resolve this situation.

"You're not supposed to be here," I inform the ghost.

A bewildered Mr Frank, who has been staring up at him in utter disbelief, suddenly turns to me.

"It's okay," I tell my teacher. "I'm used to this kind of thing."

As Mr Frank grapples with my calm reception of our guest, the ghost himself lets out a loud, "HA!"

"I know who *you* are and you can't stop me," he declares arrogantly, floating up higher and looking down his nose at me. "You don't deal with my *kind*."

"Why are you here at this school?" I ask him crossly.

"I happened to be in the area and I thought I might kill time by causing a bit of havoc. It's what I'm best at," he informs us proudly. "I HATE being told what to do, and you know who always tells you what to do? Teachers! So I saw the school and thought I'd do a bit of revolting! Time to have some FUN!"

With this declaration, he somersaults several times through the air and then floats down into the cubicles before we hear a lot of clanking and clanging. A flush handle comes skittering across the floor from under one of the cubicle doors, shortly followed by another one.

"Maggie, I know what to do," Mr Frank whispers urgently, appearing to collect himself. "I need to get a book from the library. Can you handle this on your own for a bit?"

"No problem," I say, sounding a lot more confident than I feel. "Please hurry, though."

He gives me a sharp nod and then turns to pull open the toilet door. As he does so, a small black blur comes swooping past his head, screeching indignantly. I grimace, realizing I'd left Bat-Head in my backpack in the library when we ran out. He must have escaped.

Mr Frank yelps as Bat-Head flies past his ear.

"I can explain the bat," I blurt out.

Mr Frank stares at me wide-eyed before croaking, "No need," and rushing off.

"We have a ghost problem," I say to Bat-Head, jumping as a toilet seat comes sailing over a cubicle door, landing on the wet floor with a splash.

Springing into action, I cover my head with my arms in case any other toilet parts are flung in my direction and race towards the sinks, where I frantically begin turning off the taps one by one while the ghost is distracted by the toilets.

"Oh no you don't!" He comes through a cubicle door, shrieking with laughter at my futile attempts, and turns them all back on with one quick sweep, the taps spinning so fast, they fly right off. Streams of water jet out in all directions, soaking me in the process and causing Bat-Head to jump upwards to dodge them.

"How is flooding the toilet a revolt?" I yell out, using my hands to try to stop it from at least one of the sinks. "This is the stupidest protest I've ever witnessed."

He stops mid-somersault and furiously scowls.

"What's your name?" I ask quickly, reasoning that if I get him talking, it delays further anarchy.

"I'm Nash," he divulges, looking me up and down curiously.

"I'm Maggie and this is Bat-Head."

"You're a *slayer*," Nash says, delighted with himself for knowing this key information. "One magical creature can recognize another one."

"Yeah, I've heard that before," I say, recalling a similar statement from Diana Dazzle. "But I'm not magical. I don't have cool powers like you."

I notice he reacts to this with elation, flattered by my acknowledgement of his magical nature. He likes praise, something I can use to my advantage as I continue to buy time before Mr Frank returns.

"You're not a very good slayer," Nash says pompously. "I've heard you're *friends* with them. I can see you even have one of their bats."

Bat-Head squeaks, baring his little fangs at Nash.

"You're keeping the wrong company," Nash tells me.

"Why do you say that?"

"Because ghosts are way more fun. Have you ever seen one before me?" he asks, and when I shake my head, he brightens. "Watch this."

He launches himself forwards and flies right through me, making me shiver as it feels like I've jumped into a pool of icy water.

"Pretty cool, right?" he says, hovering up by the ceiling.

"Yeah, that was ... uh ... great. Do you like being a ghost?" I ask stupidly, racking my brain for things to say.

He sniffs, considering my question. "I like haunting my old band. They kicked me out, you know, before I became a ghost. Their new music SUCKS. They don't have any presence onstage, either. Without me, they've really lost their sparkle."

"I can imagine. Do they live in Goreway?"

"No, they're in Manchester. I paid them a little visit on my way here." He sniggers. "I made one of them wet his pants."

I roll my eyes. "Very nice."

"I have to have SOME fun as a ghost, otherwise it's pretty lonely," he tells me, defensively hugging his arms across his chest. "Ghosts don't get covens or packs. And it's not like anywhere welcomes us. But hopefully soon I'll have my own home. You'd be surprised how many are already haunted, and ghosts are very territorial. It's been murder trying to find a good location for me to settle down."

"You're here to find a home? Like, an empty house somewhere?"

"A house? No, no, it's slightly grander than a *house*." He gives me a strange look. "I'm here for the same reason as all the others."

When I don't reply and merely offer him a blank expression, the corner of his mouth twists into a smile. "You don't know, do you?" he says, fascinated at this turn of events, "Oh, Maggie," he tuts, "you and your friends are in for a shock."

A loud bang of the door interrupts our conversation, and we both turn to see Mr Frank barrelling through, holding a hefty book open in his arms.

"Here! Look, Maggie!" he cries out, his eyes flickering up to Nash in fear as he jabs at a passage on the open page. "Try reading this poem out loud!"

Not completely intent on getting rid of Nash quite yet, I cautiously read the first line.

"*Unwelcome spirit of no name—*"

"*Return henceforth from where you came,*" Nash says, reciting the second line of the lengthy passage with a dramatic sigh. "Blah, blah, blah, I know how it goes. It may be effective, but that spell is factually incorrect. I do have a name, as I've already mentioned. It's Nash. And also, it proves my point right from the start. 'Unwelcome spirit.'" He throws his arms up. "Where are we supposed to go if we're unwelcome EVERYWHERE?"

"Wh-where did you come from?" Mr Frank asks nervously.

"Manchester," Nash replies breezily. "Maggie can fill you in on the pant-wetting story. Anyway, please don't read that spell out, as it sends me back to the other world and it is SUCH a long journey, especially when I'll just come back here to this human plane again. It's not like I can listen to a podcast whilst I travel, either, so it really is a drag. Look, how about this? I'll leave the school now if you don't read that thing out. Deal?"

"Can you make these taps stop running before you leave?"

In answer, he flies down and sweeps across the sinks again, somehow turning them all off, before returning to hovering above our heads.

"Thank you. Oh, and you won't freak out anyone else in Goreway?" I continue to negotiate.

"No haunting AT ALL?"

"None," I confirm.

"I mean, it's no fun, but *fine*," he huffs. "I'll leave the humans be."

I slam the book shut. "Deal."

"Pleasure doing business with you, Maggie," Nash says with a nod. He turns to Mr Frank. "You seem like an all right teacher. Put it there."

He holds out his hand for a high five, and Mr Frank

dutifully raises a shaking hand. Instead of a high five, Nash swoops down through Mr Frank and with a cackle of laughter at Mr Frank's horrified reaction, he disappears through the wall. Mr Frank and I remain standing in the flooded bathroom, processing the experience in silence.

After a while, Mr Frank gulps loudly and, with a small gesture to Bat-Head, who has come to land on my shoulder, he croaks, "Maggie, by any chance, might you be a … Helsby vampire slayer?"

"How do you know about that?" I ask, astonished.

"Because," he begins, bringing his eyes up to meet mine, "I think I'm supposed to be your slayer guide."

CHAPTER

NINE

Mr Frank sets two mugs of tea down on the library table, before sitting opposite me. I'm missing my first lesson of the day, but I've been excused due to my involvement in a "minor plumbing issue" from which I need to dry off.

The head teacher has already popped her head in, after she dealt with Jason, who had been running about the school that whole time shouting about ghosts and trying to get everyone to evacuate the building.

"It's certainly one way to get out of lessons," Miss Woods said to us, chuckling. "I assume, Mr Frank, he's been loaning a few horror books from you recently?"

He forced a laugh. "Ha. Ha. Yes. Very creative of Jason."

"He does seem to have had a fright of some sort," Miss Woods said, puzzled. "His dad has taken him home. Hopefully after some rest, he'll stop muttering about ghosts."

Mr Frank made a non-committal sound.

"Although I can see the toilets are flooded, so at least he drew our attention to that. I've already called a plumber round, they're on their way. Maggie, do you want to go home and change?" she asked, waggling a finger at my wet clothes.

Desperate to talk to Mr Frank, I assured her that I was happy to let them dry, and then Mr Frank suggested we have some hot drinks before going back to class. Miss Woods asked the school nurse to bring me a towel and then I waited on my own in the deserted library while Mr Frank hurried off to the canteen, returning with the tea.

"So then." He taps his fingers nervously on the table. "You're a vampire slayer."

I nod. "Yup. Strange, right?"

"Yes. Strange."

We fall into silence as I let him process this information.

"You know," he begins eventually, running a hand through his hair and making it stick up scruffily in all directions, "when I accepted that I was ... destined to be a guide for a Goreway slayer, I imagined that if such a role existed, it would be filled by a ... grown-up. Not someone still at school."

"I'd say that's a fair assumption."

We're both distracted for a moment by Bat-Head, who has discovered a new game of turning the pages of an open book by running really fast on them. He squeals in delight at this brand-new treadmill of his.

"How did you find out about ... everything?" Mr Frank asks, taking a sip of tea.

"It's a long story. The gist of it is, I became friends with a local vampire in Skeleton Woods, Sharptooth Shadow, and the truth came out eventually. I'm descended from the Helsby vampire slayers, but I've decided to become more of a protector than a slayer. The vampires aren't a threat to Goreway. They're cool."

Mr Frank puts his mug down. "The vampires are cool."

"Yes."

"I see. And you're friends with them."

"Ari and Miles are too. My parents are also their dentists."

Mr Frank doesn't know how to react to this

information. After a while of him not saying anything, I speak again, curious to find out his side of things.

"How do you know about the Helsby vampire slayers? You must have known who I was from the moment I arrived at this school – or maybe assumed my mum and dad were slayers – as soon as you heard my surname."

He slumps back in his chair. "No. I didn't know anything about this then. It's only recently that things started happening to me. In the lead-up to Christmas and beyond."

"What kind of things?"

"Strange things." He offers me a small smile. "I barely noticed what was going on at first, but then I gradually realized that something – some kind of energy – was pushing me towards becoming a slayer guide. The first thing was, I felt drawn to Skeleton Woods."

I sit up straight. "Me too!"

"Every time I went cycling, I somehow ended up there at the edge of the trees," he recalls as I reach for my tea. "I never set out to go there; I started actively trying to avoid the woodland, but I kept finding myself arriving there. The thing is, I've always been fascinated by Goreway, even before I moved to the town. I think deep down, I've known all along that I belong here. Then the books started speaking to me."

I choke on my drink at that one, coughing and spluttering. "S-sorry?"

"Not literally. But I'd be in here sorting things, and a book would fall off a shelf, open on a page about the vampires of Goreway, or the slayer legends and their guides. At first, I thought it was coincidence, but after the fifth or sixth time, I began to research it."

"And? What did you find out?"

He looks me right in the eye. "That alongside every Helsby vampire slayer, there was a guide to help them in their quests. Someone who lives near them, usually older. Historically, the guide has had a profession heavily influenced by the written word, something akin to a professor, writer, historian or … librarian."

He pauses, and I wait patiently as he takes another sip of tea before continuing.

"I realized that the events of last term might have some truth to them. I considered that maybe there really were vampires in the woods and, as such, there was a Helsby slayer and I was destined to be their guide. I was just trying to get my head round the fact that your mum or dad was who I was looking for, and then, when all these rumours began to spread around Goreway – the zombies, the monsters – it began to dawn on me that *you* were the Helsby always looking for answers."

He closes his eyes and pinches the bridge of his nose.

"So, you're my official guide?" I ask cheerily, when he doesn't elaborate any further. "I didn't even realize I get one!"

"You couldn't have thought you were in this alone," he says, frowning at me. "It's a big burden for one person."

"I wonder who the guide was for my Great Uncle Bram."

Mr Frank nods thoughtfully. "Yes. I wonder what happened to them." He hesitates, grimacing. "Maybe I don't want to know."

"What exactly do you do, as my slayer guide?" I ask, wanting to steer the conversation away from any hypothetical vampire incidents that may have befallen his predecessor. "Do you give me assignments? Send me to help vampires in need across the country and things like that?"

He raises his eyebrows. "Not exactly. My understanding of the role is to research vampires and their like thoroughly, so that I may be of assistance should you need guidance on how to handle a situation."

"Like how you knew what spell to read to get rid of Nash."

"Who?"

"The ghost in the toilets."

"Oh. Yes, exactly. I've been reading a lot about the supernatural recently. In fact, I've just put in a giant order for many books on the subject, and now I know that this is a thing" – he gestures at me across the table – "that a Helsby vampire slayer exists and that I am your guide, I will make a trip to the British Library to do as much research as possible, so that I can do my best to help you. Especially now that Goreway seems to be attracting so many unwanted guests."

"I don't know why that's suddenly happening," I say, leaning forwards on the table and resting my chin in my hands as Bat-Head grows tired of playing with the books and flies up to land on my shoulder. "Although, Nash seemed to think I should know. He made out as though there's a specific reason that he and 'others' are coming here."

"Others as in, more ghosts?" Mr Frank asks, his forehead lined in concentration.

"The supernatural in general, I think, which explains all the other strange sightings. I think it's something to do with Skeleton Woods. I've been sensing something odd about it recently and Diana Dazzle—"

"Who?"

"A witch I know. She was worried about the enchantments around the woods, although Count Bloodthirst—"

"Count who?"

"The Chosen Leader of the vampires, quite a scary guy at first, but great when you get to know him."

"I'm sure," Mr Frank mutters.

"He didn't seem worried about anything; he was confident this was all coincidence, but Nash pretty much confirmed that it wasn't. They're coming here for a reason."

"I can look into it," Mr Frank offers. "See if anything has happened like this before."

"Could you also look into the monster hunter? I mentioned him earlier to you, before the ghost incident. I ran into him here recently in Goreway. He seemed ... dedicated to his cause – I don't know who he's tracking specifically, but I didn't get a good feeling about him."

"I'll add it to my list."

I smile at Mr Frank. "Thanks! You know, it's very cool having a guide."

"I'm not sure how much help I'll be," he says nervously. "Helping you with vampires is one thing; I didn't know that the job would entail dealing with monsters of *every* kind."

"Me neither," I say, pulling the towel tighter round my shoulders, "but right now, I'm not sure we have much of a choice."

Ari and Miles are coming over to my house after school, but my dad messages to say he's going to be a bit late picking us up because Mrs Hollyhogg has come into the practice demanding he help Twiglet, her Pomeranian, with an emergency dental treatment. He adds that he *did* mention she should be taking him to the vet instead, but apparently she's insisting that Twiglet get "the best treatment available to humans".

We happily wait for him in a nearby café, each buying a smoothie and sitting in a table at the window, far from any other customers so we can't be overheard, before Ari and Miles both demand a full debrief of the day's events.

Ari gets out her phone, deciding she needs to take notes for her comic strip.

"Let me get this straight," she begins, "our school librarian is now your spirit guide—"

"Slayer guide," I correct her.

"—and he's meant to help you in your slayer missions," she continues, "which at the moment has something to do with a load of supernatural creatures descending on Goreway, and that, in turn, has encouraged some dude called the monster slayer—"

"Monster hunter."

"—to show up looking to trap them all in a dungeon, putting Sharptooth and the Skeleton Woods vampires at risk."

I nod. "Yeah. That's about right."

She exhales, shaking her head at me. "And here I was thinking last term was weird."

"Does Mr Frank know why you have a bat?" Miles asks. "Is that common for slayers?"

"I didn't get round to asking about that, but I'll bring it up next time. More importantly, we need to get to the bottom of why all these monsters have come here so we can work out how to get them to leave. Right now, their presence is putting the people of Goreway AND the vampire community at risk. I have to work out what to do."

Ari glances up from her phone. "It's not your responsibility to solve everything, Maggie."

"Isn't it? I am the Helsby vampire slayer." I shrug. "I'm meant to protect the town."

"From *vampires*," Miles insists. "And you've done that by becoming friends with them. I think you've already done your bit."

"Yeah, well, it doesn't feel that way. If I don't help, who will? The town doesn't even believe any of these monsters exist. It's not like they're going to be hot on the case of working out how to get rid of them."

The door to the café swings open and a boy walks in, a professional camera hanging from his shoulder on a thick black strap. As he inspects the shelves of sandwiches, I sit bolt upright, recognizing him straight away.

"That's the monster hunter's son!" I whisper to Ari and Miles, who instantly twist round to stare at him. "His name is Chase."

"He looks … normal," Miles remarks.

"You should have seen what his dad was wearing. He looked like he had stepped out of a comic book," I say.

"You'll have to give me all the details," Ari insists quietly, her eyes still fixed on Chase as he takes two sandwiches to the counter. "This is good content for my graphic novel."

Once he's finished paying, Chase turns to see the three of us staring at him. I give him an awkward wave. He frowns.

"Chase, right?" I say brightly, as he slowly walks towards the door.

"Yes," he replies warily, confused as to why I'm bothering to make conversation with him.

Which makes two of us, to be honest.

"I think I met you the other day with your dad by Skeleton Woods. These are my friends Ari and Miles."

He gives them a sharp nod.

"Nice camera," Ari says, admiring it. "You into photography?"

"Oh, yeah," he mumbles, his cheeks flushing. "It's just a silly hobby."

"Photography isn't silly," Ari tells him sternly. "I'm an artist myself. And that looks like a serious camera for 'just a hobby'."

He shrugs. "I guess. My mum was a photographer."

"Did she teach you?" Miles asks.

"Yeah. We used to go on days out and take photos of cool things we'd see. But after she died, Dad thought I should focus more on" – he hesitates – "other stuff."

"Oh. Sorry about your mum," Ari says.

"Thanks."

"My dad is always on my case about getting homework done instead of working on my graphic novel." Ari leans forward, resting her arms on the table. "What do you like to photograph?"

"Animals mostly," Chase admits, before shuffling his feet. "Sounds stupid."

"That isn't stupid!" I tell him. "Hey, have you ever photographed bats?"

He grimaces. "Actually, that's the one animal I wouldn't be interested in capturing. Bats are evil creatures."

"They are NOT," I say, bristling, while Bat-Head squeaks indignantly from my bag. "They're actually very interesting little creatures, not to mention adorable. They'd look very good in a close-up."

He shudders at the thought.

"Maggie likes bats, in case that wasn't obvious," Miles chuckles. "How long are you in Goreway for? There's a photography club here that you could join if you wanted."

Chase looks down at the floor, mumbling, "I don't think so."

"Then you should definitely visit the high street

gallery, at least," Ari says. "There's a wildlife photography exhibition that's on there for the next few weeks."

For a second, Chase's expression seems to light up with interest. But it's as though he suddenly remembers something, and his face clouds over again.

"I don't think we'll have time." He checks his watch. "I'd better go. My dad is at the theatre and he'll be wondering where I am."

"Is he in a play?" Ari asks, confused.

"No, he's checking for … uh … never mind. Anyway. Bye then."

Clutching his sandwiches, he skulks out the door.

I lean back in my chair, crossing my arms. "I bet his dad is in the theatre checking for ghosts. They like hanging out in the rafters."

We see Dad pulling up in the car outside and pick up our smoothies, ready to go.

"You know, it can't be easy for Chase that his dad disapproves of his artistic passion," Ari comments, leading the way out the café door. "I really hope he'll see that exhibition."

"Me too," I agree. "But I doubt he'll be given the chance."

Back at my house later that evening, I'm in the middle of explaining to Ari and Miles why we need to find a way of persuading Count Bloodthirst that there is a growing monster problem in Goreway, when I'm interrupted by Bat-Head, who squeaks with excitement and flits over to the fireplace, before peering up the chimney expectantly.

A moment later, a second bat comes flying out from it. She's much bigger and fiercer-looking than Bat-Head, but he seems overjoyed to see her, joining in with her activity of flying about the room and screeching. She drops a scrap of parchment on to Miles's lap and then lands on the curtain rail.

Coughing through the cloud of soot drifting down on him, Miles picks up the parchment and reads aloud: "His Excellency Count Bloodthirst is pleased to invite you to the field adjacent to Skeleton Woods this coming Saturday at dusk to take part in the highly anticipated football match of VAMPIRES vs HUMANS. Please RSVP at your convenience by return bat."

Acknowledging that Ari is as baffled as he is, Miles looks to me for an explanation.

"I forgot to mention this," I say apologetically. "Sharptooth and some of the other vampires wanted to challenge us to a five-a-side game. Us three plus my parents on the human team. They want to prove they're better than us at football, even when not using any vampire-power advantages."

Miles snorts. "As IF."

"I wouldn't be so sure," Ari says, laughing at Miles's cocky expression. "Even without their super speed and skill, they're very cunning, those vampires."

"They don't have the first clue about tactics!" Miles retorts. "We'd have it in the bag."

"I don't know, Miles, remember you'd have me on your team." I grimace. "Not to mention my parents. You'd have to give us a LOT of instruction."

Before I can stop him, Miles turns to the delivery bat and says, "Please can you tell Count Bloodthirst that we accept his invitation. We'll be there."

The bat screeches in reply, launching herself off the curtain rail and disappearing back up the chimney. Bat-Head looks sad at her leaving, so I gesture for him to fly over to me so I can give him a comforting belly rub.

"Miles, we can't go play football with them this weekend," I inform him, whilst comforting Bat-Head. "That's a terrible idea."

"Why?"

"Because it brings them out into the open! Not to

137

mention us. We have monsters running around town, remember?"

"Maggie, they're *vampires*," he says determinedly. "If anyone can protect us from monsters, it's them. There's probably nowhere safer than in their company. Plus, it's important we win." He puffs out his chest. "On behalf of humankind."

I sigh. "I should mention, the match will be refereed by bat."

"What a day!" Ari exclaims, shaking her head. "Ghosts in the loo; a librarian who's a secret slayer guide; and now a vampire vs human football match. What next? Our head teacher is a secret alien?"

"No. Although," I say, suddenly remembering there's something else I need to tell them, "I think our school friend may be a werewolf."

CHAPTER

TEN

I'm not sure this football match is a good idea. The vampires, however, are determined to go ahead with it and it's very difficult to argue with them, and not just for the reasons you'd expect, but because they're so EXCITED.

When we arrive at the field where the game will be taking place, we're all stunned into silence at the sight of the pitch they've created. In the growing darkness of the early evening, the pitch is lit by flame torches and lanterns that look as though they're from medieval times – and considering who's provided them, chances are, they *are* that old. The nets have been "borrowed" from a local football team, easily snuck out and transported by the vampires from their club once their afternoon practice was over and the sun had set. A whiteboard is propped up next to the pitch acting as a makeshift scoreboard, with "HUMANS" written at the top of one side of it and "VAMPIRES" on the other.

The vampires are busy stretching and it's difficult not to giggle as we watch them doing warm-up exercises. They're wearing a mix-match of kit that they bought from the clothes section of the supermarket and, without human guidance, they've put their own unique spin on it. Dreadclaw seems to be wearing a collared shirt that would look more suitable in a classroom, while Nightmare is sporting two pairs of shorts, one of which is on his head. Sticking to general vampire rules, they're all wearing cloaks still, but these seem to be shorter than their normal ones, jaggedly cut in half to stop at their waists.

All the bats are acting as cheerleaders, hovering above their respective vampires and screeching in what I think is an encouraging manner. In the spirit of friendly rivalry, Bat-Head, on my shoulder as usual, sticks his little tongue out at them and blows a raspberry.

"Glad that, despite your Skeleton Castle roots, you know whose team you're on, Bat-Head," Miles asserts with a nod of approval.

The teams aren't the only ones who have shown up for the match, with one side of the pitch lined with excitable vampires who have come to spectate. Some of them have made banners for the occasion, reading things like, "GO TEAM VAMPIRE!" and "HUMANS SMELL (*tasty … haha just joking, stinky humans*)" in bright red lettering that hasn't dried properly, so is dripping slowly down the card on to the grass.

Ari squints at them. "That's red *paint*, right? Because it looks suspiciously like—"

"It's paint," I state confidently, although I'm not *entirely* sure myself.

"Shame we couldn't bring any fans." Dad sighs. "It would have been fun to have people cheering us from the sidelines."

"They'd be too busy running away from the vampires and screaming to cheer, Mr H," Ari reasons.

Count Bloodthirst, who appears to have taken on the role of the vampire team's manager, is barking instructions at his team.

"Lift those knees up higher, Fangly! I said, HIGHER!" he demands.

"Yeah, look alive, Fangly!" Maggothead smirks, proudly running on the spot.

"But I'm NOT alive," Fangly points out with a huff, as she launches into star jumps. "I'm a vampire!"

Nightmare sniggers.

"What are you laughing at?" Fangly seethes, narrowing her eyes. "Yesterday during practice, you ran into the goalpost!"

Nightmare stops laughing, his expression twisting into anger. "Only because Dreadclaw knocked into me!"

"It's not my fault I slipped in the mud," Dreadclaw argues, attempting some lunges. "I was trying to concentrate on running slowly like humans do, and I'm not used to wearing these silly shoes!"

"They're called football *boots*," Sharptooth corrects him cheerily, bopping up and down as she does some squats. "I think they're really cool."

"How come mine are so bright?" Dreadclaw asks, gesturing to his neon-orange pair. "Fangly has spooky black ones."

"I studied pictures of the best football players in the world, and some of them wear really bright boots, so I thought I should order a selection!" Sharptooth tells him. "Maybe it's a tactic and they distract other players with their bright boots?"

Dreadclaw's expression lights up. "That's a great idea! I'll throw my boots at their heads! Then we'll score!"

Sharptooth shakes her head. "No, Dreadclaw, that's not allowed in football, remember? We've been through this. Just like how you can't jump on people's shoulders, either, like you did with Nightmare the other day."

Dreadclaw looks extremely disappointed at this news.

I've barely seen Sharptooth all week because they've been having practice sessions, and Miles has also been very demanding on the time of us humans. He may be shy and bookish off the pitch, but, *whoa*, Miles is competitive when he's on one. I knew he was good at sport but I've seen a whole new side to him – a highly motivated, ambitious side that comes with mildly terrifying leadership skills.

During our training the other day, he told Mum to "look lively" and she instinctively replied, "Yes, sir!" in all seriousness.

Miles turns to us now with steely determination. "All right, team, this is our time to shine. Let's get warming up, come on, jackets off!"

Ari glares at him as we reluctantly peel off our warm coats, our breath visible in the freezing evening air.

"Did we ever elect Miles to be captain?" she mutters grumpily. "Or is this more of a dictatorship?"

"Enough chit-chat, Ari," he scolds, clapping his hands and running up and down on the spot. "You'll be sweating in no time. Let's get that blood running through your veins! The other team don't have that advantage!"

He cracks a smile at his own joke.

"Yeah, but they don't feel the cold either," Dad reminds us wistfully.

As Miles forces the others into laps, Count Bloodthirst glides across the pitch to me, his arms outstretched in welcome.

"It's going to be a fascinating match," he drawls, his red eyes glinting in the light of the flames. "I only hope your team won't be too bitter when we win by an extraordinary amount of goals."

I put my hands on my hips. "I don't think we should be playing at all."

"Now, now, it's important that you at least *try*," he smirks. "What's that preposterous human saying? Oh yes, it's not the winning that counts, it's the taking part." He chuckles. "So adorable, but completely nonsensical."

"I don't mean the human team, I'm talking about ALL of us," I clear up impatiently. "You ignored my bat messages this week telling you about my meeting with the ghost."

"I'm not interested in anything ghosts have to say. There's really no need to take any notice of one ghost popping up."

"It's not just Nash that I'm worried about. If you'd read my messages that Bat-Head delivered—"

"I read about your concerns," he interrupts tiredly. "But as I've said, the vampires are perfectly safe. We are very capable of protecting our home."

"I know that, but Nash implied that—"

"Ghosts are notorious complainers, whinging away constantly. It's extremely draining. Why do you think humans allege that they moan all the time? Whatever that ghost said, he was simply trying to get inside your head, as ghosts are wont to do, and he seems to have succeeded."

"What about Diana Dazzle and her comments about the enchantments?"

"Witches are always desperate to make vampires look inferior because they're threatened by us," he says smugly. "I have respect for Diana – she's one of the few witches in the world I can stand – but don't put it past her to try to spark panic amongst our community just for a little fun. I won't let her make a fool of us."

"But Count Bloodthirst—"

"It's time to play football, unless the humans want to accept defeat now," he announces, rubbing his hands together, his fangs gleaming as his mouth twists into a smirk.

"Fat chance!" Miles shouts across the pitch, grinning as Dreadclaw practises catching a penalty from Sharptooth in goal and misses. "I hope vampires are better losers than they are keepers!"

As all the players gather together in the middle of the field around me and Count Bloodthirst, Sharptooth gives me a gentle nudge.

"Don't worry, Maggie, we won't let anything happen to you, your family or friends," she assures me, having heard our entire conversation along with all the vampires thanks to their amazing hearing.

"I know," I reply with a grateful smile. "But they're not the only ones I'm worried about." I glance over to our vampire audience, before leaning into Sharptooth and quietly asking, "Those banners aren't painted in blood, are they?"

"Don't be stupid! It's ketchup!" she says, as I sigh in relief. "It's great because if we get peckish at half-time, we can just lick the signs!"

Count Bloodthirst clears his throat. "Welcome one and all to the much-anticipated VAMPIRES vs HUMANS football match!"

The spectators cheer and whoop from the sidelines. Miles claps his hands, nodding as his eyes scan across his team, as though to say, "We've got this!"

"In the interest of fairness," Count Bloodthirst continues, "we have asked Bat-Grouch to referee."

Taking his cue, a large, greying, miserable-looking bat, with a whistle hanging round his neck, comes flying over to hover above us. He looks like he'd rather be anywhere else.

"Bat-Grouch does not belong to any vampire and he has no loyalty to the vampire community," Count Bloodthirst says disapprovingly. "He makes it perfectly clear that he holds every creature on this planet, bar himself, in contempt, and has only agreed to referee this match in exchange for a rare stamp that I have in my possession. He collects them."

Ari snorts. "He's giving up his evening to referee a stupid game in the freezing cold for a *stamp*?"

Bat-Grouch screeches at her indignantly.

"Don't anger the ref, Ari," Miles hisses.

"As I was saying," Count Bloodthirst continues, giving Ari a withering look, "the referee is completely neutral and would like a clean, respectful game from both teams. Now, if the captains would like to shake hands, we can begin."

Sharptooth and Miles step forward with outstretched hands.

"Good luck, humans!" Sharptooth exclaims brightly. "Thank you to your ancestors for inventing this beautiful game."

Miles smiles broadly at her, unused to such a sincere and kind start to a match. "And good luck, vampires. Thanks for toning down your powers today so we can play."

They shake hands – Miles gasping at her cold grip – and Count Bloodthirst balances a coin on top of Bat-Grouch's head. When Sharptooth calls heads, Bat-Grouch jerks his head back, causing the coin to flip up and in the air before dropping down on the grass. Bat-Grouch swoops down to examine the result before pointing a wing at Miles, who punches the air triumphantly.

The crowd cheers as we all run into position. Dad's in goal and I'm a defender, while Miles and Mum are taking on midfielder positions and Ari is our forward.

Bat-Grouch blows the starting whistle and the game begins.

Ari kicks it to Miles, who dribbles it down the pitch, dodging past Nightmare, but soon successfully tackled by Fangly, who passes it up to Sharptooth. Mum brilliantly intercepts, kicking it to Miles, who nudges it to Ari, who takes a shot and...

"GOAL!" Miles bellows, running to give Ari a victorious high five as our team cheers and goalie Dreadclaw buries his head in his hands.

Bat-Grouch gives a whistle and the vampire standing by the scoreboard furiously splats some ketchup from a bottle on to her hand and uses it to smear a "1" on the Humans' side, and a "0" on the Vampires'.

The game starts up again and after a very impressive manoeuvre from Sharptooth to dodge round Miles, she passes the ball to Maggothead, who dribbles it nicely towards me. I do my best to attempt a tackle, and do a surprisingly good job at putting the pressure on, but Sharptooth helps out Maggothead and manages to steer the ball to the other side of the pitch, taking a hopeful shot at the goal. The football soars just over Dad's fingertips and hits the back of the net.

Sharptooth whoops and does a somersault about ten

feet in the air in celebration.

"YES! VAMPIRES RULE!" Maggothead exclaims, while the crowd goes wild.

The vampire in charge of scoring happily wipes the Vampires' "0" away using her sleeve, and replaces it with a "1", before licking the ketchup off her clothes.

Back into position and Bat-Grouch is about to start play again when all the bats suddenly freeze, their heads all spinning in the same direction.

"What have you heard?" I ask, moving over to Sharptooth.

Her jaw clenches. "*Dogs.*"

"Aw, sweet." Mum smiles, catching her breath. She notices Sharptooth's expression has clouded over. "Do vampires not like dogs?"

"I don't think these are normal kinds of dogs," I say.

"What do you mean?" Dad asks, coming to join us from the goal.

I don't need to explain because at that moment Marrok appears at the end of the field with a woman I don't recognize. They stop still as the vampires – suddenly in attack mode, displaying their fangs, their eyes narrowed to slits – gather together in front of us, creating a fort, with Count Bloodthirst front and centre.

"Well, what do we have here?" he says in a low, threatening voice, eyeing them up before letting out a truly evil cackle that chills me to the bone.

"Wait!" I call out hurriedly before anything can happen. "He goes to our school!"

Sharptooth points her finger at Marrok. "That's the werewolf you told me about?"

"Excuse me," Mum begins, holding up her hand and giving me a stern look. "What did you just say?"

Uh-oh.

Probably should have mentioned this to my parents before now.

"You go to school with a WEREWOLF?" she practically yells. "And you didn't think to tell us?"

"It slipped my mind," I squeak as Bat-Head shudders under Mum's glare. "I wasn't certain he was a werewolf and you let me hang out with vampires so I didn't think it was that big a deal. If it helps, I think he might be a nice werewolf. Let me go check."

"Oh yes, just go give that a check," she scoffs, crossing her arms. "If he doesn't bite your head off, we'll know he's nice."

"Darling," Dad begins gingerly, putting an arm round Mum, "let's give Maggie the benefit of the doubt, shall we? After all, she can sense these kinds of things."

As Mum's face softens, I decide not to fill them in on how when I first met Marrok, the sense I was getting was actually one of caution. No need for them to know the details.

I make my way through the crowd of vampires to Count Bloodthirst.

"Let me talk to them."

He closes his eyes, inhaling deeply. "*Fine.*"

Thanking him, I walk out towards Marrok and his companion, Sharptooth right behind me.

"Ew," she whispers as we get closer, "they stink."

"Don't say that," I reply sharply. "Be nice."

"If I have to," she grumbles.

"Hey," Marrok begins, looking tense as we stop in front of them, "we thought we could hear a football game going on."

"You happened to be out on an evening walk in the area?" I ask.

The corner of his mouth twitches as though trying to suppress a smile.

"Actually, we could hear it from our house," he confesses. "We don't live too far from here."

"Ah. Good hearing, I take it."

"Not bad." He glances at Sharptooth. "You don't smell so fresh either, by the way."

She scowls at him. He turns his attention back to me.

"How long have you known?"

"About the vampires in Goreway? Or that you're a werewolf?" I ask.

"The werewolf thing."

"I've had an inkling for a while," I inform him. "Your name kind of gave it away."

He watches me curiously. "And you were *okay* with it?"

"I wanted to give you the benefit of the doubt. As you can see from my friends, it wasn't so strange an idea to me."

He relaxes his shoulders. "We don't want to hurt anyone. This is my aunt, Loveta. Aunty Loveta, this is Maggie. She goes to Goreway School, too."

Aunty Loveta sniffs the air and tilts her head at me. "What are you?"

"She's a Helsby vampire slayer," Sharptooth informs her loftily. "And I'm her best friend, Sharptooth Shadow."

"A vampire slayer and her best friend … who's a vampire," Aunty Loveta repeats, unconvinced. "Is this some kind of joke?"

"It's a long story," I answer.

It dawns on me that Marrok is wearing football shorts and is carrying his sports bag. He didn't leave his house because he was curious. He came to join in.

"You wouldn't be interested in playing football, would you?" I ask. "Because we might be able to squeeze in some more players."

Sharptooth looks horrified.

Marrok beams at me. "We thought we'd check. Right, Aunty Loveta?"

"I admit it's been a long time since anybody wanted me on their team," she growls. "But I didn't realize there would be quite so many *vampires*. I don't know what Grimmwolf would say about this."

Sharptooth recoils at the venomous manner in which Aunty Loveta says "vampires".

"Who's Grimmwolf?" I ask, growing apprehensive of the clear animosity between Aunty Loveta and Sharptooth, neither helping to win the other over.

"Grimmwolf is my dad," Marrok answers. "You met him at school."

"I didn't know his name was Grimmwolf. Must be hard to keep the werewolf identity secret with a name like that," I observe.

"Yeah, well, Marrok isn't such a common name either,"

he points out, before turning to his aunt with a pleading expression. "You promised that you would at least *consider* the idea of joining in if the vampires were involved."

"I know that, Marrok, but now I'm here" – she eyes up the mass of vampires crowded behind me, before her eyes drift to Sharptooth right in front of her – "it seems less plausible. How can we trust them?"

"How about you form a truce?" I suggest. "The vampires won't hurt you, so long as you won't hurt them."

Aunty Loveta raises her eyebrows. "How do we know they'll keep to their word?"

"Duh, we're vampires playing football with *humans*," Sharptooth says. "You know how tasty humans smell? That says it all."

"She has a point," Marrok says, while I glance over my shoulder to check that Miles didn't hear Sharptooth referring to humans as "tasty".

"The real question is, how do *we* know we can trust *you*?" Sharptooth says.

"You can trust us," Marrok assures her. "We didn't come here to cause any trouble. Aunty Loveta and I love playing football, that's all. I get to play at school, at least, but she's stuck playing with only me when I get home in the evenings. I thought it would be fun for her to have a chance to play in a team again."

"I can understand that," I say, offering Aunty Loveta a smile.

"But what about Grimmwolf?" she points out, her expression softening a little. "If we could hear the football match from the house, then he might be able to hear that we've joined in. Then what would happen? If he found out we'd made contact with the vampires, let alone played alongside them..."

"He's working late at the hair salon in town. He won't be able to hear anything from there," Marrok assures her. "He doesn't need to know."

"Your dad is a hairdresser? Makes so much sense. Your family really does have great hair," I acknowledge.

"Mostly genetics," Marrok grins, before feeling the need to explain his aunt's hesitancy. "Vampires and werewolves have been enemies for centuries; it's really an unwritten rule and, in my opinion, an outdated one. But my dad is less ... open-minded."

"Why does the magical community have so many ancient arguments?" I ask, putting my hands on my hips and turning to address Sharptooth. "I thought the vampires and witches didn't like each other. But you also have a problem with werewolves?"

"A lot of the tension between wolves and vampires comes down to who gets which territory," Marrok jumps in to explain. "There aren't that many places where our kind can live in peace. Same goes for vampires."

Sharptooth sniffs. "That, and werewolves think they're better than us."

"Oh please. Vampires declare themselves superior to everyone else at the first chance they get," Aunty Loveta snarls.

"It's not our fault that vampires are so COOL. And anyway, everyone knows that werewolves have a habit of taking what has belonged to vampires for centuries," Sharptooth retorts, her red eyes flashing with anger.

"Usually things that vampires stole from us in the first place," Aunty Loveta snaps back.

"Okay, both of you put your fangs away," I demand. "We're meant to be forming a truce here, remember?"

Glaring at each other, the two of them reluctantly back down.

Marrok grimaces. "It may take some work, but maybe there is a chance of making peace with the vampires while we're here in Goreway. I'm hoping to persuade my dad that we don't have to butt heads. We can live beside each other. Civilly."

Aunty Loveta gives Marrok a knowing look, adding, "For now, at least."

"You don't plan on staying near Skeleton Woods for long, then," Sharptooth ponders, while Marrok's eyes fall to the ground. "I suppose that might help convince Count Bloodthirst to let you play today. A temporary truce might be obtainable."

"Let's give it a try," I determine, waving over Count Bloodthirst before pointing my finger from Sharptooth to Aunty Loveta. "Play nice. We want Count Bloodthirst to know that we're all in agreement here."

"Maggie, you do know he's heard the entire conversation, right?" Marrok reminds me, looking amused.

"It's been most enlightening," Count Bloodthirst announces as he drifts over to us. "The werewolves have come to beg for the chance to play alongside the vampires."

"I'd hardly call it begging," Aunty Loveta mumbles, but Marrok nudges her sharply in the ribs with his elbow.

"We would like to join in with the game," Marrok confirms. "If that's okay with you, of course, Count

Bloodthirst."

"They come in peace," I affirm.

"So they say," Count Bloodthirst drawls.

"If you won't believe what they say, then at least consider that it would be pretty stupid for two werewolves to try to take on a whole colony of vampires, don't you think?" I point out.

"That's true," Count Bloodthirst says. "But our two kinds have never been able to see eye to eye, and there must be a reason for that, so I highly doubt that—"

He stops to listen for something at the exact same time that Aunty Loveta does.

"What is it?" I ask nervously, but Sharptooth shrugs, looking confused.

"I didn't hear anything," she says.

"Me neither," Marrok agrees.

Aunty Loveta shakes her head in disappointment at Marrok. "That's because you have no appreciation for the *bombycilla garrulous*, known commonly as the—"

"Waxwing," Count Bloodthirst finishes for her. "A lovely little bird, with a distinctive grey-pink plumage." He looks at Aunty Loveta, impressed. "You know about birds?"

"I have had a great interest in birdwatching since I

was little," she informs him proudly. "Their song brings me a sort of … peace, I suppose."

"Yes, me too," Count Bloodthirst says. "When you're a creature of the night, there is a strange comfort and harmony to be found in the study of birds, who can soar freely."

"I agree."

The group falls into silence.

"Guess you're not so different after all." I smile.

Count Bloodthirst clears his throat. "I have decided that you may join in with this football match, on the condition that a truce is officially declared and no harm will come to any of my vampires."

"Deal." Aunty Loveta nods. "Thank you."

"No special werewolf abilities allowed. This is a human-level football match," he continues. "And I trust you are happy with a bat as referee?"

"So long as the bat's fair," she replies. "I played a werewolf vs centaurs game many years ago and the referee was a horse. Talk about bias."

"I assure you, Bat-Grouch likes vampires no more than he likes werewolves, or any being for that matter. The only creature he has any respect for is himself."

"Then that's fine by us."

"Very well, let us return to the game," Count Bloodthirst announces. "You may split – one of you play with the humans, the other with the vampire team."

"Maybe it's best if I play alongside the vampires," Marrok suggests.

"No, it's okay," Aunty Loveta says, with a much warmer voice than we've heard so far, gripping his arm excitedly. "It's nice for you to play with your *friends*."

Marrok flushes. I remember his comments in the library about his last school not wanting him to play on their team, and I suddenly get the feeling that Marrok was as good at fitting in at school as I was before I came to Goreway.

This is the first place that has ever felt like home.

Marrok glances at me apologetically, before quickly emphasizing to her, "We're just at the same school, Aunty Loveta, I never said that—"

"No, she's right," I say firmly. "We're friends. Now, are you ready to play the weirdest game of football ever?"

Grinning at me, Marrok suddenly throws back his head and gives a long howl. Naturally, Loveta joins in. When they're finished, Marrok sees that I'm staring at them with my mouth open in shock.

"Sorry," he says, laughing at my expression. "Force of habit."

CHAPTER

ELEVEN

"This is all your influence, Maggie," Sharptooth tells me as Marrok and Aunty Loveta head over to the sidelines to put their football boots on.

"What do you mean?" I ask her.

"You opened our eyes to befriending humans," she explains, nudging me. "Now, other surprising friendships don't seem so strange and scary."

"If that's the case, then it wasn't just me who made it possible," I point out, smiling warmly at her. "It was a joint effort."

Miles and Ari appear at my side, looking over to Marrok.

"So, Marrok is definitely a werewolf, then." Miles

gulps. "Do werewolves ever lose control and eat their friends? Or is that just myth?"

"I'll let him answer that one. He can hear every word we say."

Miles starts. "All the way from over there?"

Marrok finishes tying his laces and catches Miles's eye, laughing.

"*Oh*," Miles whispers.

Ready to play, Marrok jogs over to us, while my parents strike up a conversation with his aunt.

"We stay in control, no matter what form we take, so you can relax," Marrok explains, giving Miles a thump on the back. "You're more likely to get a bite from one of these vampires than me. Hey, thanks for letting us play. This has got to be the coolest thing I've ever been a part of."

"Same here," Ari agrees, staring wide-eyed up at him. "I have SO many questions for you. Can you turn into a werewolf now? Does it hurt? What's your deal with the moon?"

"Let's leave the questions until after the match," I recommend, noticing Bat-Grouch getting very shirty about such a long halt to proceedings.

"I agree," Marrok says. "Aunty Loveta has offered to

take the vampires' side, so I'll play with you lot if that's okay."

Miles perks up at the suggestion. "Yeah, cool. We're lucky to have you."

Miles and Ari move away into position, and before Marrok follows their lead, he turns to thank me again.

"It really means a lot that you're letting us join in. It doesn't seem like a big deal, but this" – he gestures around the pitch – "it's really nice to feel like I can be myself somewhere. Seriously, Maggie, thanks."

"No problem."

He suddenly glances over to my parents with a strange expression.

"What is it?"

"Your dad just asked my aunt if werewolves have good dental care."

I burst out laughing. Count Bloodthirst announces that the match is ready to recommence and the teams quickly prepare themselves, before Bat-Grouch blows the starting whistle. Marrok and Aunty Loveta prove to be excellent additions, both brilliant at football, despite not using any werewolf advantages.

As it continues, it looks to be a nail-biting match with no obvious winner, both sides playing well. We get a penalty when Maggothead achieves a brilliant header with an accidental twenty-foot jump, but their team soon gets payback with a penalty of their own when Marrok forgets himself and dribbles the ball expertly fast on all four limbs.

When the scoreboard displays 3-3 with just five minutes left to play, we're all feeling equally excited and nervous. The crowd is going wild at the sidelines and the teams are feeling the pressure.

"Prepare to lose, humans!" Aunty Loveta cries, giving Fangly a high five. "You're no match for the vampire-werewolf mash-up!"

"In case you hadn't noticed, we have the stronger team!" Marrok calls back. "We are going to—"

Before he can finish his sentence, Marrok is sent flying backwards with huge force when something comes soaring through the air, knocking him over. He tumbles to the ground, tangled in a giant net.

"Marrok!" Aunt Loveta cries in horror, running over to help him.

But as she moves, another ball of rope comes soaring over, releasing itself into a net before enveloping her, sending her rolling across the ground, completely trapped.

Panicking, everyone turns to look in the direction

from where the nets are coming. A cloaked man with a string of garlic round his neck appears at the edge of the field, pushing some kind of small cannon ahead of him.

I gasp. "The monster hunter!"

He lets out a roaring laugh as he surveys us. Chase emerges from behind him.

"Well, look what we have here?" the monster hunter bellows. "An entire field of monsters. It's my lucky day!"

"Chase, it's us! From the café! Tell him to stop!" Ari calls out.

"Chase, we'll need more than a net cannon," the monster hunter barks, causing Chase to tear his eyes away from Ari's pleading expression. "Come on, don't just stand around! Pass me the Sunlight Projector! Or the stakes, if they're closer!"

Sunlight Projector. Stakes.

My heart thudding against my chest, I frantically shout for Sharptooth, who appears at my side in a flash. "Get the vampires out of here, back to Skeleton Castle, safe in the enchantments! NOW!"

"But what about all of you?" she asks, panicked, as Bat-Ears flits around beside her, just as distressed. "And the werewolves!"

"He's not after us, he's after you! We'll help the

werewolves, but you have to get out of here now! Now, Sharptooth! Go!"

She turns to address the vampires, calling out, "Everyone retreat to Skeleton Castle! Go! Count Bloodthirst, send the bats!"

She's hardly finished her sentence and the vampires have disappeared, the monster hunter no match for their speed. Count Bloodthirst retreats to the trees, but lingers, appearing to be muttering something repeatedly under his breath.

A swarm of bats rises from the woodland, a storm of fluttering wings heading straight for the monster hunter and Chase.

"Whoa!" Ari gasps. "Is Count Bloodthirst doing that?"

"*Vampire magic*," Miles adds, as much in awe, watching the bats descend in a frenzied cloud.

"Ari, Miles, help Aunty Loveta get free!" I instruct as she continues to grapple with the ropes confining her. "I'm going after the monster hunter!"

Marrok and Aunty Loveta have transitioned into werewolves, attempting to gnaw through the ropes with their huge, sharp fangs. Miles and Ari share a startled look before they quickly get over it and begin tugging and pulling at the ropes, desperately trying to free them.

In the meantime, I run at the monster hunter and Chase, with Bat-Head flying alongside me and my parents hot on our heels, declaring that they're coming to help. Having cried out in irritation at the vampires vanishing, Oscar is now using one hand to dig inside his bag and the other one to swat away the mass of bats swarming around him. Chase is yelping in horror at the bats, crying out, "Dad! Dad! Stop them!"

Oscar finds what he's looking for in the bag and holds up a large green-and-yellow spiralled egg. He pushes down on the pink button at the top of it with his thumb and it sends out an energy pulse so strong, my parents are knocked backwards and the bats are all stunned, sent tumbling backwards through the air as though in slow motion.

It doesn't work on me or Bat-Head.

I pelt towards him, while Bat-Head, as though reading my mind, flies at Chase. I throw my arms around the monster hunter's waist, catching him off guard when he's focused on stunning the bats, tackling him to the ground. I hear Chase scream at the sight of another bat and there's a thud as he drops his bag and runs away into the distance, Bat-Head in hot pursuit, screeching as loud and threateningly as he can.

"What the—" The monster hunter pushes himself up on to his elbows, staring at me, perplexed, as I scramble to my feet next to him. "What are you DOING? Why are you trying to stop me! These are MONSTERS!"

I quickly sweep up Chase's bag from the grass, grab the first thing I can find and hold it out in front of me. At first glance, it looks like an old, heavy TV remote, with a bright yellow button in the middle of it. I point it straight at Oscar, who slowly stands.

"I would be very careful with that," Oscar says gravely, fear flashing across his eyes.

"What is it?" I ask, catching my breath and pushing back the wisps of hair falling into my eyes.

"That sucks away the voice of a banshee," he reveals. "That way they can never hurt anyone again." He reaches out his hand. "Please give that to me."

"You need to leave here and never come back," I tell him, refusing to pass it over.

His forehead creases in confusion, his eyes fixed on me, glinting with a mixture of anger and fascination. "Who *are* you?"

"I'm Maggie Helsby, the protector of Skeleton Woods and Goreway."

"*Helsby*," he repeats in a whisper. "The vampire slayer.

You protect these monsters?"

"They're NOT monsters!"

His mouth twists into a sinister smile and he bursts out laughing. "Oh, this is precious! You, a little girl, think you can stop what's coming?" He sneers at me, shaking his head. "I'm not going anywhere, Maggie Helsby."

"What do you mean? What's coming?"

"Everything," he says simply. "Monsters from all corners of the country; they're all coming to Skeleton Woods."

I boldly shake the banshee voice-controller at him to make sure he answers my question. "Why are they all coming here?"

"Because, for the first time in centuries, the enchantments have been weakened. Rumours travel fast in the world of monsters; they're all talking about it. The treasure of Skeleton Castle was a lost cause before, but now, they're coming for it, and I'll be here, ready to catch them."

I stare at him. "*What?* There's no treasure there!"

"The monsters think there is and they want to steal it. No ordinary treasure either, but ancient relics that can solve all their monster problems: money beyond their wildest dreams; long-lost books of ancient spells; rings of vampire magic that can make them human again." He snorts. "They'll believe anything. It's pathetic. You didn't think those wolves are here to simply make friends, did you?"

"Marrok *is* our friend!"

The monster hunter throws his head back and laughs menacingly. "HA! I thought the Helsby vampire slayers were meant to be clever! Was it you who asked for the enchantments around the woods to be tampered with so your family and friends could all be *buddies* with the vampires?"

He reads my expression and tuts loudly, shaking his head.

"Oh dear, Maggie Helsby, the downfall of Skeleton Woods and its vampires will all be because of you. If only you had sought the advice of someone who actually knows about these things." He places a hand on his chest. "Humans like us and monsters like them can never be friends. It's our destiny."

I'm so shocked, I can hardly breathe. I stand numbly, unable to say a word.

He smirks. "You know what, Maggie, I'll do as you say and leave, because this is just the beginning and I need to go prepare myself for all the monsters who are about to descend upon your quaint little town and these legendary woods."

He crouches down next to the net cannon and pulls on a lever sticking out its side, which allows it to be folded up neatly, like a bizarre wheelie case. Throwing his holdall over his shoulder, he gestures to Chase's bag.

"I'll let you keep the banshee voice-controller and all those monster-repellent goodies in there," he says, throwing me a pitying look as he turns to walk away. "You're going to need them."

CHAPTER

TWELVE

I've never been to a witches' council meeting before.

I'm not sure what to expect, but I'm very nervous and glad that Sharptooth is here with me. Count Bloodthirst invited both of us to join him in attending the meeting, which has been set up by Diana Dazzle as a matter of urgency. It takes place at midnight in the middle of another woodland a few miles away, much smaller than Skeleton Woods, but just as daunting in the darkness. My parents have insisted on coming, too, but Count Bloodthirst asks that they wait in the car at the edge of the woods. Considering I'm flanked by two vampires, they don't really need to worry about my safety.

They just need to worry about me getting told off by a coven of witches.

Or, rather, that's what I'm worried about.

"It will be fine," Sharptooth whispers as we make our way through the woods.

The leaves rustle in the wind, twigs crack under our feet, owls hoot eerily, hidden in the branches of the trees, and somewhere in the distance a fox lets out a blood-curdling cry. Bat-Head, hanging from my jumper, tucks himself further away under my coat.

"Oh, sure, absolutely nothing to be nervous about," I repeat with heavy sarcasm. "Just a load of magical people whose homes are now threatened thanks to me having lowered enchantments for a *party*. And then again for a castle tour. But, yeah, I'm sure they'll understand."

"I believe it was me who organized the celebration and then the tour," Count Bloodthirst says calmly, striding ahead of us, the bottom of his cloak sweeping leaves along as he goes. "The witches don't intimidate us."

"Speak for yourself," I mutter.

He stops abruptly as we reach the location of the meeting. The moonlight shines down on the seven gathered witches, all sitting cross-legged on the ground in a semicircle with their animal familiars by their side.

Peering out from behind Count Bloodthirst, I realize that the witches are not actually touching the ground, but floating just above it.

Cool.

"You made it," Diana Dazzle says, sitting to our right at the very end of the curve.

"And you're on time," another witch comments with a wry smile. "I seem to remember from the last instance you were called to join us, Count Bloodthirst, that you kept us waiting at least an hour."

"Ah yes, that's right," he replies coolly. "This time, the directions given to me were correct."

The witch scowls. "That was me who gave you the directions last time and they were perfectly good. It's not my fault that you clearly can't—"

Diana clears her throat. "I don't think we should waste any time. It's important that we focus on the larger problem at hand. Do we all agree?"

There's a ripple of murmured agreements, and, satisfied, Diana looks to the witch in the centre of the semicircle, sitting directly opposite us. She's tall and willowy with long wavy grey hair flowing over her shoulders and bright green eyes.

She speaks, her voice soft but authoritative.

"You're very welcome, Count Bloodthirst," she begins, before tilting her head to look past him at me. "And your friends, Sharptooth Shadow and Maggie Helsby. My name is Savannah Hex, and I am the chair of this council. Thank you for joining us tonight."

"I take it Diana has explained the current situation of Skeleton Woods," Count Bloodthirst says. "We hope we can work with you to resolve things swiftly."

Savannah gives a small smile. "I'm afraid there's rarely a swift solution to tampering with magic of such a complex nature as the enchantments surrounding Skeleton Woods. You really should have consulted us before attempting such a feat."

Diana Dazzle's eyes drop to the ground guiltily.

"Vampire decisions do not rely on approval from witch councils," Count Bloodthirst says drily.

"They should when they involve witch magic," Savannah tells him, a flash of irritation passing across her expression. She collects herself and gently adds, "Diana has expressed her regret at not consulting her fellow witches, but I understand why she was reluctant to do so – we're not the easiest of communities to persuade when it comes to aiding vampires."

"Let us not forget the countless occasions the

vampires have graciously helped the witches," Count Bloodthirst says haughtily. "Wasn't it just last year that you requested my aid in tracking down and stopping the witch who'd cast a spell turning a hundreds-strong audience of a concert hall into a bat army?"

Savannah flinches. "A small hiccup."

"When we found her, she was planning her takeover of No. 10 Downing Street," he reminds her, taking great pleasure in the recollection. "Without me, she would have succeeded."

"I don't know why she'd choose an army of bats," one of the witches mumbles with a sigh. "Surely if you can pick anything, you'd go with something frightening, like lions."

"Oh, I'm not so sure, bats can be *ferocious*," Sharptooth declares, gesturing to Bat-Ears, who is fast asleep on her head. He lets out a cute, squeaky snore. She quickly adds, "You should see him when he puts on his scary face."

"Anyway," Savannah says loudly, "this isn't about who does what for whom. This is about the enchantments of Skeleton Woods. Are they completely down, Count Bloodthirst?"

"Not yet. But it would seem they're significantly weakened."

Savannah looks to me thoughtfully. "Isn't this what you want, Maggie Helsby?"

I place a hand on my chest in surprise. "Me? No way! I want the enchantments back up and running, protecting the vampire community and the people of Goreway."

"A Helsby vampire slayer *protecting* Skeleton Castle. I never thought I'd see the day. You're very different to your Great Uncle Bram," she informs me. "He did a good job of keeping the communities separate and safe. I heartily approved of his approach."

Feeling chastised, I look at the ground. "I didn't mean for this to happen."

"But you're friends with the vampires, aren't you?" she points out, gesturing to Sharptooth with her hand, gem-set gold rings on each of her long, delicate fingers. "Why should it be a problem if anyone is free to roam the woods? I thought your community was *vegetarian* now" – she fails to hide a sneer at this – "so I don't see why the witches should go out of their way to solve your mess."

Count Bloodthirst looks to the sky impatiently.

There's clearly a big divide between the witches and vampires, something I was aware of but still feel uncomfortable witnessing first-hand.

Although I do think there's hope to change that. After all, the vampires played football with the werewolves, their greatest nemesis, right? And Diana seems to be able to hang out with Count Bloodthirst without the two of them making mean jibes the *whole* time.

Maybe working on this will help bring them together!

Or it could make their relationship much worse.

Oh well. Let's hope for the best.

"Look," I begin, stepping forwards, "I trust the vampires not to hurt anyone, so that's not the issue here. The problem is, there are rumours about treasure hidden away in Skeleton Castle that seem to be attracting a variety of … uh … creatures. And that, in turn, has brought the monster hunter to Goreway."

"The monster hunter." Diana's eyes widen in horror. "He's *here*?"

"Yes."

"How could he have made his way to the region without any of our scouts raising the alarm?" the witch next to Diana asks. "It's not possible."

"He has the means of going unnoticed, even to us," Savannah says, looking uneasy. "The tools and equipment at his disposal have been honed by monster hunters for centuries. He is able to sneak up on the supernatural without warning."

"Something we witnessed first-hand when he disturbed our football match recently," I inform them. "The vampires got safely back to the castle, but he managed to capture two werewolves and—"

"Werewolves were playing football with the vampires?" Diana asks with great interest. "How can that be?"

"We looked past our differences," Sharptooth says brightly, giving her a wonky smile. "Did you know that werewolves can lick their elbows? None of us can! Honestly, give it a go and you can't!" She does a demonstration, sticking her tongue out and bending her arm towards her, attempting to reach. "See? But werewolves can do it no problem! Since learning that from Marrok, I have a newfound respect for werewolves, don't you?"

There's a pause as the witches stare at her in baffled silence.

Sharptooth beams back at them.

Eventually, Savannah clears her throat. "Do go on, Maggie."

"Yeah, so, the monster hunter got two of the werewolves with this net-cannon thing, but we managed to get one of his bags off him that contained special knives that could cut through the rope – it was werewolf-proof. They couldn't use their fangs or claws to free themselves. It was terrifying. Even with the amazing hearing of the vampires, bats AND werewolves, he was able to get close enough to attack us."

For the first time in our conversation, Savannah looks genuinely worried.

"The monster hunter recently captured a witch who was visiting London from Transylvania," she informs us gravely. "We think he has imprisoned her somewhere in the city, but we haven't had any luck in tracking her down. Do you know where he is now?"

"No, but I know he's in the area. He's lying in wait for the swathes of monsters he predicts will start to make their way here in the hope of getting to Skeleton Castle. We've already met a few of them, and I'm scared they're all in danger."

"You're scared *for* the monsters?" Savannah checks in surprise.

"Of course!"

Her piercing eyes bore into mine. "You are … unusual, Maggie Helsby. I hope the path you've chosen is the right one. Change has its consequences, you know."

The monster hunter's words that have been haunting me since I spoke to him flash across my mind: *Humans like us and monsters like them can never be friends. It's our destiny.*

I won't let him be right. I have to save the vampires.

"Please help us to restore the enchantments," I plead, addressing all the witches there. "With them back up and running, the monsters won't come and then the monster hunter will go away."

"He won't go away. He'll just hunt them elsewhere," Diana adds pointedly.

"I guess. But my job is to protect Goreway and Skeleton Woods." I turn back to face Savannah. "If you won't restore the enchantments for the vampires, then at least consider the local witches who are currently under threat from the monster hunter, too. Making things back to the way they were also benefits your community."

She listens to my case, then informs us that they'll need a moment to confer.

"Very well," Count Bloodthirst says, spinning round with an expert vampire swish, his cloak cracking as he turns.

He walks just a few paces away, encouraging me and

Sharptooth to follow him. We huddle together as the witches do the same. I watch them curiously.

"They're not talking," I complain, frowning over at the witches, who are silently standing together, looking from one to the other.

"Oh yes, they are," Count Bloodthirst says. "They're using a spell that allows their minds to communicate."

I gawp at them. "*Seriously?* Cool."

"Not as cool as vampire magic," Sharptooth says loftily.

"Obviously," I assure her.

After what feels like a long time of kicking around leaves and watching Bat-Ears and Bat-Head squabble over an acorn – as usual, Count Bloodthirst's bat ignores them, much too superior to join in on such nonsense – the witches finally conclude their silent conversation and we're invited to join them back in the clearing.

"We've decided that the enchantments will need to be restored to Skeleton Woods," Savannah says abruptly, but holds up her hand before I can start thanking her. "However, as we have been discussing at length, it's not a simple spell to put them back the way they were. These are no ordinary enchantments, they're delicate and complex, created a long time ago in harmony with the trees themselves and the creatures that they protect."

"Okay." I nod. "So what does that mean?"

"It means, in order to do the spell, we're going to need the magical item with which the spell was created all those years ago; it's a priceless and powerful relic of vampire magic," she says, fixing Count Bloodthirst with a steely gaze.

He narrows his eyes at her. "We don't have it. I've told you, there is no treasure in the castle. Those rumours are false."

"I know you don't have it, Count Bloodthirst, but that doesn't change my answer. You're going to need to get it. Then we can do the spell."

"What is this item?" I ask, looking between them.

She takes a deep breath. "Dracula's Ring."

Sharptooth jolts next to me. "*Dracula's Ring*," she repeats in amazement. "That's what was used to create the enchantments of Skeleton Woods."

"It's the only magical item that can create such specific magic," Count Bloodthirst informs her matter-of-factly, while Sharptooth gazes up at him in disbelief. "I should have known that it would be necessary to restore the original enchantments. I naively assumed that they could be lowered and returned without it once they were in place."

"Don't beat yourself up. I was under the same impression," Diana sighs.

"Okay, so we need this ring and then you can do the spell and everything will be fine! Great!" I exclaim enthusiastically, my spirit lifting. "Where do we find it? Count Bloodthirst, you once implied Dracula is a real vampire – does he have it? Are you pals by any chance?"

Count Bloodthirst flinches. "*Pals* might be a stretch. There was a time that we were great enemies – he's always been threatened by me as a much younger, more powerful vampire. Now he seems to have accepted it, and I suppose you could say we tolerate one another."

"So you're frenemies," I say, much to his distaste. "He might lend you the ring, then, if you ask nicely."

"He doesn't have it," Count Bloodthirst tells me impatiently. "It's simply named after him because he helped to forge it. Something he loves to boast about. I have been instrumental in forging several magical vampire items, but do you hear me bragging about them? No." He pauses, adding, "I suppose I must give him credit for his branding and marketing skills."

"If Dracula doesn't have it, then where is it?" I ask.

"We're not sure," Savannah replies.

I blink at her. "Huh?"

"Some believed it to be under the care of the Skeleton Woods' vampires—"

"Which it's not," Count Bloodthirst emphasizes.

"So then it's likely to still be with the witch family," she concludes.

"What witch family?" I ask, clasping my hands together. "Please say one of yours."

She offers me a sympathetic smile. "Afraid not. As you'll know, Count Bloodthirst, the last official known use of the powerful vampire magic of Dracula's Ring in this country was the Skeleton Woods enchantments – either the ring is with the vampires who required those spells, or it was left in the hands of the witch who helped to create them. She came over from Transylvania to conjure the spells. It wouldn't surprise me if the ring was taken back to Dracula's homeland."

"So, it's in the hands of witches, even though it's a *vampire* relic," Count Bloodthirst mutters in disgust, receiving a sharp look from Savannah.

"Transylvania," I say slowly, trying to process this information and not freak out. "We need to go to Transylvania to get the ring we need to do this spell."

"You'll also need to persuade the witch who has inherited the ring, and therefore become its protector, to loan it to you. I warn you now, that might be the tricky part. Unlike us, some witches aren't so welcoming to vampires."

"Because you've all been a hoot," Count Bloodthirst says sarcastically.

"Can't one of you get it on our behalf?" Sharptooth suggests hopefully. "I know it's a lot to ask, but they're much more likely to loan it to a fellow witch, right?"

"That idea did come up in our conferring," Savannah acknowledges, glancing at Diana, "but it's impossible. None of us can spare the time … and to be honest, we'd rather not advertise to our international friends that we're in league with vampires. It might destroy our relationship. If you want to return Skeleton Woods to how it was, you'll have to find a way to get Dracula's Ring yourselves. Once you have the ring, Diana is willing to attempt to restore the enchantments with it."

"There's only a small chance it will work for me," Diana adds. "According to legend, an item of that kind of vampire magic selects its sorcerer."

"Okay, let me check I have this right," I announce. "We need to find a way to get to Transylvania, and once we're there, we then need to persuade a witch to loan the vampires her ancient, priceless, magical ring. Then we have to bring the ring to you and then see if said ring even works. And if it doesn't…"

I trail off, looking to Savannah expectantly.

"We'll have to work out a plan B before monsters take over Skeleton Woods and the castle, whilst also ensuring we're not wiped out by the infamous monster hunter," Count Bloodthirst finishes.

"Wonderful," I croak.

"You'll be pleased to hear that we do have the name of the witch family and where you can find them in Transylvania," Diana says, attempting to sound positive. "I'll send Count Bloodthirst the details by bat and I can alert them when you're coming."

I give her a weak smile. I suppose that is *something*. "Thank you. And thanks for agreeing to help us when we have the ring."

"We'll do what we can," Diana promises.

Savannah clicks her fingers and seven broomsticks appear from thin air. Each witch steps forward, grasping the broomstick lined up for them.

"It's time for us to go," she declares. "We wish you luck in your endeavours."

"Thank you," Count Bloodthirst says. "May the bats be with you."

With a curt nod, Savannah calls out, "I declare this council meeting adjourned."

With that, the witches mount their brooms and disappear into the night. Once they're gone, I lean back against a tree and bury my head in my hands.

"Don't worry, Maggie, everything is going to be all right," Sharptooth assures me, placing a hand on my shoulder. "We'll work it out together."

"First things first," Count Bloodthirst says, stroking his chin, "we must plan a trip to Transylvania. It will be difficult for us to go, we'll need to travel at night only, which of course makes things a lot more complicated. And then—"

"A trip," I repeat quietly, lifting my head.

Sharptooth reads my expression and her eyes light up. "You have an idea!"

"I think I know how to get to Transylvania," I say, nodding slowly as a plan begins to form. "Although we're going to need some help."

The next day, Mr Frank opens the door of the head teacher's office to find me, Ari and Miles waiting for him outside. We leap to our feet as he emerges.

"Well?" Ari asks, holding up crossed fingers.

"It wasn't easy to persuade her," Mr Frank admits, before a smile creeps over his lips. "But I'd better let the parents know the school trip will no longer be to Rome."

"YES!" I cry, high-fiving the others. "Transylvania, here we come!"

CHAPTER

THIRTEEN

"This is going to be a *disaster,*" Mr Frank whispers.

I might just agree with him. Not because we've changed the trip last minute from Rome to Transylvania, prompting a HUGE barrage of questions from parents and students, and not even because Mr Frank has had to come up with a completely new itinerary, hotel and restaurant bookings for fifty students in Transylvania at the last minute.

The reason the school trip is probably going to be a disaster is because we're bringing a vampire.

Sharptooth is coming.

There was no stopping her. As soon as I told her and Count Bloodthirst that the school trip to Transylvania had been approved, she insisted that she come with me.

"I'm not letting you meet that witch and try to get that ring on your own, Maggie," she told me stubbornly, folding her arms. "Magical creatures aren't all as friendly as vampires, you know."

I tried to talk her out of it, largely for practical reasons, as I really didn't fancy her turning into a big pile of dust the moment she stepped out of the woodlands for the day, but she decided that she would risk irritating the local witch council one more time by asking if they could provide her with the magic that allows vampires to be in the sun unharmed.

Sharptooth must have done a good job persuading Count Bloodthirst to agree that she should accompany me on the Dracula's Ring quest, because he managed to get Diana Dazzle on side, too. She's agreed to do the daylight spell for Sharptooth.

Understandably, we're all a bit nervous. I'm terrified for Sharptooth, keeping everything crossed that Diana's spell will work for all three days, whilst Mr Frank is struggling to relax over the idea of heading up a school trip that secretly includes a werewolf, a vampire and two bats.

"It will be *fine*," I insist, standing next to him as he wrings his hands nervously whilst the other students begin to climb into the coach that's just pulled up to the school. "What's the worst that can happen?"

He stops fiddling and turns to stare at me in disbelief.

"Okay," I say, holding my hands up, "I suppose there are some bad things that could happen. But it's very unlikely. We know now that Marrok is a nice werewolf, and there's no chance that Sharptooth is going to hurt anyone. Plus, I've had a very stern word with Bat-Head to stay hidden when we're in public, and I'm sure Sharptooth will have done the same with Bat-Ears."

"Do bats always do as they're told?" he asks.

I hesitate, thinking about my spat with Bat-Head last night when he decided that ripping up my homework with his bat claws was a fun new game. Before I can say anything, Mr Frank reads my expression and closes his eyes with despair.

"I'm going to get fired after this, aren't I?" he whimpers.

"Hi, Maggie," Marrok says, strolling over to us after passing his bag to the coach driver to load up with the others. "Hey, Mr Frank."

"How is your aunt doing?" I ask him, worried about the effect the monster hunter's appearance may have had on the pack. "Is she okay?"

"It will take more than being captured in a net to upset her," he comments, just as Jason, the boy who first saw the ghost, walks past. He gives us a strange look and Marrok quickly explains, "I'm talking about … my pet fish."

Jason nods and then goes to join Toby and Jenny, who are about to board the coach. The three of them have become close friends over their shared experience of the supernatural. Ari told me that she overheard them talking about filming a documentary that would include interviews with Jason about the ghost, Toby about the monster, and Jenny's grandmother about the zombies. Word on the street is the postman had a run-in with a goblin over the weekend, so he's keen to tell his story, too.

"Any news on the monster hunter?" Marrok continues in a low voice, once Jason is safely out of earshot. "Do we know where he is?"

"No. Are your dad and Aunty Loveta going to be all right, knowing he's around somewhere?"

Marrok nods. "They've put precautions in place. We can cover our tracks now we know we're being hunted. I've made them promise to send me regular updates; they insisted I come on the school trip. Have you got a plan yet as to what to do about him?"

Mr Frank and I share a glance. We've agreed that we can't tell Marrok about Dracula's Ring and restoring the enchantments. We know that his pack need to live in an isolated area near a woodland, so that they're able to transform and run free when they can, without being seen by humans. Large woodlands like the one in Goreway offer the perfect cover. Aunty Loveta did say something about the werewolves and vampires learning to live with each other only "for now", so it must only be a temporary plan, but I also get the feeling that Marrok has found his place here in Goreway. Maybe they'll think of staying.

I don't want to break it to Marrok quite yet that we are hoping to solve everything by kicking them out, too. It feel terrible about it, but there's no other solution.

"We have a few ideas," I say breezily, looking away from Mr Frank, who is visibly upset about lying to Marrok. "One thing is for sure, we have to do what we can to get the monster hunter to leave Goreway."

"I couldn't agree more," Marrok says. "Let me know if I can do anything to help. I'm here if you need."

I nod, feeling too guilty to say anything else. Oblivious to anything amiss, he notices two people approaching the school and gasps.

"Is that … *Sharptooth*?"

When we see her, Mr Frank groans and I have to clamp my hand over my mouth to stop myself from laughing. Accompanied by Diana Dazzle, who seems to be guiding her with constant encouraging words, Sharptooth looks absolutely ridiculous, bulked out by what must be several layers of clothes covered by a huge puffer coat that is so long it covers her feet and trails along the ground. Wearing thick woollen mittens, she has the coat's hood up over her head and, on top of that, is wearing a gigantic, wide-brimmed, floppy woven sunhat and big bug sunglasses that take over her face. She's carrying an open floral umbrella over her shoulder like a parasol to block out any sun.

She's also walking at a snail's pace, shuffling along as though her legs are tied together, too terrified to take a longer stride that might expose her feet to a glimpse of sun outside of the umbrella's shade, despite wearing wellington boots.

"He-ey, Sharptooth," I say, biting my lip to stop myself from giggling. "Wow. Look at you!"

"I know!" She hobbles over to us. "I'm outside! In the daytime! And I haven't turned into dust! I'm like a Normal Human Being!"

"You sure are." I elbow Marrok in the ribs as he sniggers, his eyes watering from doing his best not to laugh out loud. "Does the spell not work without all these" – I gesture to the hat and umbrella – "safeguards?"

"It works perfectly without them," Diana answers through gritted teeth. She has obviously had a tiring time persuading Sharptooth to take her first steps into the light. "But Sharptooth wanted to be extra safe."

Glancing around to make sure no one else is listening – although Sharptooth is beginning to get a lot of strange looks from those still getting on to the coach – Diana holds out a small vial of bright, sparkling orange liquid hanging from a silver necklace.

"I've told Sharptooth, but to remind everyone, she'll need to take two drops of this every four hours to keep the spell topped up. Don't lose this vial – I had to ask a warlock to mix up this potion for me and witches hate warlocks, so I won't be asking for any extra."

"How many enemies do witches have?" I ask, trying to keep up.

"We'd have fewer if people we helped simply listened to us without asking unnecessary questions," she replies, narrowing her eyes at me.

"Sorry. I promise we won't lose it, right, Sharptooth?"

"Of course not." Sharptooth smiles. "I don't want to be dust. I like being alive! Even though I'm not alive. Because I'm a vampire, if you get what I mean."

"Please try not to say things like that in front of anyone," Mr Frank begs.

"Here's her passport." Diana holds it out to Mr Frank. "Quite proud of the magic I conjured to create that. It has excellent detail."

"How come you're coming on the school trip, Sharptooth?" Marrok asks, amused.

"She wanted to experience human culture," I quickly reply, at the same time as Sharptooth says, "In case the monster hunter comes looking."

Marrok frowns in confusion, and Sharptooth and I glance at each other, panicked.

We probably should have discussed our cover story beforehand.

"Both those things," I explain, forcing a laugh. "She wanted to experience human culture AND make sure we're okay if the monster hunter tracked us on the trip. Anyway, we should get on the coach and get to the airport, right, Mr Frank? Don't want to miss our flight! And remember, Sharptooth, if anyone asks, you're my visiting cousin."

"Got it," Sharptooth states, before practising her line:

"I'm Maggie's human cousin, who is visiting. And also is human."

Bat-Ears pokes his head out from the top of her coat and squeaks impatiently. Bat-Head, tucked away in my backpack, responds with a screech.

Mr Frank sighs, repeatedly muttering, "I'm going to lose my job" as he walks away.

"Good luck," Diana says, passing Sharptooth the vial of potion.

Sharptooth takes it gratefully. Ari and Miles finally show up, running through the school gates. They're busy squabbling as they rush over to the driver and help him to load their bags on to the coach, the last two to arrive.

"I knew I'd forgotten something," Ari is saying crossly. "If you hadn't been yelling at me to hurry up, I would have remembered my toothbrush. Now what am I going to do?"

"You can buy one in the airport," Miles snaps. "And I wouldn't have been yelling if you'd been ready on time. Why didn't you pack the night before instead of leaving it until this morning?"

"You are SUCH a grandpa sometimes, Miles," she huffs, walking over to our group.

They suddenly spot Sharptooth and both freeze. Ari breaks into a wide grin.

"Well," she begins, her eyes sparkling with joy, "this is going to be interesting!"

Sitting next to me on the coach, Sharptooth slams her hands against the window, her face squished against the glass as we pull away from the school.

"WHAT'S HAPPENING?" she cries.

"The coach is moving," I whisper, noticing heads swivelling to look at us. "Remember, this is how humans get around. By vehicles."

"THIS IS CRAZY!" she marvels loudly. "WHEEEEEEEEEEEEEE!"

I slide lower in my seat, cringing.

If this is her reaction to a bus, what is she going to be like on a plane?!

"Maggie! Maggie! Look at me!"

Having stealthily set Bat-Head and Bat-Ears free to fly up to the rafters of the airport building and hide there until we board the plane, I turn just as I'm about to go through security to see Sharptooth has jumped up and climbed into one of the trays along with the hand luggage, liquids and her giant coat.

She is about to be scanned through the X-ray machine.

"Sharptooth! Get down!" I hiss, as the security guards echo my instruction.

Mr Frank facepalms in despair behind the queue of people gawping at her, and she cheerily hops off, exclaiming, "That was fun!"

Ari and I are busy spritzing perfume in duty-free when we hear a piercing scream and spin round just in time to see the guy working at the sunglasses shop faint, flopping dramatically to the floor.

Sharptooth stands next to him, looking VERY guilty as she places a pair of sunglasses back on the rack and then comes shuffling over to us, while his colleagues run to his aid.

"He was helping me to find a pair that suited my face," she confides in us. "Then he told me to look in the mirror, so I did! I forgot that I don't have a reflection so all he saw was a pair of sunglasses floating in the air."

"Maybe just stick with us from now on," Ari advises, putting an arm around her and guiding her away.

The air steward stops the trolley at our row and smiles down at us.

"Would you like any drinks or snacks?"

Sharptooth, who has had the time of her life experiencing taking off in a plane, beams up at him.

"Yes, please! Do you have any ketchup?"

"What would you like it with?"

"I would like ketchup on its own, please."

"Oh." He falters. "Uh … we do have some ketchup sachets."

"I'll take the lot," she says brightly. "How much will that be in human money?"

Astonished, he digs into a tray and pulls out a handful of ketchup sachets.

"There's no charge for these," he informs her, before moving along.

"Wow! You get these free on planes?" She tears open a sachet and squeezes the ketchup into her mouth. "I LOVE flying!"

Bat-Head and Bat-Ears, both hidden in my bag under the seat in front, screech in agreement. When someone in the row ahead of us curiously peers back through the seats, I act as though the noise came from me, by unconvincingly going, "SQUEE! SQUEE! I'm VERY excited about our holiday! SQUEE!"

His eyes then shift across to Sharptooth, squeezing

the ketchup straight on to her tongue and smacking her lips, before tearing open another sachet.

He recoils in horror.

I might pretend to be asleep for the rest of the flight.

Waiting for our bus to pick us up from arrivals, a woman taps Sharptooth on the shoulder.

"Excuse me," she begins, looking Sharptooth up and down, "are you, by any chance, from the tourism board?"

"No, I'm from Goreway! I'm a visiting human cousin!"

The woman seems confused. "You're not dressed up like a vampire to welcome tourists here, then?"

"I am not a real vampire," Sharptooth says, gravely serious. "Not at all. I am a human. A real-life HUMAN."

"Would you mind taking a selfie? You really look like the real deal," the woman asks coyly, holding up her phone.

"What's a selfie?" Sharptooth frowns. "I don't like taking things. That's stealing."

Chuckling at her, the woman holds her phone up, standing close to Sharptooth and smiling at the camera pointing down at them. "One – two – three!"

As she presses the button, her phone suddenly combusts, bursting into flames.

She screams, dropping it to the ground.

"Oh look, our bus has arrived!" I croak, dragging Sharptooth away as the woman stares after us, her mouth open in shock. "I hope you've got insurance!"

I slump down on my bed in the hotel room and close my eyes, as Bat-Ears and Bat-Head fly out the open window to stretch their wings.

"We made it to Transylvania. I can't believe it," I say in wonder.

Ari and Sharptooth, who are sharing the room, drop their bags – or in Sharptooth's case, her umbrella – and both come to lie down in relief next to me.

"Wow!" Sharptooth exclaims, wiggling around. "Beds are a lot more comfortable than coffins!"

"Who would have thought it?" Ari smiles, catching my eye.

We burst into infectious giggles and don't stop until Mr Frank knocks on our door and tells us it's time for lights out.

We've got a big day tomorrow.

CHAPTER

FOURTEEN

"What do you mean we're not coming?"

Ari stops in her tracks, frowning at me.

"Sharptooth and I have to visit the witch alone," I emphasize, careful to keep my voice down. I don't know where Marrok is, but I hope he's out of werewolf-hearing distance.

I meant to wait until later to tell her and Miles that I didn't want them to join us in finding Dracula's Ring, but Ari has been going on and on at me about what the plan is all day and I can't put her off any longer.

So far, despite all obstacles, the trip has been a success. Before we left, Diana had made contact with the witch coven here to prepare them for our arrival, and it had been agreed that we'd meet them late tonight, which meant that we could spend the day with the rest of the school group enjoying the sights of Transylvania.

Our first stop has been Braşov, an amazing medieval city of Gothic architecture. We spent a long time admiring this huge square called the Piaţa Sfatului, where Mr Frank told us all about how it was the place of public trials and executions during the Middle Ages.

"I can sense a vampire presence here," Sharptooth had said excitedly, receiving odd looks from our peers. "I think they must have pretended to be executed and then just gone about their night when everyone went home!"

Ari was eyeing up some street food and didn't look all that impressed when Mr Frank announced we had to move on to visit a Gothic church, but she brightened when he mentioned that afterwards we'd be going on a cable car to see the view. After a delicious lunch where we took over a café and the waiters looked perplexed at the number of us descending upon the tables, we have been allowed some time to explore the quaint shops.

"Why don't you want us to come with you tonight?" Miles asks.

"I'm not going to put you in any danger," I say firmly,

walking onwards. "We don't know this witch or how she's going to react."

"But you might need our help," Ari points out, falling into step with me. "We don't want you to be in any danger, either."

"I'll have Sharptooth. Seriously, I think it's better if there are only two of us. She might not be so welcoming if we arrive as a big group. And none of this is your responsibility. I'm the Helsby slayer, who has to protect everyone. This is all on me. I have to be the one to sort out this mess."

Ari and Miles share a look.

Miles sighs. "If you're sure."

"Don't worry, I'll protect Maggie," Sharptooth assures them, inspecting a stand of Transylvania key rings. "Should anything happen, I'm good at taekwondo. Also, I'm a vampire. We'll be just fine!"

She promptly selects a key ring, but forgets her vampire strength, accidentally pulling the whole stand toppling towards her. Yelping in surprise, she defensively headbutts it, sending it flying back the other way, knocking into the other stands lining the side of the shop. There's a ripple of crashes as the stands fall one after the other like dominoes, sending key rings, fridge magnets, mugs, postcards and ornamental souvenirs scattering across the floor of the shop.

We survey the damage in horror.

"Oh, yes," Ari breathes, "I'm sure you'll be *just fine*."

Sharptooth and I wait until everyone is asleep before creeping out through the hotel with Bat-Head and Bat-Ears flitting along above us. Mr Frank has come to wave us off, making me promise that I'll call him at the first sense of any danger.

"Remember, Dracula's Ring is an ancient relic of unparalleled value," he whispers anxiously, walking us to the front door. "If she has it, it's unlikely that she'll simply hand it over. And if she gets insulted by you asking, don't push her on it, just come back. We can work out a different way of persuading her; we still have time here to work it out. You're not in this alone, Maggie."

"Thanks, but we'll be okay," I assure him with a confident smile. "She wouldn't have agreed to meet us if she wasn't willing to at least hear us out."

He nods, his forehead creased. "Here, I want you to take this," he says, holding out a small pocketbook.

It's old, bound in faded brown leather. I flick through it; each page contains what looks like a poem – some a few lines, others much longer – illustrated with intricate symbols and patterns.

"What is this?"

"Wow!" Sharptooth exclaims excitedly, looking over my shoulder, along with Bat-Ears and Bat-Head, who both fly down to admire it. "That's vampire magic!"

"Yes, it's a book of what's believed to be vampire enchantments," Mr Frank reveals. "As far as I can tell, it was first published in the 1500s; this copy of course dates much later than that, the 1900s. They're only basic spells, but interesting all the same."

I look up from the book. "Where did you get this?"

"It took me a while," he reveals, "but eventually I tracked it down in a second-hand bookshop in central London. I took a trip there and managed to get a very good price. I don't think the seller really knew what it was."

"Mr Frank, you know even if I read out these spells, I can't conjure vampire magic, right?" I remind him.

"Not even *I* can do vampire magic," Sharptooth adds, taking the book from me and examining the first few pages. "It is very rare, and chooses the vampires who can conjure it. Count Bloodthirst is one of the lucky few."

"I know all that, but I also believe in trusting my gut,"

Mr Frank asserts. "I knew I had to get my hands on this book and, once I had it, every feeling was telling me to give it to you, Maggie. You never know, it might come in handy somehow."

I smile at him. "Thanks, Mr Frank."

"Just doing my job," he says, glancing nervously out at the darkness through the window. "Promise me you'll be careful."

"Promise."

I tuck the book into the pocket of my coat and follow Sharptooth out into the cold night air to make our way to the address Diana gave us. It's quite far from where we're staying, but as it's the dead of night, Sharptooth is able to use her vampire speed, carrying me over her shoulder, zipping through the streets so quickly that the ground beneath me turns into a dark blur and I have to shut my eyes tightly to stop myself from feeling dizzy.

When she stops and sets me down, I have to take a moment, not just to steady myself, but also to double-check she's got the right address. We're not in a woodland or anywhere near one – this is a built-up area and right in front of us is a modern block of flats. You'd expect a witch to live in some kind of spooky haunted house. Although I guess they are supposed to blend in.

Bat-Ears and Bat-Head come swooping down from the sky to land on our shoulders, having enjoyed flying freely above us.

"Diana said to press the buzzer for number thirteen," Sharptooth reveals, strolling up to the door. "Are you ready?"

"I think so."

She reaches out and presses the button next to "13", and a crackling voice comes out of the intercom. We can't hear what they're saying, but the door emits a low whirring, signalling it's unlocked. We push it open and start the climb to the third floor, where we find number 13 at the end of the corridor. Confused by this setting, which is not what I expected at all, I lift my hand and knock gingerly on the door.

It swings open and we're confronted by a woman in a long-sleeved black dress. Wearing striking black eye make-up, she looks in her twenties and has a purple-streaked peroxide-blonde pixie-cut hairstyle.

"Sorry," I say quickly, "I think we've got the wrong—"

"Maggie Helsby, I'm guessing," she says to me. "I've been expecting you."

She gives me a good look over and then her eyes drift across to Sharptooth. She scowls, jutting out her chin, while Sharptooth refuses to flinch under her glare.

"And you must be the *vampire*," she adds, not bothering to hide her disdain.

Sharptooth opens her mouth to reply, but before she can say anything, Bat-Head and Bat-Ears swoop over the witch's head and into her home.

"Sorry!" I wince as she ducks in surprise, prompting Sharptooth to snigger at her reaction. "They're very rude."

"It's fine," the witch seethes, glancing over her shoulder to see them flit about the apartment. "As long as they don't disturb my familiar. She doesn't take kindly to pests."

"Pests?" Sharptooth looks furious. "I'll have you know that vampire bats are—"

"Is there any way we can come inside," I interrupt, aware that we're still standing in the corridor. "We might be overheard here."

The witch reluctantly stands aside to allow us in. I step into her flat and take in the brightly decorated interiors of the open-plan space.

All her furniture is modern, with bold, block-coloured sofas, patterned rugs and gold-framed glass coffee tables. There are glossy home and interior magazines stacked on the bottom shelf of her overfilled, busy bookcase that sits in one corner of the room, and on the other side is a large wide-screen TV. Several candles are lit, dotted around the room, filling her home with a musky, floral fragrance.

"You look surprised," our host comments, coming to stand in front of me after closing the door. "What were you expecting? Some kind of spooky underground lair? Perhaps a haunted castle. I'm afraid only the vampire community go in for such dramatics."

"Whatever," Sharptooth huffs. "Haunted castles are awesome."

"We blend in with humans," the witch continues to me, ignoring her. "Witches are able to live just like they do, but with the added advantage of casting spells."

"Some might see that as *trickery*," Sharptooth comments.

I turn to Sharptooth and whisper sharply, "Remember why we're here."

Sharptooth purses her lips grumpily. Whether she likes it or not, we need this witch to grant us a favour. There's a sudden loud hiss and angry meow from a corner of the room as Bat-Head flies too low and disturbs a snoozing black cat, curled up on her bed.

"That's my familiar, Glinda," the witch says. "And I'm Elena."

"Are familiars like witch companions?" I ask, watching the black cat curiously.

"We're much more than that," Glinda answers herself. "We guide our witches and set them on the right path. Of course, our witches can choose to ignore our advice; for example, I told Elena that it would be a bad idea to welcome a vampire into our home, but she decided not to listen."

"I'm very pleased you didn't," I tell Elena enthusiastically. "Thank you so much for giving us a chance to speak to you."

She gestures for us to take a seat on the teal sofa, while she sits down on the bright orange armchair next to it. Having got a fright from Glinda, Bat-Head joins me on the sofa, hopping up on to my lap, while Bat-Ears, content with having explored Elena's flat, comes to land on Sharptooth's knee, wrapping his wings around himself and clasping her trouser material with his feet before contentedly toppling forwards and falling asleep.

"I was intrigued," Elena admits. "Normally I wouldn't even consider hosting a vampire, but Diana mentioned that it was regarding a matter to do with the monster hunter. She wouldn't tell me anything else."

"You know about the monster hunter, then."

"How do *you* know about him?"

"He's in our town, Goreway, now. We need to get rid of him and, in particular, keep him away from the vampire community in Skeleton Woods," I explain. "He is very dangerous. Vampires have very good hearing, but they can't hear him sneak up on them, and neither could the werewolves. Two of our werewolf friends were captured recently, but luckily we were able to help them to escape with a knife the monster hunter left behind."

She frowns. "You are friends with werewolves as well as vampires?"

"I'm friends with the werewolves, too," Sharptooth informs her proudly. "They can lick their elbows."

"How strange," Elena drily remarks. "So you want to stop the monster hunter. But why would you need to come all the way to Transylvania for my help to do that?"

"There are ancient enchantments around Skeleton Woods and they've been weakened. A lot of monsters seem to think there is treasure hidden away in Skeleton Castle—"

"I've heard of those rumours, and they don't surprise me." Elena narrows her eyes at Sharptooth. "Vampires keeping a hoard of treasure for themselves. Sounds right up your street."

"The only treasure we have at Skeleton Castle is the tomato ketchup I've been stockpiling. You can buy the bottles in bulk," Sharptooth announces indignantly. "And don't even think about coming for the ketchup. You won't get through me."

Elena wrinkles her nose. "Why would I want *ketchup*?"

"Why WOULDN'T you want it more like?" Sharptooth retorts.

"The point is," I continue, raising my voice and shooting Sharptooth a warning glance, "because the enchantments are weakened, monsters are coming to Goreway, hoping to get a share of the treasure. That, in turn, has attracted the monster hunter. It's not just the vampires who are in danger, it's the magical community. Witches will be in danger too if we don't stop him."

Shifting in her seat, Elena looks down at her hands in her lap. "I'm aware of that. It would seem we have a common enemy. I've been planning a trip to England to track him down. The monster hunter has captured my aunt."

I gasp. "*What?* When?"

"Recently. I didn't realize she'd been kidnapped at first; I thought she was enjoying her holiday and being useless at staying in touch. But he found her in London and has imprisoned her there, I believe."

"The witch council did say that a witch from Transylvania had been captured," Sharptooth recalls. "I'm sorry about your aunt, that's not very nice. If Count Bloodthirst or one of the vampires from the castle was captured by the monster hunter, I'd be very upset."

Elena looks confused by Sharptooth saying anything nice, so hesitates before she speaks, as though she's waiting for Sharptooth to burst out cackling and yell "JOKING".

When she can see that Sharptooth is perfectly serious, she replies a little softer than before, "Yes. Thank you. It's been upsetting."

"You can help us to protect our community from him, and we can help you to find your aunt," I assure her.

"How are you going to protect the vampires from him?" Elena asks curiously.

"We need to strengthen the enchantments around Skeleton Woods. Return them to how they used to be, before we tampered with them."

Elena nods. "That kind of spell is very powerful. It is created in harmony with the trees. Not an easy bit of magic."

"That's why we're here," I state. "We think you may have something that we need to recreate those enchantments. The ones that were created by someone in your family centuries ago."

She scrutinizes my expression. "Hang on. You're talking about…"

"Dracula's Ring," I confirm. "We were hoping you would help us to find it."

She throws her head back and laughs, startling both bats, before they fall back asleep again. Sharptooth and I share a look, surprised by her outburst. We wait for her to finish giggling.

"You're joking. You want me to hand over Dracula's Ring to a vampire and a young girl with a bat sidekick?" Elena shakes her head. "Did you really think I'd be able to simply give it to you?"

"We would look after it, I promise," I say.

She snorts. "There's no chance I'd trust the word of a vampire."

"I'm not a vampire."

"No, but you do have a bat," she says, her eyes twinkling with curiosity. "Why is that?"

"I don't know and it's not important," I snap impatiently. "You said yourself we have a common enemy.

If you could lend us Dracula's Ring, then we could stop the monster hunter and protect—"

"The vampires," she jumps in. "That's who you're protecting. What about once you send him away? Goreway will be protected, but the magical communities around the rest of the country won't be helped."

My shoulders drop as I deflate, well aware that she makes a good point. I have to try to appeal to her a different way.

"Elena," I begin, leaning forwards, "please consider the fact that all those centuries ago, a witch in your family worked alongside the vampires to create the spells surrounding Skeleton Woods. I know it was a long time ago, but your family is connected to the vampires – that witch wanted to protect them. Maybe you weren't always enemies."

Elena doesn't say anything.

"If you help us, then we can at least do *something* to stop the monster hunter," I continue, spurred on by her silence. "And maybe, now that we know he is in Goreway somewhere, we might even have the chance to get through to him and persuade him to choose a different career. Help us to stop him from using Skeleton Woods as his hunting ground – from there, we might have some hope of stopping him altogether."

As I finish, Sharptooth catches my eye and smiles. Elena takes a long, deep breath.

"*Fine*," she whispers eventually.

"You'll ... you'll help us?" I check, sitting up straight. She nods.

"THANK YOU!" I cry, leaping to my feet and rushing over to give her a hug, disturbing Bat-Head, who begins screeching in irritation, flying around our heads with Bat-Ears.

Elena is too startled to push me away at first, but when Sharptooth yells out, "VAMPIRES LIKE HUGS NOW, TOO!" and hurries over to pile on top of me, Elena lets out a muffled "Oof!" and I release her, pulling away.

"I may have decided to help you, but I draw the line at hugs from a vampire," she asserts.

Unperturbed by the insult, Sharptooth throws her arm round my shoulders and squeezes me into her, as Bat-Head and Bat-Ears land grumpily on our shoulders.

"How exactly do you intend to use Dracula's Ring?" Elena asks, folding her arms across her chest.

I hesitate. "We're not sure exactly. My slayer guide, Mr Frank, is reading up on it, and the witches we met hinted that it may not work. But Diana is going to try her best to recreate the original spells for the woods."

"Not much of a plan," she remarks.

"I know." I shrug helplessly. "But all we can do is try."

"Can *you* use the magic of Dracula's Ring?" Sharptooth asks Elena. "After all, it was a witch in your family who used it all those years ago."

"I wouldn't know. The ring chooses its own protector."

"You haven't tried to use it?" I ask, baffled. "Why wouldn't you check to see if it works for you?"

"Because I don't have it," Elena states.

The surge of elation I'd just felt evaporates instantly. Sharptooth turns to me in bewilderment.

"What?" I whisper, my mouth dry. "But ... but you said..."

"I said I'd help you," Elena reiterates, "and I will. I'm going to tell you where you can find Dracula's Ring, information that no one but me knows. If you manage to get it, I'll chaperone it back to England with you. As it technically should belong to my family, I will take it back once we've attempted the spell. Then I'll travel to London to free my aunt. That's the deal."

"If you don't have it, where is it?" Sharptooth asks.

"If I tell you, you have to agree for me to chaperone

the ring if you manage to get hold of it, wherever it goes. If you try to take it from me, I will find you."

I hold up my hands. "We wouldn't do that. Yes, you can chaperone the ring."

She nods and then gestures for us to sit back down on the sofa. She waits until we're sitting before she clears her throat to speak.

"It's in Bran Castle."

"Wait." I brighten. "That's on our itinerary for tomorrow! It's supposed to be Dracula's castle, right? We're already due to go there!"

"Getting to the castle is easy, but getting the ring is near impossible," she warns. "In fact, no one in my family has managed it. My ancestor brought Dracula's Ring back to Transylvania after a stint performing magic with it over England. Then, when she found out that some evil witches knew of its existence and would come after it, she hid it in Bran Castle and protected it using its own magic."

"Whoa." Sharptooth looks impressed. "She sounds like a very good witch."

"Too good," Elena sighs, leaning back in her chair. "No one from our family has been able to retrieve it since."

"*No one!*" My heart sinks. "Are you sure?"

Elena nods. "Every witch in my family since has attempted to get it, but none of us have been successful. I tried just last year, thinking I might be powerful enough now, but I failed at the first hurdle, as always. The secret of where it is hidden is passed down to each generation in my family in the hope that one day, it will be found."

"If you can't get your hands on Dracula's Ring, there's no chance that Sharptooth and I will be able to do it!" I wail. "We can't use magic!"

Elena shrugs. "I'm sorry, Maggie. It would be easier if I could hand it over to you, but that's not possible. If you want Dracula's Ring, you're going to have to somehow break the spells that protect it."

I bury my head in my hands. "What are we going to do?"

There's a moment of silence before Sharptooth gently says, "It's like you just said to Elena, Maggie. All we can do is try. Right?"

Lifting my head, I turn to look at her bright red eyes staring back at me hopefully.

"Right, Sharptooth," I say, trying to muster as much optimism I can manage. "All we can do is try."

CHAPTER

FIFTEEN

I'm not sure how thrilled Mr Frank is about a witch joining us today, but he's going to have to put up with it for the sake of Skeleton Woods. I know it's a lot to ask when he's already responsible for a vampire and a werewolf, but he's not the only one who's making sacrifices – my reputation has taken a hit over all this. My classmates think that I've invited a random family member on my school trip, and she happens to be distinctly weird thanks to her insistence on wearing five jumpers and a sunhat, even on a cloudy February day.

Elena said that she'd meet us here at the castle, and I'm desperately hoping that she is a little bit more practised than Sharptooth at blending in with the humans.

"Don't you think if you were going to become a pile of dust, you would have done so already?" I point out to Sharptooth when she opens her umbrella the moment we step down from the coach at Bran Castle.

"I'm not taking any chances, Maggie," she says stubbornly, checking her sunhat is on properly. "Who knows how trustworthy this spell is? It's difficult for me to put my life completely in the hands of a witch."

"Whoa, this castle is so cool!" Ari gushes, gazing up at it.

Perched atop a cliff, Bran Castle is an imposing, pale stone fortress with tall turrets and striking red rooftops. It's different to the dark, jagged towers of Skeleton Castle.

"Maybe I could include this in my graphic novel," Ari continues, getting her phone out to take pictures. "It definitely has a vampire vibe to it."

"Yes," Miles agrees nervously. "Sharptooth, Dracula doesn't still … um … live here, right?"

"He uses it as a holiday home," a voice behind us says.

We spin round to see Elena standing there with an amused expression. She's wearing a green long-sleeved, knee-length dress with tights, silver-studded ankle boots and a black fedora hat. She looks like she's the lead singer of an indie pop group. Ari beams at her.

"*You're* Elena?" she asks in amazement.

Over breakfast in our hotel, I had told Ari and Miles about our meeting with Elena by writing what she'd told us down on a napkin – I couldn't risk Marrok overhearing any mention of Dracula's Ring. I could come up with an excuse as to why I'd met a witch should Marrok ask, but the ring would be difficult to explain.

Ari was impressed at the idea of Elena being a young witch – Diana Dazzle was the only witch she'd ever met and she hadn't considered the idea that there are witches of every age living amongst us. She'd immediately begun to point out people in our class who could be witches, but Miles pointed out that she already had a slayer, a werewolf and a vampire in her friendship group, so shouldn't be greedy.

"Who are you?" Elena replies cautiously.

"I'm Ari, and this is Miles. We're friends of Maggie and Sharptooth, so you don't need to worry, we know about *everything*. Can I ask you a question? If legendary vampires like Dracula exist, does that mean legendary witches, like the Lady of the Lake, exist too?"

Elena's mouth twists into a smile. "Now that would be telling."

"They SO do!" Ari squeals excitedly to Miles.

"Great." Miles gulps. "More scary magical people to fear."

"Thanks for coming, Elena," I say, before noticing the cat winding its way around her feet. "You too, Glinda."

"I'm not here by choice," Glinda corrects me, promptly.

"Like I said, I'm here in case by some miracle you are able to get … what we discussed, so I can come back with you and watch over it," Elena reminds me, as Glinda hisses at my bag, likely sensing Bat-Head's presence in there. "But I won't be of any help when it comes to actually recovering it."

"I know," I say, nodding. "I'll do what I can."

"We're here to help too," Ari says determinedly.

"Yeah, whatever you need," Miles agrees.

I thank them, but there's no way I'll be asking them to help me in this. I've already put enough people in danger, I'm not going to risk getting them mixed up in the daunting task of retrieving Dracula's Ring – according to Elena and her family legend, Dracula's Ring lies in a dark dungeon beneath the castle. As none of them have been able to get past the first protective spell of the sealed entrance, they don't know what magic is waiting beyond it, and it could be very dangerous.

Elena also mentioned that the only people who have attempted to retrieve the ring before have been witches – she wasn't sure what might happen if a non-magical human like me tried. The magic might be insulted I'd even try to get past it and repel me.

"How can magic be insulted?" I'd asked.

"Magic has its own ways," Elena had replied mysteriously.

"And what do you mean by it repelling me?"

She hadn't answered that one, pretending to be distracted by Glinda, which didn't exactly fill me with confidence. I keep having visions of knocking on a door and being instantly catapulted backwards through the air.

"Come on, everyone! This way," Mr Frank announces, gesturing for us all to follow him from the car park up a stone paved road towards the castle.

As we begin the climb, the other students notice Elena has joined our group. When Jason asks me who she is, I explain that she's a distant relation, who happens to live in Transylvania and offered to help Mr Frank by providing some local knowledge.

"What's with the cat?" Jason asks, watching Glinda trot along ahead of us next to Elena and Ari.

"Uh ... she's a stray," I say. "Clearly."

Glinda comes to an abrupt stop and swivels her head round to hiss furiously at me.

"She's very well groomed for a stray," Jason observes.

Satisfied at this response, Glinda happily returns to her strutting.

When Jason has moved away, I find Marrok falling into step with me.

"What's with the witch?" he asks casually, and I have to shush him.

"Would you mind keeping your voice down?" I say, slowing down until we've fallen behind, right to the back of the group.

He holds his hands up. "Sorry. I'm a little bit curious as to why a Transylvanian witch, who has no relation to you whatsoever, despite what you're saying, has joined our school trip to Bran Castle."

"She's a friend of a friend."

"Maggie, have you forgotten that I'm a werewolf?"

"That hadn't slipped my mind, no."

He reaches his hand out to gently nudge my arm, slowing me down to a complete stop. "Then you'll remember that I have really good hearing, right? What was that witch talking about when she said that she wouldn't be able to help you and Sharptooth 'recover it' in the castle? What are you trying to get?"

I sigh irritably, annoyed at myself and the others for forgetting ourselves and talking about it all so openly.

"Nothing," I say breezily. "Something from the gift shop."

He frowns at me.

Pretending not to notice his sullen expression, I glance up the hill to see the rest of the class are way ahead of us now. I decide to take advantage of being away from the crowd and swing my backpack off my shoulder to unzip it. Bat-Head shoots up through the gap, swooping through the air.

"Good time for a quick wing stretch," I explain, watching him go.

Marrok looks up, too. "He seems happy. Lucky he found you."

"I've got so used to having him around, I'd be lost without him now," I admit. "Although I could do without his dribbling when he sleeps on my pillow."

"It's nice that he found where he belongs. That's important," he adds with such sincerity that I'm taken aback.

"Yeah. It is, I guess."

"You weren't talking about something from the gift shop earlier, Maggie," he blurts out. "I heard her saying that whatever it is you're looking for in there, if you find it then she's coming back home with us to watch over it. That makes it extremely precious, so I'm going to go ahead and take a guess that it's not a postcard or fridge magnet."

"Okay, fine," I say, my stomach churning at the stress of this conversation as I desperately try to avoid telling him the whole truth. "Elena has an aunt who has been kidnapped by the monster hunter and she wants to come with us to rescue her."

"That doesn't explain what you're looking for today here at the castle." He lowers his eyes to the ground and shakes his head. "Maggie, I know why Elena is coming back to England with us. I knew you and Sharptooth were up to something when I could hear you leaving the hotel to find her yesterday. She's going to help you put back the enchantments around Skeleton Woods, isn't she?"

A lump builds in my throat. I should have known that he'd work it out.

After a few moments, I give in and nod.

"So, there's something here in the castle that is going

to help with those enchantments," Marrok surmises dismally.

"It's the only way to get things back to the way they were," I say gently, feeling terrible. "Things are getting out of control in Goreway. We have to put them back."

"What if there was another way?" he asks, his eyes gleaming. "What if we could get rid of the monster hunter without putting up the enchantments? All that does is send all the non-humans away and him chasing after us still."

"It's not that simple. We don't know how dangerous the other supernatural creatures are. What if they hurt someone in the town? Or the vampires? I'm supposed to protect everyone. I can't risk that happening."

"I highly doubt they're going to hurt anyone; they've come for the treasure," he declares, refusing to back down. "Maggie, do you know why we came to Goreway in the first place? There was a reason Dad wanted that treasure. Our home is going to be destroyed by property developers. They kicked us out because they owned the land. They're going to tear down our house, along with our local woodland, in order to build a private golf course. Our woods wasn't saved in the end like yours was."

"I'm sorry, Marrok."

"Then Dad got it in his head that if we could get our paws on some of Skeleton Castle's treasure that was going to waste, hoarded out of sight by the vampires, then we'd be able to get our home back and save the woodland. That was the plan." He takes a deep breath. "But then we got to Goreway and everything changed."

I fold my arms. "How?"

"For the first time in my life, I found somewhere I belonged. I've never fit in anywhere, but in Goreway, I was right at home. It was like we'd always meant to end up there somehow. No one thought I was a freak. I made friends; I got to play on an *actual* football team. I'm part of something now. The very first person I met at school made me feel welcome. I'd never felt welcome anywhere."

He pauses. I suddenly realize just how much Goreway means to him; it's exactly the same for me.

"When we'd been there for a while, Dad decided to check out whether the enchantments of Skeleton Woods had weakened further," Marrok continues. "But I followed him and persuaded him to leave it alone. He eventually agreed to turn back."

"Sharptooth heard you," I recall.

"My dad is VERY stubborn," he says affectionately. "He had his mind set on getting into Skeleton Woods so he could get that treasure – he knew that with the enchantments down, our pack could take on the vampires. The plan was to live in Goreway temporarily until the enchantments were down completely. Then we'd attack."

I flinch at the idea of the werewolves taking on Sharptooth and the rest of the vampires.

"But," Marrok continues quickly, "things change. I don't want to leave Goreway. Aunty Loveta wants to stay, too. Not instead of the vampires, but alongside them. She and I secretly came up with a much better plan – we would communicate with the vampires, and find a way to work together. We realized we didn't need to take advantage of weakened enchantments. We could persuade them to *change* the enchantments to allow us to share the woodland, too. That way, we could all stay in Goreway, with no hostility. We could be neighbours."

"That's why you came to join in the football when you heard us play," I realize. "It was a good way to begin a relationship with the vampires."

"For that reason, and Aunty Loveta really did want the chance to play with a team," he says with a shrug. "I'm not the only werewolf who has felt out of place until now."

"What about your dad?"

He offers me a weak smile. "Like I said, he's a stubborn wolf. But I persuaded him to leave the woodlands alone once. I think if I had the chance, I'd be able to bring him round to a new way of seeing things. He loves his job at the salon in Goreway. And Skeleton Woods is on our doorstep – we have to live near woodland that we can use."

"Marrok—"

"We have to be able to run properly," he interrupts pleadingly. "We have to be isolated so that we can transform without terrifying the neighbourhood. I don't want to leave Goreway. But if you put up those enchantments, our pack will have to find somewhere new. And the monster hunter will follow us."

My stomach twists into knots as I say, "But I don't have a *choice*."

"Your plan protects the vampires. What about everyone else?"

"There are zombies hanging out in playgrounds! Monsters chasing people down streets! We're lucky those people only lost their hats and not their heads. Things have got out of control. I'm sorry, Marrok, but we have to put those enchantments back. I have to protect Skeleton Woods. It's what I'm *meant* to do."

"It's your destiny."

"Exactly," I say, waving down Bat-Head to return to my bag.

"You're wrong," he counters, lifting his eyes to meet mine. "Your destiny is to slay vampires."

He's got me there.

"Maggie! Marrok!" Mr Frank calls out all the way down the hill, his voice echoing off the cliffs. "Come on, you're keeping the whole class waiting! The tour will start soon!"

"If you changed your destiny, Maggie Helsby," Marrok concludes, walking away, "you can change anything."

CHAPTER

SIXTEEN

Sharptooth looks as glum as I feel.

"You overheard our conversation, then," I say, sidling up to her once I've completed the trek up the hill to the castle entrance and Bat-Head is safely stowed away again.

"It is a bit sad," Sharptooth admits, pushing her sunglasses up her nose. "Marrok may be very stinky, but being asked to leave somewhere you call home sounds terrible. I hope wherever his pack goes next, there are decent ketchup supplies."

She gives me a comforting pat on the arm, before we huddle through the door of the castle, joining Ari, Miles and Elena, while Mr Frank introduces himself to the tour guide. Marrok isn't standing with us, choosing to be on his own in the corner, even when Miles catches his attention and waves for him to come join us.

"What did you say to Marrok?" Ari asks, nudging me. "He looks like his former self. You know, all serious, like he was when he first came to the school. Like he's auditioning for the role of a brooding werewolf in a lame teen movie."

"Remember, he can hear what we're saying," I remind her.

"Oh yeah. Sorry, Marrok," she whispers, giving him a little wave across the room. "I meant that in a nice way. You would definitely be the cool werewolf in a movie."

We see his scowl wobble, breaking into the smallest of smiles.

Mr Frank asks us all to listen in as the tour guide takes charge, welcoming us to Bran Castle, home to the world's most famous and deadliest of vampires, Count Dracula.

"HA!" Sharptooth cackles, causing everyone to swivel their heads round to look at her.

Clearing his throat, Mr Frank apologizes on her behalf and asks the confused tour guide to please continue with her introduction.

"What?" Sharptooth shrugs when I give her a pointed

look. "Dracula may be famous to you humans, but he's not the deadliest in our history. Yes, he's got the most merchandise and a human book of fiction, but does he live in a dungeon of bones? No. That vampire is WAY more dangerous."

Ari opens her mouth, but Miles stops her from speaking by quickly holding up his hand and saying, "Please, don't ask her to expand on the bones. *Please*."

"Don't worry, Miles, that vampire doesn't live here in Transylvania, so you're perfectly safe," Sharptooth says cheerily. "He lives miles away in England!"

Miles's eyes grow wide as saucers. "Sharptooth, that's where WE live."

"Oh yeah." Sharptooth looks thoughtful for a moment. "Do we live in the north of England or the south?"

"The north," I answer gingerly. "Why, where does the dungeon-of-bones vampire live?"

"Never mind," Sharptooth says hurriedly, avoiding our eye contact.

"You know, having a vampire as a friend isn't all it's cracked up to be," Miles says under his breath, closing his eyes in despair.

The tour begins and we duly follow the guide, as she admirably attempts to keep our class as interested as possible by telling all the myths of the castle surrounding Count Dracula, as well as the boring factual and architectural stuff that only Miles is keen on hearing.

We reach a staircase and, while everyone else makes their way up to the next floor of the castle, Elena signals that this is our opportunity to slip away. Sharptooth and I hang back, faking an interest in an intricately carved wooden chair sitting at the bottom.

"The detail on the legs is fascinating," Miles says enthusiastically, until we tell him that it's all a ruse to sneak off and he can join the rest of the class if he wants.

"Are you sure you don't want us to come with you?" Ari asks. "What if you need us for something? What if you get in trouble?"

"Then there certainly won't be anything you humans can do to help," Elena replies matter-of-factly. "You'd all be goners."

"Again," Miles croaks, "I'd like to reiterate how fun it is to hang out with you magical folk."

"Please be careful," Mr Frank whispers urgently, having purposefully announced that he'd be bringing up the rear of the group so that he could wait with us. "I'm still not sure this is the best idea."

Marrok has paused halfway up the stairs and he

turns to look down at us, listening in to every word we say.

"It's the only idea we have," I state, refusing to acknowledge Marrok. I already feel guilty enough. "We'll be fine. I promise. Now you lot go, before people get suspicious."

They reluctantly leave, while Elena and Sharptooth stay lurking around the bottom step with me. Marrok's shoulders slump forward as he heads up the final few steps, disappearing round the corner, followed closely by Ari, Miles and Mr Frank.

"This way," Elena instructs.

The castle is a maze of corridors, but Elena knows exactly where she's going, marching determinedly ahead of us and telling us when to hide at the sound of someone's footsteps. We reach a cordoned-off area and she unclips the rope, ushering us to duck quickly through an old, heavy door behind it. It's locked at first, but after a quick spell from Elena, opens with a loud creak. She shuts it behind us and mutters another spell. I hear the clunk of the door locking itself again.

I feel a drop in temperature in this small, dimly lit room. Its stone walls are crumbling, there are cobwebs in the corners and squeaks from a mouse scurrying in the corner. An old fireplace on the other side of the room is so neglected, it looks as though it might cave in on itself at any moment. The only sign that anyone has walked into this room *ever* is an old, used candle that is on its side, surely discarded now that it's so melted down and all that's left is the small bit of wick sticking out from the leftover wax.

As Bat-Ears flies out from under Sharptooth's coat, I let Bat-Head free from my bag. They explore the room with a couple of swoops about it and then come back to land on our shoulders.

"Wow," I say, my teeth chattering, "this room really isn't meant for tourists, is it?"

"I think this is very tasteful interior decorating," Sharptooth remarks. "Could do with a spooky chandelier and maybe some old splashes of blood, but I like it!"

"They closed it off, because it's boring," Elena explains, ignoring Sharptooth, "but looks can be deceiving. This is the most interesting room in the whole castle."

She steps over to the fireplace and picks up the candle, using a spell to light it. As she does so, a crack appears down the front of the fireplace and it splits in two before crumbling to dust completely, transforming into an archway, revealing a hidden passage behind it.

Elena smirks at my startled expression. "That's why no one would be able to find it without the help of magic. Lighting the candle with a certain spell opens the door."

"So, that's the first protective spell?" I ask, eyeing up the darkness in the passageway ahead. It doesn't look particularly welcoming.

"No," Elena says, amused at my misunderstanding. "This is just how you get downstairs to the secret lair under the castle where the ring is hidden. There's a staircase at the end of this passageway. At the bottom of those steps, you'll find your first challenge. Here." She hands me the candle. "You'll need this to see your way."

"I can use my phone torch," I point out.

Elena shakes her head. "You can't use any kind of light but this. Nothing else works. And this flame dies out by the time you hit the last step."

"Where there's another magical candle waiting for us?" I ask hopefully.

"No," she says.

"Cool!" Sharptooth exclaims. "I love the dark!"

"No one has managed to get any further than the bottom of those steps," Elena says wistfully, looking down the passageway. "No lights work down there, not even magical spells to get any light. I don't want to sound pessimistic, but if witches haven't been able to do it—"

"Then we're unlikely to get anywhere," I acknowledge. "At least this way, we'll know for sure. Thanks for getting us this far, anyway."

"I'll wait for you in the courtyard," Elena replies.

"You're not going to wait here for when we come back up the stairs?"

"You only have a certain amount of time to crack the first spell. Then you're spat out into the courtyard."

"Spat out," I repeat. "Sounds … uncomfortable."

"I'll see you soon," Elena concludes, taking a step back.

"If the gift shop sells ketchup, could you please buy me a couple of sachets?" Sharptooth asks her brightly. "I'll owe you. Right, Maggie, I'll lead the way because I don't need any stinky witch candle. Why do all candles smell like lavender? BLEUGH. When are they going to make ketchup candles?"

Chattering away, Sharptooth strolls through the archway.

"Good luck," Elena says, watching her go. "I think you might need it."

"Thanks," I say, holding up the candle ahead of me. "I'll see you later."

I walk carefully down the passage, feeling strangely comforted by Sharptooth's prattling on about ketchup. I probably don't feel as scared as I should – being a slayer, I'm really at home in the dark.

Sharptooth waits for me at the top of the spiral staircase and then makes her way down with Bat-Ears fluttering just ahead of her. Bat-Head and I follow close behind. In the last flicker of candlelight, we see that it's a dead end.

There's about two feet of space between us coming off the final step and a stone wall right ahead. Crouching down in the darkness, I place the useless candle at my feet and straighten, hoping that my eyes get used to this pitch-black as quickly as possible.

Just in case Elena is mistaken, I reach for my phone and try to get it to work, but it's switched off and won't come back on.

"Are you okay, Maggie?" Sharptooth asks beside me. "Can you see anything?"

"Nothing."

"I can see everything! I'll be your guide, don't worry."

"But there's just a wall in front of us," I say, putting

my hands out in front of me and blindly reaching for it. I find it and place my hands up against the cold stone, feeling for a door handle or a draught or any kind of clue. "This is so ridiculous."

"You do *look* quite ridiculous," Sharptooth giggles. "Are you hugging the wall?"

"I'm trying to work out if it's a secret door," I huff. "How is anyone meant to get past this if the witch who created it won't allow us to see anything? Not even magical light will work."

"We could try using the torch over there," Sharptooth says breezily.

I freeze. "There's a torch in here?"

"Yes, a medieval flame torch. We have them in Skeleton Castle!"

"Sharptooth, why didn't you say?!" I cry. "Where is this torch?"

"It's in the right-hand corner of the ceiling."

"Can you reach it?"

"Duh! It's an easy jump."

I hear a whoosh as Sharptooth leaps into the air, landing without barely making a sound. Just as I'm about to ask how we can light it, the flame of the torch bursts into life, filling the space with light.

"How did you do that?" I ask in awe.

"I didn't do anything!" she claims, peering at the long handle of the torch in her grip. "Oh, hang on, it has a transcription etched in here. The writing is all swirly – typical witch, they always have to go over the top with their calligraphy. It says, 'only the undead'."

Sharptooth brightens, exclaiming, "I'm undead! Technically. You know, vampires aren't really alive or dead. Maybe this torch is only for vampires."

An idea strikes me. Suddenly I'm filled with hope.

I grab her arm. "Remember what Elena said about the witch who created these spells to protect Dracula's Ring? She wanted to hide it from *evil witches*."

"That's right." Sharptooth nods.

"Sharptooth," I continue, "maybe the reason none of Elena's family could get to it, even though they were witches, was *because* they were witches! These spells protect the ring from witches. And you know what kind of magic Dracula's Ring creates?"

In the flickering light of the flaming torch, I see Sharptooth's eyes widen.

"*Vampire magic*," she says.

There's a rumbling sound as a row of red flames bursts out from the ground at the bottom of the wall and it begins to crumble away to dust, just like the fireplace before. As the stone falls away, a long corridor stretches out in front of us, with candlelit chandeliers hanging from its ceiling.

At the very end is a coffin-shaped door.

Sharptooth grins at me. *"Cool."*

"These spells were never meant to be broken by witches," I conclude, feeling like I might burst with excitement. "They were created to welcome vampires."

CHAPTER

SEVENTEEN

The sound of our footsteps echoes off the walls of the dimly lit corridor.

"What if we have to do vampire magic?" Sharptooth asks apprehensively. "I can't do that! We'd need Count Bloodthirst."

"I just hope we don't have to do any riddles," I admit. "I'm so bad at stuff like that."

Reaching the door, I stop Sharptooth before she can turn the handle.

"Do you think you need to do this alone? I'm not a vampire after all, and if this is only meant for vampires, I might scupper our chances of getting Dracula's Ring."

"I'm not doing this without you, Maggie," Sharptooth

says, balking at the suggestion. "Besides, how do you know that we won't need a slayer? We have no idea what is waiting for us behind this door."

"Maybe we've done the hard bit and the ring is in this room, sitting on a nice cushion," I say hopefully, but Sharptooth looks unconvinced.

"Ready?" she asks me.

"Ready," I reply.

Sharptooth turns to Bat-Ears and repeats, "Ready?"

He squeaks.

She then looks to Bat-Head on my shoulder. He squeaks, too.

"Good. We're all ready."

She turns the handle and pushes open the door.

Once we've all intrepidly stepped through, the door shuts behind us and then disappears completely. There's no going back.

We're in what looks like an empty room at first, but then hear a noise coming from the left-hand corner behind us. On high alert, we spin round to see three cloaked vampires huddled together.

Sharptooth greets them with a joyful, "Hi!", but they're not taking any notice of her, because floating inches away from their heads is a large garlic bulb, suspended in mid-air.

Sharptooth has told me before that the legends about garlic and vampires really are true. They can't stand it. When my mum cooked it once at our house, not realizing that a vampire had joined us for dinner, Sharptooth fainted.

As she notices the garlic bulb, Sharptooth yelps and jumps backwards, flinging herself against the far wall, while Bat-Ears screeches at the sight, hiding himself under her coat. Bat-Head stays put on my shoulder, but wrinkles his little nose.

"GROSS!" Sharptooth cries in a panic. "Maggie, be careful!"

"It's all right, Sharptooth," I say, before calling over to the vampires. "Don't worry, I'll try to move it."

I stride over to the garlic bulb and try to swipe it out of the air, but it darts out of my reach. The vampires, quivering in fear, flinch at the sudden movement, pressing themselves as far into the corner as they can manage. I try again and again to catch the garlic bulb, but it escapes my grasp each time, flitting backwards and forwards, up and down.

"How long have you been in here?" I ask the vampires, still trying to catch the garlic bulb and having no luck.

The vampires don't answer me. The only sounds that

come out of their mouths are cries of horror when the garlic bulb moves closer to them. I feel horrible for them. They must have made it this far to get the ring and then been cornered in here. I hope they haven't been stuck like this too long.

"Maggie," Sharptooth calls out, "look!"

A door has appeared in the wall on the opposite side of the room and it swings open. All I can see through it is darkness. We have a clear path into the next room.

"We can't leave them," I say to Sharptooth, and she nods miserably.

"I know. Why won't that garlic bulb leave them alone?"

"I don't know." I address them directly. "Do you know why it's so focused on you? Did you use vampire magic before it got like this? Maybe we can undo the spell."

But they still don't respond. They're so scared by the garlic bulb, they won't even look at me. As it continues to evade capture, I have an idea.

"Sharptooth, pass me your sunhat. I can use it as a net."

She peels it off her head and throws it to me. I attempt to swish it through the air towards the bulb, but to no avail. After trying from all angles, I appeal to Sharptooth.

"I need your help. This garlic bulb is moving with vampire magic; I think it needs vampire instincts to catch it."

"You want me to go near that thing?" Her bottom lip quivers. "But it's FOUL."

"I know, but I don't know what else to do. Will it really hurt you if you touch it?"

"It will sting." She hesitates and then wails, "But I would be better at catching it than you. You're terrible."

"It's harder than it looks," I mutter defensively.

Sharptooth addresses the vampires in the corner. "And it doesn't seem to have it in for me, like it does for you, so I think I should be the vampire here to make the sacrifice of helping the useless human to do an easy catch."

"You know, I can hear you," I remind her, putting my hands on my hips.

"Okay, I can do this," she says.

"Remember, you're the kind of vampire who has been walking around in the sun the last couple of days," I say, to build her up as much as possible. "Compared to that, this is nothing. You're the bravest vampire I know."

"Really?"

"Yes."

With a fresh wave of determination, she pushes herself off the wall and eases her way over, edging around me as she nears the floating bulb. As she gets closer, she looks as though she might be sick, wobbling on her fleet slightly.

"The smell of it is making me feel dizzy!"

"You're doing really well," I encourage her, hoping she doesn't bottle it now that she's so close. I hand her back her hat. "Okay, here's the plan. Bring the hat down on the bulb from above and I'll help you pin it down on the floor. Then, all of you vampires run straight through that door to the next room."

"But what about you?" Sharptooth says. "You might get locked in here with that ... that ... THING!"

"A floating garlic bulb isn't scary to humans, don't worry," I chuckle. "The most important thing is we get all the vampires to safety. I'll deal with the garlic bulb. Got it?"

Sharptooth nods.

"Okay, on the count of three, bring the hat down on to the bulb and force it to the floor," I instruct. "One ... two ... THREE!"

It happens in a blur. Sharptooth jumps forward and, lifting the sunhat into the air, brings it down on top of the garlic bulb quick as a flash. I've barely finished my count of three before Sharptooth has it pinned down on the floor, yelling, "MAGGIE, MAGGIE, HELP!"

I kneel next to her and place my hands on the brim of the sunhat, pinning it to the floor as the garlic bulb bustles around inside the crown of the hat.

Jumping to action, Sharptooth instructs the other vampires to follow her, but they don't react. It's as though they've been cowering there, frightened, for so long, they're stuck in a trance. Sharptooth tries pulling at their cloaks, but they refuse to budge.

"They're too frightened by the garlic bulb!" I yell to her, putting all my energy into holding it captive in the hat. "We have to destroy it. Can you jump on it and try to crush it?"

Groaning, Sharptooth holds her nose and then takes a running jump, landing directly on top of the bulb in the hat. It doesn't flatten. She tries stamping on it repeatedly, but that doesn't work either.

Another idea flashes across my mind. I grimace at the thought.

"There's only one thing to do," I announce.

Obviously knowing what I'm thinking, Bat-Head squeaks in solidarity, giving me the courage to act.

In one swift, fluid motion I lift the hat ever so slightly with one hand and use the other to grab the garlic bulb, before taking a large bite out of it, my eyes watering as I chew quickly.

"ARGH!" Sharptooth squeals, recoiling. "DON'T, MAGGIE! SAVE YOURSELF!"

The taste is overpowering and disgusting, but I keep chomping until the whole garlic bulb is gone, Sharptooth watching on in utter dismay, her hand clamped over her mouth. Swallowing the last mouthful, I sit down on the floor while Bat-Head fans me with his wings, as though I've just completed a marathon.

"I can't believe you just did that!" Sharptooth says.

"At least everyone is safe now," I wheeze. "Let's hope there's water in the next room. And lots of mints."

Sharptooth holds out her hand to help me up and as I get to my feet, we turn to assure the other vampires that they are now safe, but, right in front of our eyes, they flicker and then evaporate into thin air.

"Where ... where did they go?" I ask, glancing around the room in confusion. "They ... *vanished*. Can vampires do that?"

"No," Sharptooth replies, her brow furrowed. "They weren't vampires. They were ... magic."

"What?" I whisper.

"They must have not been real! They were an image of vampires." She clicks her fingers as something dawns on her. "That's why they didn't talk to us or move! Wow, they seemed so real, didn't they? I even touched their cloaks and it felt normal! That is some very impressive magic right there."

I narrow my eyes at her. "You mean to say, I just ate a whole GARLIC BULB to save vampires who didn't EXIST?"

"If it helps, I think this means we passed the test," Sharptooth says, nodding to the door that appeared earlier.

It has started to crumble into dark dust, while another door appears on a different side of the room. This time light is shining through the doorway. I breathe a sigh of relief.

"True. I wonder what would have happened if we'd have left those poor vampires behind and run through that other door."

"We'd have probably been spat out into the courtyard," Sharptooth reasons, before clapping me on the back. "Well done, Maggie! You did it!"

"*We* did it. I couldn't have done it without you catching it in the first place."

"Let's go through," she encourages, before adding, "Maybe try not to breathe too heavily."

I clamp my mouth shut and give her a thumbs up. We wander through the door into the brightness of the next room. Again it disappears once it's closed behind us and the light of this new room swiftly fades to darkness. There is no ceiling in here, but instead a pitch-black night sky with a near-full moon glowing dimly above us.

Along the walls of this long dark space, rows and rows of shelves appear, filled with books. A bright white coffin-shaped door forms in the wall at the other end of the room and a clock hangs just above it. It says the time is two minutes past midday, which can't be right.

"This is weird," I comment, striding past the books to the far wall.

"Look at all these books!" Sharptooth says, her eyes twinkling with admiration.

As I get closer to the door, words appear across it, written in bold black ink.

"Sharptooth, check this out," I say, waving her over as she continues to gaze around all the shelves in wonder. "It looks like a poem."

I read the lines out loud as they appear:

Hindrance to this vampire's path,
An obstacle so frail and slight,
Whether you be wood or iron,
Nought can stop a vampire's might.
The moon commands we move this way,
To lurk in shadows is our plight,

...

...

"And then it looks like two lines are missing from the end." I put my hands on my hips as I glance over the poem again. "What do you think it means?"

"I think we have to finish the poem," Sharptooth says. "Maybe the last two lines are in one of these books."

"You're a genius! That must be it."

"But there are hundreds of books in here," Sharptooth points out. "It would take us ages to try them all. We could be here all day."

The clock over the door starts ticking, but the hands are going the wrong way. It's going backwards. It's counting down.

"Sharptooth!" I yell out, tripping over my feet as I run to the books to the right of the room. "We only have two minutes! Quick! Start looking! We need your vampire speed!"

"What am I looking for?" she cries, rushing over to the left.

"I'm not sure! Some kind of poetry book maybe?"

She immediately becomes a blur as she races around the room, sweeping books off the shelves that look like poetry books, flicking the pages and reading through at super-speed. The bats join in to help her, swooping along the shelves and screeching if they see a book that fits the bill. Feeling particularly useless with my slow human speed, I still try to help, examining the shelves as fast as possible. In the time it takes for me to pull one of the shelf and flick through its contents, she's done fifty.

"One minute!" I shout, as she continues to work.

"None of these contain *vampire* poetry!" she wails. "Why do humans write poetry about flowers and fruit?! HELLO. Where's the creepy content?"

"Maybe it's a poem written by a vampire, not a human," I suggest, looking out for a name on the spines that sounds spooky.

"Vampires don't really write poems..." Sharptooth trails off and then suddenly zips over to me, arriving at my side in half a second. "Vampires have written spells, though! Maggie, what if it's not a poem? What if it's a spell for vampire magic?"

"The pocketbook that Mr Frank gave me!"

Before I can even raise my hands to find the book in my pocket, Sharptooth has lifted it from my jacket and found the page.

"Read out the whole spell just in case!" I instruct.

She begins:

Hindrance to this vampire's path,
An obstacle so frail and slight,
Whether you be wood or iron,
Nought can stop a vampire's might.
The moon commands we move this way,
To lurk in shadows is our plight.
Open to the dark beyond,
Allow the undead through this night.

The clock stops ticking and the last two lines appear on the door, completing the spell. The door swings open. We both cheer, jumping up and down on the spot, while Bat-Ears and Bat-Heads do a couple of celebratory somersaults through the air.

"Come on," Sharptooth says, grabbing my arm and pulling me towards the door. "We have to be getting close."

We race through into the next room, which is small, dark and cold, as though we've walked into a cave.

"Great interiors," Sharptooth says to me.

"Yes, very welcoming," I reply drily, my eyes darting around as we wait for the next challenge. I was right to be nervous, but not for the reason I'd imagined.

There's a loud clang from above our heads and before we have time to react, two small cages came hurtling down straight on top of Bat-Ears and Bat-Head, trapping them both in individual cages that clatter on to the ground. Sharptooth and I both scream and get on our hands and knees to desperately try to free them, while their wings flap against the bars in a panic.

A soft voice floats through the air: "Welcome."

We pick up the cages and scramble to our feet, turning to see a woman calmly watching us. Wearing a green, hooded cloak, she has long black hair, dark eyes and bold red lips.

"I created all this to protect the most precious item in my possession. And to get this far, you have proved yourself – you have shown you will protect my dear friends, the vampires, and that you have the knowledge to wield vampire magic. Now, I will give you what you really want."

She lifts her hands to her neck and removes her necklace, a swirling blue stone on a long gold chain.

"This stone is filled with water from an enchanted realm," she explains, dangling it from her fingers. "It is the most powerful item of magic in existence. With this stone, you can be rich and powerful beyond your wildest dreams. Any possession you've ever wanted will be yours. You will be hailed like a queen, worshipped like a goddess. Magical creatures will bow in your presence."

I notice Sharptooth's eyes have glazed over as she gazes at it. "Wow. It's beautiful."

"The most precious gem ever created," the woman states. "You can take it, if you want. It's all yours. I only ask for a small offering in return. One to add to my collection."

She lifts her eyes to the top of the cave. A colony of bats emerges from the darkness, swirling over our heads, the cave echoing with the flutter of the wings.

I recoil in horror, clutching the bat cage tightly.

Sharptooth is mesmerized by the necklace, as though

it's trapping her in its spell, but I can see that she's fighting against it, her eyes twitching as though she's trying to tear them away.

"N-no," she says, as though it pains her to speak. "N-not Bat-Ears."

The woman tilts her head at her. "A small price for receiving everything you've ever desired in return. *Wouldn't you agree?*"

It must be a very powerful magic in that stone and, somehow, I'm immune to it – but these tasks were created for vampires, not human sidekicks.

"Fight it, Sharptooth," I hiss at her, willing her to find the strength to shake herself out of its hold. "Don't let the magic win."

"This stone is what you *really* want. You don't need that old ring. This has more to offer you," the woman insists, the gem glowing brightly as she speaks. "Riches will flow!"

"That's not what we want!" I shout, hoping Sharptooth can hear me. "We've come here for Dracula's Ring."

The witch gestures to the blue stone. "That ring is nothing to this. Don't you want to be rich? Don't you want to snap your fingers and get whatever you want? Don't you want to bathe in gold?"

Suddenly Sharptooth cries, "I'd rather bathe in k-ketchup!"

I beam at my friend as she blinks over and over, shaking her head vigorously, trying to shake the spell she's under right out of her head.

"You heard her!" I tell the witch. "We don't want any riches. We want to protect our friends and we can do that with Dracula's Ring. That's what we came here for, nothing else."

She looks from my stubborn expression to Sharptooth's, and then breaks into a wide smile. The necklace turns into dust, spilling across the floor. With her other hand, the woman holds out the most dazzling ring I've ever seen: a large, oval-shaped swirling-red jewel set into a thick gold band.

Without moving her lips, I hear her voice in my head:

"It is yours. Protect it."

The room begins to sway and everything around me twists into a blur of colour. I wrap my arms tightly around Bat-Head's cage, determined not to let him slip away from me, no matter what happens. I'm falling backwards and the ground disappears from under me.

Everything goes dark.

"Maggie? Maggie, are you all right?"

I open my eyes to see my reflection in the large bug sunglasses right above my face. "Sharptooth?"

I go to push myself up off the floor before I realize that I'm not lying down. I'm sitting up on a bench. Sharptooth is standing in front of me, crouched to peer at me.

"Where are we?"

"The courtyard of Bran Castle," Sharptooth says, coming to sit down on the bench, adjusting her sunhat to make sure she's well covered. "We weren't spat out, which is good!"

"That *wasn't* being spat out? Euch, whatever that was, it was bad enough." I suddenly sit straight up. "The bats!"

But Sharptooth points up into the sky. Bat-Ears and Bat-Head are swooping freely around each other, enjoying being out in the fresh air.

Slumping back in relief, I look around to try to spot anyone from the school trip. "Do you think they left without us and went back to the hotel?"

"No, we've only been gone a few minutes according to them," Sharptooth answers brightly. "I checked and they're still on the tour. I can't believe all that happened and no one even noticed we were missing. Elena's not even bothered to come wait here like she said, she's wandering about the gift shop."

As I go to push my hair from my face, I notice something cold on my finger brush against my forehead.

I slowly lower my hand so I can see my fingers.

There, on my right hand, is Dracula's Ring.

CHAPTER

EIGHTEEN

I should be happy.

Against all odds, Sharptooth and I retrieved Dracula's Ring, and now we have a real chance at restoring the enchantments to Skeleton Woods. Elena can't believe it. I think she's still in shock. When she finally left the gift shop to come find us and saw me inspecting the ring, she could barely speak, and she hasn't spoken much since.

Ari and Miles made us tell them everything about the magical tasks we had to face to get the ring, gasping and cheering at all the right moments, saying how much they wished I'd let them come, too. Mr Frank took us to one side to quietly tell us he was very proud and blushed when I said that him giving me that book was one of the keys.

But all of it is dampened when I think about Marrok.

Obviously overhearing the hushed conversations of our triumphant quest as we left the castle, he looked crestfallen. He hardly engaged with anyone else and avoided our group for the rest of the trip, but not because he looked mad. It was more that he seemed lost in his own world again, as though he was shrinking into himself.

As though any hope he'd been holding on to had been extinguished.

On the way back home from the airport to Goreway, I sit on the coach, every now and then patting my pocket to check the ring is still there. It's in a secure box that Elena created for it with a spell. I clutch my bag to my chest so Bat-Head can be close. He sticks his nose out the gap in the zip, his big eyes gazing up at me, and lets out a quiet squeak to try to comfort me. I gratefully give him a pet on the head with my finger.

"This is rubbish," I whisper to him.

"How can you say that?" Sharptooth says, tearing her eyes away from the window. "We are in a big tin box and it's MOVING. This is incredible!"

"I'm not talking about the coach journey, Sharptooth," I say with a hint of a smile. "I mean about … Marrok."

"Oh," she responds. "Maybe he can let us know where he moves to and we can all go visit him."

I lean my head back against my seat and close my eyes, signalling I don't want to talk any more about it, partly because it makes me feel too sad, but also because I know he can hear every word we say, even if he's sitting a few rows behind.

"What if only the werewolves stay?" Miles said thoughtfully when we'd attempted to brainstorm ideas that might help Marrok before we left Transylvania. "Maybe Diana could redo the enchantments to allow them to cross them."

"That would be a very difficult spell. It's already going to be extremely intricate, and that's if we can even get the magic from Dracula's Ring in the first place," Elena replied. "If we tampered with it even more to allow the werewolves, who knows what we might create? It could make everything worse."

"We can't risk that," I sighed, resting my chin in my hands.

"And how do you pick who gets to stay?" Ari pointed out with a shrug. "How come the werewolves would be allowed but not that green slimy monster? The other supernatural creatures might be insulted and take their vengeance."

"I hadn't even thought of that," Miles said, grimacing. "We don't want a load of rebelling monsters on our hands."

"Is there any way Marrok and his pack could stay even without being able to use Skeleton Woods?" Ari asked hopefully.

"Werewolves like to live close to a woodland so that they can run freely," Sharptooth told us. "It can be very dangerous if a werewolf doesn't transform regularly. They can start to lose control of their abilities, changing without warning. Humans have never taken kindly to werewolves – they tend to instinctively think they're dangerous, so stop them before anything can happen. I don't think Marrok's pack would want to risk that happening."

"We'd still have the monster hunter to deal with, too," I added. "I don't think it would matter to him how nice the creatures are. He's not going to give up easily."

We all sat in miserable silence, trying to accept that by saving Skeleton Woods, we'd be sending Marrok away.

Now, having landed back in England, the journey home feels sombre. Even if the best thing happens and the enchantments work, saving Goreway and Skeleton Woods, we still have to say goodbye to Marrok.

The coach slows down as it pulls into the town, trundling up the high street towards the school. I open my eyes to look out the window.

Something is wrong.

The street is empty. There are no pedestrians strolling along the pavements, hardly any cars on the road, the shops are all boarded up and all the curtains and blinds down the street are closed. I frown, leaning over Sharptooth to peer out properly.

"Where are all the humans?" she asks, pushing her nose up to the glass. "Is it normally this quiet?"

"No."

I crane my neck over the rows of seats ahead of us. Mr Frank has undone his seat belt and is peering out the front of the bus. We park up next to the school and the doors swing open. Mr Frank is the first to rush down the steps and we see him standing next to the entrance gates, his hands on his hips as he looks around, bewildered.

The school has a big "CLOSED" banner pasted across its sign.

As we all get off the bus and the bags start to be unloaded, the parents waiting to pick up their children from the trip emerge from hiding away in the main school building. They gesture to their kids to come to them quickly, before they rush away home, or call out to them from the safety of their cars, zooming off down the road as soon as the student has shut the car door behind them.

"What's going on?" Ari asks, as she and Miles huddle together next to me. "Something is off."

"I think we all know what's going on here," Marrok growls from behind us, looking distraught. "It's because of creatures like me."

"I'm sure that's not it," Miles says quickly.

"You were right, the enchantments need to be put back to how they were," Marrok continues. "Clearly, the monsters have overrun your town and now everyone is hiding from them, terrified. I'll tell my dad and aunt, and we'll go somewhere else."

"Marrok, maybe—"

"It's okay, Maggie," he interrupts. "I really appreciate you trying your best to come up with a solution that works for us, too. I know that you really do wish it could be different and that means a lot. But" – he gestures at the empty high street – "us staying is not worth this. It's not fair to force everyone to hide away." He pauses, before offering us all a sad smile. "Good luck with the enchantments. And thanks for a great trip, Mr Frank."

He turns and strides away, moving too fast for any of us to stop him.

I sigh heavily. "This seems so unfair."

"I don't want Marrok to leave," Miles says, speaking for all of us.

"I was even getting used to his stink," Sharptooth adds glumly.

A shrill voice suddenly calls out across the car park. "Mr Frank! Mr Frank!"

We turn to see the head teacher, Miss Woods, scurrying over to us from the school, darting round the parents still gathering their children to rush home.

"There you are," she wheezes, her large, dangling earrings swinging frantically. "We need to make sure everyone gets away safely and" – she hesitates, doing a double take at Sharptooth – "oh! I see you encouraged the students to get into character out in Transylvania. You look like a real vampire, dear. And what an interesting ... style. I think I have the same sunhat. ARGH!" She jumps, looking down as Glinda uses her leg as a scratching post. She clutches her heart and exhales in relief. "Oh, phew, it's just a cat. Sorry. I'm a bit on edge, I'm afraid."

"Why is the school closed? What's going on?" Mr Frank asks.

"I'll explain it to you, but we must get everyone home. No dilly-dallying!" she instructs, ushering other students towards their parents. "If we hang around, the interrogations begin!"

Ari scratches her head. "Interrogations. What does she mean?"

My parents' car pulls up behind the coach and I wave at them as they come hurrying over, wearing serious expressions.

I greet them with a hug, before asking what's going on.

"Things have been a bit ... uh ... odd around here," Mum begins, pulling away from me and giving a smile to the others. "Ari and Miles, we told your parents that we'd get you safely home – we thought that we'd insist on picking you up so that we could talk freely about—" She nods to Sharptooth and then notices Elena. "Hello! Are you the witch?"

Elena nods curtly.

"Sorry you're not seeing Goreway at its best," Dad says. "We've had some difficulties around here and now everyone is too frightened to leave their homes."

"Why did no one call or message us about this?" Mr Frank asks.

"None of the parents wanted to alarm any of you," Mum divulges. "We thought it best to let you get home and then explain things."

"It must have got really bad," I say, biting my lip. "Were the monsters everywhere? And which ones were the worst ones?"

Mum glances at Dad in confusion. "What?"

"Zombies, slimy monsters, ghosts – which were the ones that really scared everyone?" I ask again. "Or was it more chaos than fear, in which case I'm guessing Nash was part of it? Did any of them mention the treasure of the castle? I hope Marrok's family are okay. Did anyone cotton on that they were werewolves? No one hurt them, right?"

"Oh, also, did anyone see any goblins?" Ari adds. "Apparently some of those are lurking around somewhere. What are they like?"

"Whoa, whoa, whoa." Dad holds up his hands. "You think everyone is shut inside because of monsters?"

I pause. "Um. Yes?"

"No!" He shakes his head in disbelief. "Maggie, the monsters didn't do this."

"There haven't been too many sightings of monsters, and aside from those involved, most people don't believe any of the stories about them anyway," Mum adds.

"Then what is it that everyone is afraid of?" Ari asks.

"The monster hunter!" Dad exclaims, as though it's obvious. "He's been a nightmare, scaring off everyone until we're all afraid to set foot outside our doors!"

"The monster hunter," I repeat, astonished. "I don't understand."

"He's been interrogating everyone to make sure they're not in league with the monsters," Mum tells us, glancing around nervously. "And that's not the worst of it. He stomps around town, shooting nets and all sorts at any sudden movements or at the first sign of something unusual."

"Poor Mrs Hollyhogg came out wearing her green raincoat yesterday. She turned a corner and BAM" – Dad claps his hands together – "she found herself covered head to toe in a horrible syrupy orange goo! It froze instantly so she couldn't move a muscle! The monster hunter said he thought she was a green monster. Her husband has been using the hairdryer to attempt to melt it off ever since. We rang yesterday and it's still not off yet, but she can at least wiggle her toes and fingers now. Twiglet, the Pomeranian, keeps trying to eat the goo, which isn't good for his sensitive stomach."

"A schoolboy a few years above you got hoovered up

into a glass box with a Ghost Removal Machine when he was asked by his parents to bring in a bed sheet off the washing line," Mum sighs. "He got a bit caught up in the sheet as he pulled it away from the pegs and the monster hunter thought he was a ghost. Luckily, he let him go, but still! It wasn't a nice experience, as you can imagine. Everyone's too scared to go out."

"Speaking of which, you need to all go hide," Dad says hurriedly, "especially you, Sharptooth and Elena. Who knows where the monster hunter is now?"

"Hiding is the last thing we need to do," Sharptooth declares. "We have to stop him!"

"How do we do that?" Miles asks.

"Mr Frank, there must be something you can find out on the monster hunter," I tell him determinedly. "We need all the information we can get. Anything that might be useful to stop him."

"I can try, Maggie. So far, I haven't been able to learn anything about him that might be helpful," he divulges. "But I'll do my best."

"What can we do?" Ari says, looking to me for instruction.

Before we continue, a bat comes swooping down from the sky. I recognize her straight away.

"It's Count Bloodthirst's bat," Sharptooth gasps, holding out her hands so she can land, before speaking to her directly. "You never stray from him."

The bat launches into a tirade of screeching, causing Bat-Ears and Bat-Head to poke their heads out from Sharptooth's coat and my bag to listen. They both start squeaking in response, sounding panicked.

Sharptooth snaps her head up. "It's a message from Count Bloodthirst. He says not to return to the castle. The monster hunter has all the vampires trapped in there!"

I gasp. "*What?* How did he get into the woodlands?"

"The enchantments must have completely failed now," Sharptooth wails. "He's captured many other creatures and he's got them all there, too. But I have to go back to Skeleton Woods! I have to help them! And I don't have any more potion. The spell keeping me out in the daylight is going to wear off soon."

"Don't worry, Sharptooth," I say, as calmly as I can, my mind racing. "It's going to be okay." I address Count Bloodthirst's bat. "Tell him that we've got a plan and we're going to work it all out."

The bat nods to me and then jets off through the air, heading out of town in the direction of the woods. Everyone turns to me for direction.

"Mum and Dad, you need to take me, Elena and Sharptooth to Skeleton Woods now. We have to try to do the enchantments with Dracula's Ring," I say firmly.

"Of course! Get in the car," Mum says, jangling the keys from her fingers.

"Actually, even though your moving tin boxes are fascinating feats of engineering, I think I can get us there faster," Sharptooth reminds me. "It will be no problem carrying you and Elena over my shoulders."

"If it's all the same, I'd rather travel by broomstick," Elena says, Glinda sniggering by her feet. "There's got to be one in the school somewhere that I can use, and I'll use an invisibility spell once I'm in the air."

She clicks her fingers and a broomstick comes soaring through an open window straight into her outstretched hand. Thankfully, almost everyone has gone home by now and Miss Woods is too busy telling the coach driver to save himself and drive away from Goreway to notice a broomstick floating behind her.

"Great," I say, as Elena prepares to leave with Glinda. "Mr Frank, do everything you can to get us information on the monster hunter. Once the enchantments are up, he should run off in a trance, so we can help the vampires. But we'll need to know what to do once he's out the woods."

Ari and Miles share a look.

"What about us?" Miles asks. "What can we do?"

"You need to stay *safe*," I emphasize.

Ari recoils. "What?"

"I'm not going to let you come with me into a wood where there's a monster hunter and a load of monsters. It's not safe. Mum and Dad can make sure you get home okay. Sharptooth, let's go."

"Wait, Maggie!" Ari grabs my arm. "We're not going to let you do this alone."

"Absolutely not," Mum agrees, Dad nodding along beside her. "We'll all come with you."

"You can't. I'm the Helsby slayer. This isn't your responsibility, it's mine. I'm not going to put you in any more danger."

"You keep saying that, but we're a team," Ari insists, gesturing to Miles. "If it's your responsibility, then it's ours, too.

"There must be *something* we can do to help," Miles says, glancing to Mr Frank as though he might suggest an idea, but he stares back at him blankly.

"I have to go," I say apologetically. "I'm the only one who might be able to change the monster hunter's mind."

Not wanting to waste any more time, Sharptooth picks me up and the next thing I know, the ground is a blur underneath me and the wind is roaring in my ears as we leave my family and friends behind and head as fast as we can towards Skeleton Woods.

CHAPTER

NINETEEN

Skeleton Castle is bathed in sunlight.

It doesn't make any sense until I creep closer through the trees to see several giant spotlights dotted around it, shining artificial sunbeams all over the castle. Not only will the vampires not be able to step outside, the light will be pouring in through the windows and all the nooks and crannies of the door and walls.

"We have to turn them off!" Sharptooth says from our position tucked away behind a tree, throwing off her sunglasses, hat and coat now that we're safely in the woodland. She's about to move forwards when I grab her.

"Wait, we need to find Elena first," I say, pulling her back. "The most important thing is to set up the enchantments so we can flush out the monster hunter and get him safely away from everyone else. Then we'll turn off all those lights."

Bat-Head, who's keeping lookout along with Bat-Ears, gives a warning squeak and both of us spin round, grateful to see Elena creeping towards us, Glinda at her feet.

"Good, you're here. You both need to come see this," Elena whispers with a grave expression, urging us to follow her back the way they've come.

"Did you find the monster hunter?" I ask, trying to step as quietly as possible, which is near to impossible in a woodland. Everything seems to crunch beneath my trainers.

"No," she replies, as we crouch down behind a moss-covered boulder on her instruction. "I found the monsters."

Peering over the top of our hiding place, I can hardly believe my eyes. Supernatural creatures, caged or bound, are gathered in a clearing amongst the trees.

There are two monsters, round and green, each with four spindly legs and ten googly eyes, trapped in iron barred cages, lined up next to much larger caged pink-haired monsters, who have yellow spikes down their spine and just one giant eye in the middle of their faces – bizarrely, they are all wearing different kinds of hats that don't fit their heads properly. An orange goblin with pointy ears and gentle yellow eyes sits hunched over in another cage nearby, hugging his knees. A family of zombies sitting on the ground, their ankles chained together, are attempting to entertain themselves by throwing up the leaves and watching them float down again; a tall, strong ogre is tied to the trunk of a tree with thick, glowing yellow rope; several ghosts, including Nash, are impatiently bouncing off the walls of individual glass cylinders; a colony of bats flutter frantically in a big glass box; and three gagged witches are in separate cages nearby with steel contraptions over their hands so that they can't do magic, their familiars trapped in boxes next to them.

I gasp as I recognize two of the witches: "Diana and Savannah!"

"He must be good at his job to have captured them. Look at all these creatures. How could he do this?" Elena seethes. Glinda hisses in agreement.

"We have to do the spell now," I say determinedly, reaching into my pocket and pulling out the ring box. "If it works, we can free them and they'll all escape straight away out of the forest. The enchantments will help them to leave as quickly as possible, too."

"I hope this works," Elena says. "Diana is a more experienced witch. It really should be her trying this. Do you think I can go over there and try to speak to her?"

I shake my head. "Knowing the monster hunter, he'll have laid traps. He'll be ready for others to try to rescue the creatures he's already captured. Can you hear where he is, Sharptooth?"

"I wish," she sighs. "He's able to move silently around us, remember?"

"What about his son, Chase?"

"I can't hear him anywhere near her."

Opening the box, I pass Elena Dracula's Ring and she slides it on to the middle finger of her right hand. She takes a deep breath, anxiously looking down at her hand as she flexes her fingers. She catches my eye.

"A spell that hasn't been done in centuries with a ring that's been viciously protected from witches. No pressure, eh? What if its magic won't work for me?"

"You're the best chance we've got. Whatever happens, we won't let the monster hunter win," I say.

"Never!" Sharptooth declares. "What's that human phrase? We won't go down without a fright!"

I can't help but smile at her. "I think it's, we won't go down without a *fight*. But actually, your version seems more appropriate in the circumstance."

"We won't go down without a fright," Elena repeats, steeling herself. "Okay, let's try this incredibly complex, very rare, extraordinarily difficult spell. Bat-Head and Bat-Ears, are we good to go?"

The bats circling overhead check our surroundings once last time before signalling that the coast is clear. Elena pushes herself up from behind the boulder and, standing tall, drops her shoulders and closes her eyes, inhaling deeply through her nose. Glinda moves to sit valiantly at her feet, taking great pride in her brave witch.

I jolt at the ice-cold hand that takes mine – Sharptooth huddles close, both of us watching Elena, as her lips begin to move while she quietly incants a spell.

The trees around us start to creak and shake, and leaves pick up off the ground, twisting round in a gentle breeze that becomes stronger and gustier. Sharptooth's red eyes widen in hope, her silver hair blowing across her face, my fingers crushed in her strong grip. Bat-Ears and Bat-Head flutter down to us, tucking themselves safely away under our collars.

Elena lifts her right hand, clicks her fingers and…

Everything stops.

The leaves flop to the ground. The trees are silent.

Elena opens her eyes.

"Did it work?" Sharptooth asks excitedly, as we get to our feet.

I know the answer before Elena says it. "No."

"But … but it felt like it was working!" Sharptooth cries, gesturing around her.

"Yeah, the spell itself was working, but" – Elena holds up her hand to show us the ring – "this didn't."

"We have to try again," I say, refusing to give up. "And quickly. If he didn't know we were here before, I think that may have given us away."

"Yeah, our cover is definitely blown," Elena confirms, glancing over my shoulder.

I turn round to see all the captured magical creatures staring at us. I give them a small wave and then bring my focus back to Elena. "Are you ready to try it again?"

"Yes," she says, trying not to appear defeated. "I suppose so."

"Like cloak swishing, it just needs a bit of practice," Sharptooth encourages. "If it helps, I think you're a good witch, and I don't even like witches." She hesitates, before turning to quickly call out, "Diana and Susannah, you're quite good witches too!"

We hear the chief witch sigh heavily and, with her mouth gagged, say something that sounds like, "HIS-HA-NA-NA."

"It's *Savannah*," I translate.

"Whoops." Sharptooth grimaces. "Why don't you have normal names, like Sharptooth or Bloodthirst?"

Elena shakes out her hands. "You two stand back and let's try this again."

We do as instructed and give her and Glinda space. I cross my fingers and wait as Elena mimics what she did before, chanting the spell and causing the woodland to spring to life. It's amazing to watch the tall, thick, gnarled trees that seem unmoveable begin to sway gently from side to side, creaking and groaning as though they're communicating with us.

Eventually reaching up to the sky with her right hand, much higher than last time, Elena lifts her chin and then clicks her fingers.

It all goes still. My heart sinks. Nothing has changed.

Elena drops her head. "It didn't work."

"Maybe … maybe the ring needs a polish," I suggest,

and as soon as I say it, I know it sounds stupid, but I'm clutching at straws, terrified of moving to plan B.

And that's because I don't HAVE a plan B.

Dejected, Elena pulls the ring off her finger and holds it out in her palm, inspecting it closely, before glumly reminding us, "It chooses its protector. And it's not me."

"I'm going to go turn off that artificial sunlight," Sharptooth announces. "If we can't put the enchantments back, then we at least have to free everyone. Count Bloodthirst will know what to do and he's no good cooped up in the castle!"

"Wait!" I call out, but she ignores me, bolting forwards.

She doesn't get very far. She's barely a few metres away when there's a loud SNAP as she steps right on to a trap. A net hidden on the ground envelops her and pulls her up into the air, leaving her tangled and helpless, hanging from a tree.

"SHARPTOOTH!" I cry, as she squirms around.

Elena gasps in fright, dropping the ring on the ground. There's a sudden swishing sound as a metal contraption flies past and then a loud clang as it fastens itself round Elena's hands, clamping them together. She stumbles backwards, trying to get it off and is knocked off her feet by another trap net that ensnares her and Glinda, pulling them up off the ground.

As Sharptooth and Elena dangle above me, the monster hunter emerges from the shadows with a thin-lipped smile.

"Nice to see you again, Maggie Helsby," he says loftily.

"Wish I could say the same, Monster Hunter."

He sneers. "I must say, you've made some silly choices up until now. I, on the other hand, am exactly where I wanted to be. On the winning side."

"I don't see how this is winning," I say, gesturing to the magical creatures.

"Thank you for bringing this vampire and witch to me," he says, glancing up at Sharptooth and Elena. "This vampire seems special somehow. Why is that?"

"She's the next Chosen Leader after Count Bloodthirst," I tell him, deciding that at least if I keep him talking, I can buy some time to work out what to do.

"Ah." He tilts his head at her. "Shame you won't have a community of vampires to lead. They'll all be locked up like you, once I've transported all of them to my lair."

"Let me go!" Sharptooth grumbles, squiggling around in the net.

Bat-Ears, who has been trying to cut through the rope with his teeth and clawed feet, gives up and lets out a frustrated screech. He looks like he's about to fly at the monster hunter in anger, but Sharptooth stops him.

"Don't," she instructs, halting him in mid-air, before jabbing her finger in the direction of the box of bats sitting with the other trapped creatures. Heeding the warning, Bat-Ears dips into the net to sit on Sharptooth's head instead.

"Wise," the monster hunter sniggers.

Bat-Head tucks himself further under my coat.

"As I was saying, Maggie, I'll be taking all these monsters away from Skeleton Woods," he announces pompously. "The people of Goreway will be safe, thanks to me."

"They're more scared than they've ever been *because* of you," I retort, but he doesn't seem to hear me, continuing on with great pride as though he's about to be awarded a medal for his service.

"Just like the monster hunters before me, I too have continued the great fight against these terrifying creatures. You understand my drive better than anyone, surely, Maggie Helsby."

I make a face at him. "No way! I don't understand you at all!"

He lifts his eyebrows in surprise. "You're a slayer."

"A protector, you mean. I don't want to be a slayer."

"You don't get to make up the rules," he snaps, as though I've touched a nerve somehow. "If your destiny is to take on a title then that's that! My mother told me right from the start what I was destined to be: a great monster hunter, the next in line after her. And even when things were difficult, I reminded myself that it wasn't up to me. It was up to destiny."

"You can choose your own path," I insist, thinking back on what Marrok told me. "You don't *have* to do this, you know."

"What do you mean?"

"I didn't want to be a Helsby vampire slayer, so I rearranged things a bit."

"That's true!" Sharptooth cries, as her net spins round in slow circles. She waits for it to spin again until she's facing us to add, "She's a really terrible slayer."

"And Sharptooth's a vampire, but she's chosen to be vegetarian!" Elena calls out.

"Because of our decisions, the vampires AND the Goreway residents are happy. We're working together.

You could do the same!" I say, allowing myself to hope as his stern expression softens. "Are you even happy going round the country, capturing monsters?"

"Of course I am," he says, shifting his weight from one foot to the other.

"I'm not so sure. And I don't know whether Chase is all that keen on being a monster hunter, either."

He pauses, lost in his thoughts.

Then suddenly he scrunches up his face and bellows, "Stop trying to confuse me! You're twisting everything!"

"I'm trying to make you see things a different way!"

"I'm tired of this chit-chat!" he shouts. "I have the whole of Skeleton Castle under siege! I have gathered these monsters up and made Goreway safe again. Monsters are monsters. End of. You should be thanking me! Now, this" – he bends down to pick something up from behind a tree that looks like a VERY intense super-soaker water gun with retro-coloured tanks – "is a Goo Blaster!"

"I've heard of it," I say crossly. "You know, Mrs Hollyhogg, who works at the post office, is a very nice person. She did not deserve the goo."

"That was a misunderstanding," he grumbles, put out by my reminding him of the incident. "It's not my fault she dresses like a green monster."

One of the ten-eyed monsters shouts out some gobbledygook from its cage.

"He says that he thinks Mrs Hollyhogg dresses very stylishly," Elena translates.

"I couldn't agree more," I add, smiling at the monster. He grins back, flashing long rows of sharp blue teeth.

"ENOUGH!" the monster hunter barks. "It's time to pick a side, Maggie Helsby. Either you choose to side with me, the winning side, or you chose the losing side, the monsters."

I clench my fists, staring him down to show I'm not afraid.

"If all of these creatures are monsters, then I guess so am I," I declare. "I choose to side with them."

"In that case," he sighs, shaking his head in disappointment, "you choose THE GOO!"

He lifts the Goo Blaster and presses the trigger.

CHAPTER

TWENTY

A globule of bright purple goo flings through the air and narrowly misses as I jump out of the way, flinging myself across the ground. It splats across the trunk of the tree behind me, splashing Elena.

"Ew! Gross!" she squeals, trying to wipe it off her cheek with the metal contraption binding her hands.

"Sorry!" I cry out, scrambling to my feet as the monster hunter presses a button to revolve the tanks round on the blaster, loading up a red one.

While he's distracted, Elena whispers, "The ring!" nodding to it lying next to my shoe.

I quickly sweep it up, gripping it tightly as I race to jump behind a tree as a gigantic blob of red goo is flung in my direction. I make it just in time, hearing it hit the tree, a red treacle-like substance splattering across the leaves and twigs on the ground. I push Dracula's Ring on to the middle finger of my right hand so I don't lose it. Bat-Head, clinging tightly to the inside of my coat, pokes his head out quickly to admire it.

"You can't hide!" the monster hunter cackles, and I peer round the tree to see him dig into his pocket and pull out an odd-looking green tennis ball. "I'll simply smoke you out!"

He throws it forward and it rolls across the ground before emitting a neon-green, foul-smelling vapour. As a putrid stink fills the air, I try to pinch my nose, but somehow it still makes its way up my nostrils and it's so horrible it makes me sneeze. A disgusted Bat-Head screeches at the smell, trying to scrape his tongue with his wing.

"BLEUGH!" Elena cries. "What is that smell?! That is DISGUSTING! It smells like death! Like zombies!"

"Oi!" one of the zombies huffs, as they cough and wretch, before emitting a series of groans.

"Oi!" a green, ten-eyed monster balks, spitting out some gobbledygook.

"Oi!" replies the goblin, rambling in a different language.

"Oi!" shouts the ogre. "SMELL LIKE VAMPIRE!"

"Oi!" Sharptooth yells. "No it doesn't! It smells like stinky wet werewolves!"

"What's going on?" I wheeze, my eyes stinging from the smell.

"Well, I said it smelt like zombies," Elena begins to explain, "and then the zombies said it smelt like slimy monsters. One of the slimy monsters said it smelt like a goblin, who said it smelt like an ogre, who said it smelt like a vampire, and then Sharptooth said it smelt like werewolv–"

"I MEANT WHAT IS GOING ON WITH THE MONSTER HUNTER!"

"Oh, right, sorry!" she says, before gasping loudly. "Uh-oh, he's right beneath me! Maggie, run!"

I push away from the tree, racing forwards just as he appears wielding the Goo Blaster. Dodging through the trees, I'm not quite fast enough and, as a giant blob of purple goo comes launching through the air at me, it lands at my heels. It freezes round my shoes, throwing me forwards, and I fall flat on my face. Thankfully, Bat-Head flies out from my coat just in time and the layers of leaves on the ground provide me with a soft landing.

In a bit of a daze from the fall, I shake my head and then struggle to sit up, brushing the dirt from my face. The slime has hardened round my shoes, solidifying like a heavy purple bowling ball, so I can't get up and run away.

"You chose the wrong side," the monster hunter declares, moving towards me as I desperately try to free my feet whilst shuffling backwards on my bum.

He raises the Goo Blaster at me again. I shield my face with my arms.

Suddenly a blur of dark fur comes out of nowhere, tackling the monster hunter to the ground and sending the Goo Blaster flying from his grip. As the monster hunter yelps in shock, hitting the ground, I lower my hands to see a huge wolf pinning him down. The wolf glances back at me and I recognize his light blue eyes.

"*Marrok?*"

He nods to me before turning to snarl down at the monster hunter. I return my attention to trying to get free of the goo by wriggling my feet out of my trainers. Bat-Head lands on one of my knees, giving me squeaks of encouragement.

Squirming beneath Marrok's heavy paws, the monster hunter manages to reach his hand into a deep pocket of his coat, pulling out a silver chain necklace decorated with glowing blue charms in the shape of crescent moons and stars.

"Marrok, watch out!" I call, still trying to yank my feet free. "He's got something in his hand!"

The chain entwined through his fingers, the monster hunter holds it up, letting it swing back and forth like a pendulum. Marrok takes one glance at it and leaps off the monster hunter. Whining loudly, he backs away from him, his eyes filled with alarm and his tail tucked between his legs.

Grinning from ear to ear, the monster hunter gets to his feet, holding the chain aloft. Marrok can't take his eyes off it and he cowers low to the ground, his paws slipping and sliding through the dirt.

"Thought I wouldn't be prepared for werewolves, did you?" the monster hunter says, bristling.

"Leave him alone!" I yell, pulling my legs with all my might.

"This, Maggie, is a Werewolf Repeller," he continues, nodding to the chain as Marrok is forced to keep moving backwards away from it. "You see these little charms? They contain a magic that strikes fear into the hearts of werewolves. Do you know who created this magic a very long time ago? The monster from whom my ancestor took it? A vampire."

Marrok has shifted so far back now that he's near to Sharptooth, who remains suspended helplessly above him. I continue to frantically wriggle my feet from my shoes, feeling them slowly start to slip out as the monster hunter rambles on.

"Do you see what I'm trying to say, Maggie?" he asks, glancing back at me. "I'm trying to open your eyes to the fact that these monsters cannot even get along with one another! You may like to think that we can all be friends, but it's not possible. There's no point in even trying."

"They can get on! You saw us playing football together!" I point out, trying not to make it too obvious that my right heel has come loose from the shoe as I attempt to do the same with my left.

"I visited Egypt once with my mother, when she was tracking a deadly monster. I ended up forging a friendship with a mummy," he recalls, seeming momentarily melancholy. "I thought we were friends and then the mummy tried to put a terrible curse on me and my family. Once my mother had rescued me, she said she hoped I'd learnt my lesson. I had. I would never trust a monster again. I suggest you do the same."

"Oscar, don't do this," I plead, hoping that by using his actual name, he might be more inclined to listen. "It sounds like you don't really want to."

He sighs and then reaches down for the Goo Blaster, picking it up off the ground.

My left foot finally comes loose.

The monster hunter clicks a button on the Goo Blaster, loading a double-goo tank into place. He points it in the direction of both Marrok and Sharptooth.

"Once these two have been gooed, I shall imprison them in a cage and they will be transported to my lair in London where they will never see the sunlight again," he declares.

"HA! I don't like sunlight!" Sharptooth retorts. "So THERE!"

"Fine." The monster hunter rolls his eyes. "You will be stuck in prison and never see your friends or vampire family again."

Sharptooth's face falls. "Oh. That *is* bad."

Cowering beneath her, Marrok lets out a heartbreaking whine.

Behind the monster hunter's back, I shuffle my feet out from the goo bowling ball. I stand up and begin to creep towards him quietly in my socks, Bat-Head now on my shoulder, his eyes narrowed determinedly.

"Finally, I have caught a werewolf, and I get a vampire at the same time. Two for the price of one!" the monster hunter cackles, oblivious to my approach. "TIME TO BE GOOED!"

I barely think about what I'm doing. As the monster hunter points the Goo Blaster at my friends, I cry, "NO!" and jump out in front of them, shielding my face with my arms, preparing to be catapulted backwards by a deluge of goo.

But I'm not.

What happens next seems to occur in slow motion.

A sudden searing burst of red light blasts out from where I'm standing, rippling through the trees and bathing the woodland in a rich crimson glimmer. A wall of sparkling red flames whooshes up from the woodland floor, circling around the creatures and forming a protective wall between us and the monster hunter. His Goo Blaster backfires and he's knocked off his feet by the double whammy of the burst of flames ahead of him and a shower of green goo.

There's a chorus of amazed gasps, oohs and aahs from the supernatural creatures as they witness the brilliant blaze of red. My hands feel as though they're tingling with heat and I lower them to see the red gem of Dracula's Ring glowing brightly on my finger.

The flames begin to die down, fading to embers before vanishing, leaving no mark, burnt leaves or any sign of soot. It's as though they were never there. The glow of the ring softens, growing dim before vanishing, the gemstone returning to its usual mesmerizing swirl. I turn in shock to Bat-Head on my shoulder. He stares back at me in wonder.

Drenched in the hardening goo, the monster hunter emits a strangled cry. I ignore him, my heart thudding so hard against my chest there's a ringing in my ears, as I try to make sense of what just happened. A rustle from nearby alerts me to the presence of Mum, Dad, Ari, Miles and Mr Frank stepping forwards through the trees, all of them astounded by what they've just witnessed.

"Maggie," Ari grins, "how did you *do* that?"

"That was AMAZING!" Miles cries, his eyes so wide they look like they might pop right out at any second.

"I don't understand," Dad whispers, his hands gripping the sides of his head. "One second you were jumping in front of the goo and the next second ... the next second there was FIRE! And it was sparkly and red! Now it's gone! It's disappeared! HOW IS THIS POSSIBLE?"

Mum comes running over and wraps her arms

around me, squeezing me so tight I can hardly breathe. "Are you all right? What happened?"

"I'm not sure," I whisper back, as Dad joins in on the hug, too. "I really don't know."

"You did it, Maggie!" Mr Frank exclaims proudly, as my parents eventually let me go so I can breathe again. "You saved everyone!"

With the monster hunter safely gooed and the Werewolf Repeller chain hidden from sight somewhere beneath the slime, Marrok is able to stand and transform back into his human self. Ari and Miles gawp at him.

"I meant to say this at the football match, but the way you do that is so *cool*," Ari says enviously as he comes over to us. "I want to be a werewolf!"

Miles hushes her, but Marrok just laughs before beaming down at me.

"Thanks for saving me from the goo, Maggie."

"Thanks for saving *me* from the goo before!" I point out. "I hope he didn't hurt you with that charm necklace thing."

Marrok glances over to where the monster hunter is rolling about, immobile in his goo glob, like a tortoise stuck on its back.

"GET THIS GOO OFF ME!" he shouts to no avail.

"He can't hurt anyone any more," Marrok observes with a low growl.

Ari shoots her hand to the sky. "I have a question!" she declares. "What just HAPPENED? What was the fire thing? It looked MAGICAL!"

"That's because it was magic," Elena says from her net. "This explains the bat."

"Which bat?" Marrok asks.

"Maggie's bat. You know slayers aren't supposed to get bats, right? They choose vampires," she explains.

Diana shouts, "HI-HOL-HER-HAT" through the cloth gagging her mouth.

Elena translates: "She says, she told you that."

"So, what are you saying?" Mum asks apprehensively. "That Maggie is somehow a kind of ... *vampire*?"

"WOOHOO!" Sharptooth cries.

"No, that's not what I'm saying," Elena clears up.

"BOO!" Sharptooth huffs.

Elena chuckles. "What I'm saying is that what you all just witnessed, with the flames and the light, was a protective *spell*. It was magic."

"M-magic?" I repeat, bewildered.

"Not just any magic," she emphasizes. "Vampire magic."

I look down at the ring on my hand, my fingers still tingling from its power.

"You conjured vampire magic through Dracula's Ring – it's chosen its protector," Elena smiles down at me. "Maggie, the ring has chosen you."

CHAPTER

TWENTY-ONE

I don't understand.

Me? Why would Dracula's Ring choose me? It doesn't make any sense.

"It makes total sense!" Sharptooth declares instead. "Maggie, of COURSE the ring chose you. You protect vampires! And humans!"

"HEEZ-HER-HIR," Diana calls out.

"Can you repeat that?" Elena replies.

"HEEZ-HER-HIR!" she repeats.

Elena shakes her head. "Nope. Still can't understand what you're trying to say."

Bat-Ears swoops down from Sharptooth's net and

screeches at Bat-Head, who hops up and down on my shoulder impatiently.

"Yes, I agree, we really need to free everyone," I announce, realizing that we're all standing around marvelling over the ring while all the creatures remain tied up.

"If that's the same kind of rope that caught us at the football, it will be fang-proof," Marrok says, pointing at Elena and Sharptooth. "You need the monster hunter's knife to cut through it."

"There must be one somewhere," I say, putting my hands on my hips. "Can anyone see a bag of his stuff?"

A voice emerges from the trees.

"Looking for this?"

Chase steps out into view, walking towards us and holding the monster hunter's bag. He drops it on the ground and lifts up the special knife we need to cut through the rope.

His dad lets out a triumphant "HA!" rolling on to his side so he can look up at him.

"It's your big moment, Chase!" the monster hunter encourages as Chase strides up to Elena's net. "You can do it! You were born for this!"

I yell out, "Chase, no!" as Chase lifts the knife and...

…cuts her free.

The rope snaps as he swipes through it and she can let her legs drop down through the gap he's created. He holds out his hand so she can steady herself as she jumps down on to the ground with Glinda cradled in her arms. They both thank him profusely.

"W-what are you doing?" the monster hunter whimpers, watching this play out in horror. "Don't let them free, Chase! Capture them! Capture them all!"

"Actually, Dad, I'm not going to be a monster hunter," he says tiredly, as Elena helps Sharptooth get free of her net. "I've had a chat with Ari, Miles and Mr Frank and they've helped me realize that I don't want to capture creatures. If anything, I want to help them."

"What are you talking about?" his dad seethes, furious. "GET THEM!"

Crossing his arms stubbornly across his chest, Chase shakes his head.

"You spoke to Chase?" I ask Ari and Miles in amazement. "When?"

"When you, Sharptooth and Elena came here to Skeleton Woods," Ari reveals. "We decided to completely ignore your instruction to go home and 'stay safe', and instead realized that there was a way we could help."

"I was wondering out loud how I was possibly going to find any further information on the monster hunter, like you asked me to, Maggie," Mr Frank explains, "and then these two had the genius idea that, instead of trying to find facts within the pages of old, dusty books, I should try speaking to the one person who knows the monster hunter best of all. And who knows him better than his own son? Ari knew exactly where to find Chase."

"We found him looking wistfully at the photography through the window of the art gallery," Ari says, smiling encouragingly at Chase. "A true artist can never resist the chance to study and enjoy other people's work."

"To be honest, it was you who gave us the idea to find him, Maggie," Miles reveals, grinning at me. "When you left, you said that, as the Helsby slayer, you were the only one who might be able to make the monster hunter change his mind. But that isn't true, is it, Chase?"

"I hope not," Chase sighs, kneeling down on the ground and appealing to his dad. "The whole town is in hiding because of us."

"The people are afraid of the *monsters*!" Oscar hisses.

"These creatures are not the monsters, Dad," Chase retorts sternly. "We are."

Oscar's eyes widen in shock. "*What?*"

"Just because Granny was a monster hunter doesn't mean you have to be, and it doesn't mean I have to be, either," Chase says, sitting back on his heels. "The whole thing is completely outdated! We've never bothered to get to know these supernatural creatures. I think if we did, we might like them. Ari and Miles told me all about how they hang out with the vampires and it sounds kind of fun. They've even inspired Ari to create a graphic novel."

"And I'm the STAR!" Sharptooth cries, throwing her arms out before taking a bow. "Thank you! Thank you!"

"Aren't you tired of all this hunting and tracking and *yelling*?" Chase asks his dad, looking pained. "I think that when Mum died, you threw yourself into your work, believing this was your vocation. Maybe it was a distraction from how hard it is without her."

Oscar's jaw clenches.

"I've been too worried about upsetting you by telling you the truth," Chase continues, "because I know how difficult it's been for you and I didn't want to do something that might remind you of her, but I want to learn more about photography. I think Mum would have wanted me to. But more than anything, I think she would have wanted me to be happy. And I'm not really happy chasing monsters. Dad, you deserve to be happy, too. *Are* you happy doing what you do, Dad? Have you ever even questioned it?"

"But … but … I have to be a monster hunter," Oscar says unconvincingly, his eyes dropping.

"No, you don't. That's what Ari and Miles have helped me to understand," Chase insists. "We get to make our own choices. I'm choosing not to be a monster hunter and you can choose that, too."

Oscar is astounded, grappling with this information. "What else would I do? Being a monster hunter is all I've ever known!"

"I found those Costa Rica leaflets in the bottom of your bag," Chase divulges with a smile. "The ones about saving the turtles? I remember Mum used to talk about going there."

His dad blinks at him.

"I think that deep down, you've always known you don't want to ensnare monsters in nets," Chase continues. "I think you want to save turtles from them. Why don't you realize that dream? And leave these creatures to get on with theirs?"

"I *have* always wanted to go to Costa Rica," Oscar finally admits in a small voice. "But I didn't think it was my destiny."

"I think it's definitely your destiny if you want it to be," Ari says, nodding vigorously. "You simply have to make a choice. Helping turtles in Costa Rica, or stomping round England in those horrible boots. What would you like to do?"

He takes a moment to consider everything and then lets out a long sigh, before a smile creeps across his face. "I would like to spend the rest of my life helping the turtles in Costa Rica."

"YES!" Ari cheers, giving Miles such an enthusiastic high five that he winces in pain, cradling his hand with his other one.

"Thanks, Dad," Chase says, his cheeks flushed with excitement.

"No, thank *you*," Oscar insists, with a much more genuine and softer smile than he wore before, as though he's been plastering the wrong one on his face for years. "I never had the courage to stand up to my mum and tell her that being the monster hunter wasn't what I wanted to do. After a while, I became so focused on being the person I was supposed to be, I forgot who I really am. Your mother would be proud of you. And so am I."

Oscar reaches over and gives a comforting pat on

the top of the hardened goo, before pushing himself up off the floor and picking up the bag of monster-hunting equipment.

"I'd better start freeing everyone," he says, nodding at all the creatures happily watching everything unfold from their cages.

"What about my aunt?" Elena reminds them. "And all the other creatures you've got locked up in the London lair. Can we free them, too?"

"Yes, of course," Oscar says, looking embarrassed. "I'm so sorry. I'm sorry to all of you for everything I've done."

"Things will be different now," Elena says. "That's what matters."

"Once we've let all these creatures out, I'll give you the keys and the directions to where your aunt is," Chase promises her. "I'm guessing you can get there quicker than us. You can go free her yourself."

Ecstatic, I pull Ari and Miles into a giant hug as Chase and Elena set about opening up the cages and untying the witches.

"You did it!" I exclaim, jumping up and down with them. "Thank you for ignoring me about going home and going to find Chase instead!"

"Like I said, we're a team," Ari laughs, clapping me on the back. "We're never going to let you handle stuff as important as your DESTINY on your own."

"Mr Frank played a big part in it, too," Miles points out, causing Mr Frank to look down at the ground modestly. "You have a pretty awesome slayer guide."

"Although I think it's official that you're definitely not a slayer," Mr Frank points out, gesturing to Dracula's Ring. "You really are a protector."

"She's the bridge," Diana informs him, coming over to us now that she's been freed. "That's what I was trying to say when Elena couldn't understand me. You're the bridge connecting the vampires and the humans, Maggie. That's why Bat-Head is sticking with you. And why Dracula's Ring chose you as its protector."

Bat-Head squeaks, nuzzling against my cheek.

As Chase and Elena continue to liberate the non-humans, they all make their way over to thank us for helping them out.

"I'm very impressed," Savannah admits, rubbing her wrists now that the magic-prevention contraption has been removed from her hands. "Perhaps I underestimated you, Maggie. And you too, Sharptooth. I apologize for being rude about the vampires."

"No worries!" Sharptooth says cheerily. "I'm sorry for telling you that witches were boring, smelly know-it-alls!"

Savannah frowns. "I don't remember you telling me that."

"Oh. I must have said it to someone else," Sharptooth admits guiltily.

"Thanks for rescuing us, Maggie!" Nash declares, doing somersaults through the air as he flies over. "Before the monster hunter got me with his Ghost Removal Machine, I was considering spending some time haunting your house, but I've decided against it, because I quite like you now."

Dad looks alarmed. "Pleased to hear it!"

"We already have a slayer and a bat under our roof, I'm not sure a ghost would have caused much more trouble," Mum points out, nudging Dad playfully.

"Actually, Nash can cause a LOT of trouble," Mr Frank informs them. "You should see the plumbing bill that the school has been left with."

"Sorry about that." Nash winces. "Want me to haunt the plumber?"

"How about you take a holiday from haunting?" Mum suggests. "You could just hang out with your friends instead."

"Ah, but you forget that ghosts don't have any friends," he says, the other freed ghosts nodding along beside him. "When I heard the enchantments of Skeleton Castle were down, I thought at least I could have a nice castle of my own to haunt – that might soften the blow of being a lonely ghost."

"You won't be a lonely ghost any more, Nash. We're your friends," I inform him proudly, gesturing to the group. "So long as you don't haunt us or destroy any more bathrooms."

His face lights up. "Really?"

"Yeah!" Ari agrees. "Having a few ghosts as friends sounds pretty cool."

"Oh sure," Miles mutters, "throw the ghosts in with the werewolves and the vampires and the witches."

"He loves you all really," Ari assures the non-humans.

"MAGGIE NEW FRIEND!" The ogre bellows as he stomps his big feet, making the ground shake and irritating the zombies, whose balance is a little off in the first place as they lumber over to us, free from their chains.

Crawling across the ground with amazingly fast and agile movement, the orange pointy-eared goblin appears at my feet, holding a leaf. He offers it up to me with bright, gleaming eyes.

"For goblins, leaves are gifts that they like to put around their homes and look at," Sharptooth whispers to me. "A bit like what you told me humans do with pretty flowers."

"Oh, right! Thank you," I say to the goblin, admiring it. "This is a really nice leaf."

He nods shyly and then, embarrassed by all the attention, crawls away up the nearest tree and sits crouched within the branches, watching the proceedings from there.

Next to approach is the group of single-eyed pink-haired monsters, who remove their hats from their heads and give me very sweet little bows, speaking in roars that I don't understand.

"Uh … anyone know what they're saying?" I ask, looking to Elena hopefully as she joins us after freeing them.

"They're thanking you and emphasizing that they never meant to harm anyone in Goreway," she translates, before explaining their predicament. "Hats are like treasure to this species of monster. They collect them. They were only ever running after those people to ask if they could have their hats."

"That makes so much sense!" Miles exclaims. "The

two people who reported it both said their hats were swiped from their heads before the monsters left them alone. A complete misunderstanding."

"It's very nice to meet you," I say to the pink-haired monsters.

There's a loud barrage of gobbledygook as the green, slimy monsters totter over, fixing me with all their eyes and speaking at me continuously. I look to Elena hopefully.

"They're also thanking all of you for rescuing them," she says, "and asking if there are any good bins you know of that might have last-minute availability, as they're hoping to stay in the area for another few days."

They launch into another speech, both talking over each other. Elena waits for both of them to finish before smiling up at Sharptooth.

"If the vampire community wouldn't mind, they'd love to have a tour of Skeleton Castle. Not because they think any treasure is in there but because apparently there's a medieval bin there they'd like to see."

"I'm sure Count Bloodthirst would be happy to show you the bin," Sharptooth says before clasping a hand round her mouth. "Count Bloodthirst! The vampires! We have to turn off the artificial sunlight!"

"I can help with that," Chase calls out, opening the final cage to let the bats free. They whoosh upwards out the box, soaring round and round, dancing through the air in celebration of being free.

"I can only apologize again," Oscar mutters, chagrined. "I would help Chase turn the sunlight off, but—" His eyes flicker down to the globule of goo preventing him from moving. "This takes a while to get off. Chase, you'll need to fetch me my Goo Melter when you get a moment, but go free the vampires first."

While Chase rushes off towards Skeleton Castle, Ari picks up my hand in hers to examine Dracula's Ring closely.

"I can't believe you conjured vampire magic, Maggie," she says, admiring the swirling gem. "Did you know what you were doing?"

I shake my head. "Not at all."

"It was a very powerful protective spell," Savannah informs me.

"If you can do vampire magic, like Count Bloodthirst," Miles begins thoughtfully, "does that mean you can command all the bats like him, too?"

We turn to the witches and Sharptooth for answers.

"Possibly," Savannah reasons. "You might need to

track down a book of vampire spells to see what you can do. But they're rare and—"

"I have one," I inform her, pulling it out from my pocket and nodding to Mr Frank. "My slayer guide got it for me."

"Ah." She smiles. "Well then. You'll have to do your homework."

"I hope you can grow fangs," Ari says wistfully. "That would be *awesome*."

"They're actually quite high maintenance," Marrok informs her, running his tongue along his teeth. "Not easy keeping fangs shiny and white."

"Ah, now, we can help you there," Dad says, stepping in. "How often do you floss? Because, as a werewolf, you should be flossing at least two, or even three, times a day."

"Not that I don't enjoy chat about dental care," Diana says, "but before we get into that, perhaps we should let Maggie restore the enchantments of Skeleton Woods."

I jolt my head up. "What?"

She gestures up to the trees. "Isn't that why you sought out Dracula's Ring in the first place? You wanted to get the enchantments back up and running so that the vampires can live here in peace."

Sharptooth's expression falls. "Oh, yes. That's right."

"Now that the ring has chosen its protector, we should be able to do the spell." Diana hesitates, watching me curiously. "That is, if that's still what you want."

I glance across the group of supernatural creatures standing with me. Their many eyes – and I mean *many*, because some of them have ten each – blink back at me, filled with hope.

"You know what," I announce, an idea starting to form in my brain as Count Bloodthirst emerges from the shadows, "maybe there's another way."

CHAPTER

TWENTY-TWO

I never would have guessed that Count Bloodthirst loves to throw a party.

Sure, he hosted one in Skeleton Castle a few months ago when we chased out Mayor Collyfleur, but I thought that was a one-time thing. I was wrong. According to Sharptooth, he's been extremely dedicated to the party planning for today's celebration in Skeleton Woods and, since I've arrived a little earlier than everyone else to help out, I get to witness his party-planning skills first-hand.

"Maggothead, why are you wearing the bunting?" he snaps, gliding over to the group of vampires who are supposed to be decorating the trees. "It's not clothing, it's decoration."

Maggothead puts his hands on his hips, the colourful bunting wrapped all around him, wound tightly from his head to his feet. "Why didn't someone tell me that BEFORE I put it on?"

Nightmare, wearing a party hat on his nose, sniggers. "You look STUPID!"

With a heavy sigh, Count Bloodthirst begins barking orders at them, intent on making everything look just perfect, while I help Sharptooth check over the food tables. The vampires have really put a lot of effort into the occasion, trying to cater for the various dietary requirements necessary for such a guest list.

"Is this ... rubbish?" I ask, pointing to a pile of bin bags, as Bat-Ears and Bat-Head start bouncing up and down on them.

"Yes, it is," Sharptooth replies proudly.

"Do you want me to ask my parents to take it to the tip?"

"No! We went to the tip to retrieve them! You never told me tips were so much fun, Maggie. The cardboard crate was the best one. We had to drag Fangly out of there, she was having so much fun burrowing in all of it."

"Sharptooth," I say, giving her a strange look, "why

would you go to the tip to get a load of bin bags full of rubbish to bring to your party?"

"What else are the slimy green monsters going to eat?" She eyes up the pile. "Do you think we got them enough?"

Realizing that the monsters sit in the bins in order to consume the bags thrown into them, I assure Sharptooth that they've got plenty to snack on. I wave over Mum and Dad, who arrive with Ari and Miles. Carrying a crate of ketchup bottles, Dad carefully sets it down on one of the food tables.

"Thank you!" Sharptooth gasps in excitement, zooming over to him. "I might need one or two bottles now, just to keep me going. Decorating requires a lot of energy."

"Sure," Dad chuckles, passing her one. He nods to the large box of rocks on the table next to the crate. "What are those for?"

"Snacks for the ogre. We tried to collect as many as possible, but if he eats them all and he's still hungry, then we have a bucket of earwax over there," she explains, pointing at a bucket of yellow lumps nearby. "They're partial to it, apparently. You have no idea how difficult it was to source."

Dad promptly turns green.

It was Sharptooth's idea to have the party in the woods rather than the castle, mainly because she didn't think the ogre would be able to fit in the front door and we didn't want anyone to feel left out, especially now that Skeleton Woods is open to everyone.

The enchantments are gone. Officially, this time.

And in their place, we've created a brand-new contract.

When I had the idea, I thought the vampires would need a lot of persuading, but they were on board right from the start. Instead of a contract that comes with enchantments keeping everyone out and the vampires in, we've drawn up a new agreement whereby supernatural creatures are welcome to make their home in Skeleton Woods and in the surrounding areas, so long as no harm comes to the other woodland residents OR the people of Goreway town – and there's an added clause that the creatures should do everything in their power not to be seen by any humans, so as not to cause panic.

Just like the old contract bound all those centuries ago, this one was also overseen by the Helsby vampire slayer.

The contact, written by quill on old parchment

(with just one inky bat footprint in the corner – Bat-Ears's doing before Sharptooth could stop him) was signed by Count Bloodthirst, on behalf of the Skeleton Castle community, and Marrok's dad, Grimmwolf, who represented all other supernatural creatures new to the woods.

According to Marrok and Aunty Loveta, it didn't take as much persuading as they'd imagined to get Grimmwolf to agree to the idea of sharing a woodland with vampires. He had been stunned to hear about the football match, finding it hard to get his head round the notion that neither the vampires nor the wolves had attacked each other on sight. But Marrok talked him through everything that had happened since then and once Grimmwolf accepted that his son was determined to hold on to his friendship with the vampires of Skeleton Woods and wouldn't let the pack attack Skeleton Castle – and with Aunty Loveta's backing – he began to consider that it might be possible to live nearby them in harmony.

Apparently, after a little bit of thought, he declared that he would let the pack stay here and find a way to share the woodland with the vampires, purely for Marrok's sake.

But, Marrok informed us with a smile, everyone knows he's pretending it's a sacrifice on his part, when in fact you couldn't drag him away from Goreway Hair Salon if you tried – he's their star stylist.

In the end, he didn't seem reluctant in the slightest to sign the new contract.

Diana Dazzle and I signed as witnesses, and then I had to bind it using Dracula's Ring.

Having practised the spell with Diana a few times beforehand, I nervously placed my hand on the contract and, closing my eyes to concentrate, I recited the enchantment.

The parchment burst into red flames, but didn't seem to be burning.

The blaze quickly died down into a round, glowing ember at the bottom of the page where it vanished, leaving a red wax seal in the shape of a bat.

"That is AMAZING!" Ari had blurted out, prompting all of us to laugh and then cheer as Count Bloodthirst announced the ceremony had finished and to celebrate the new agreement, he would be hosting a party that very evening in Skeleton Woods.

In the spirit of the contract, everyone is invited.

"What happens if a creature breaks the contract?"

Miles asked him as he ushered us out the castle this morning so he could begin preparing for the party.

"They'd be cursed, of course," he answered.

"C-cursed?"

Count Bloodthirst loomed over Miles. "This agreement is bound by the powerful magic of Dracula's Ring. Should anyone break it, the ring's vengeful curse would be swift and deadly." He let out a blood-curdling cackle. "Anyway, off you go. I need to start fitting the bats for their party shoes."

Since then, Miles keeps looking at my hand warily as though the ring might suddenly attack him, no matter how much I reassure him.

The vampires eventually finish the decorating with some help from Ari, Miles and me in time for the party to begin. The three of us humans had to blow up all the balloons because vampires don't have any breath, a process that was significantly slowed by Dreadclaw, who had never burst a balloon before. Once he popped one accidentally, it was very difficult to get him to stop digging his fangs into all of them. I had to ask Bat-Head to have a word with his bat, who managed to distract him with party poppers – we consequently don't have any left for the party guests, but there is confetti all over the ground, which, in Dreadclaw's defence, adds a nice splash of colour.

Sharptooth cranks up the music on the speakers Ari's lent her for the party, and the monsters all start to arrive. Nash is very excited to introduce me as one of his "MANY new human friends" to another ghost he bumped into at a gig.

"We've decided to form a ghost band," Nash informs me excitedly, as the other ghost nods along. "What do you think of the name 'The Phantoms'?"

"I think that sounds brilliant!"

He high-fives the other ghost, their hands just going through the other's.

"Perfect, we'll be sure to invite you to our first performance. We're going to have a lot of time to practice, now that we're both haunting the same place – we've moved into the rafters of the local music venue." Nash grins at me. "And don't worry, the human bands won't know we're there. Much."

I leave the ghosts to discuss the sound they want to create and, passing the pink-haired monsters, I compliment them on their fabulous hats – a couple of which I recognize from Mum's wardrobe. I wonder if Dad asked her permission before handing those out.

I see her showing the slimy green monsters and the orange goblin the postcard we received this morning from Oscar and Chase, and make my way over to join them.

"They say that it's lovely and hot in Costa Rica and that so far Chase has managed to photograph four of the six species of toucan there," Mum informs her audience, showing them the front of the card. "This is one of his pictures. Look, that's what a toucan looks like."

Taking the postcard from her, they examine the bird on the front in wonder, before one of the green monsters snatches the card from the goblin's hand and chomps on it, letting out a resounding burp.

"Oh!" Mum says in surprise. "Well, I suppose that might count as recycling."

"Maggie!" Dad waves me over where he's standing with Grimmwolf and Aunty Loveta. "I've just been filling these two in on our new business plan, and they're very enthusiastic about the endeavour."

"A new dental practice in Skeleton Woods for supernatural creatures. I think it's brilliant," Grimmwolf declares, before tapping his teeth. "It's been a nightmare to find any dentist that understands these fangs."

"We've already made huge progress with the vampires' dental care," Dad assures them. "Once they stopped destroying the toothbrushes, things became a lot easier. We're currently developing a beetroot-flavour toothpaste."

Aunty Loveta raises her eyebrows. "I think we'll stick to mint."

I laugh. "The new dental practice is going to be a huge success, Dad."

"It's certainly going to be busy," he says, smiling as Mum joins our conversation. He puts an arm round her shoulders. "Especially as you'll be out, running about town fixing things, as the new mayor."

Mum rolls her eyes. "I'm not the mayor."

"*Yet*," I add, giving her a hug round the waist, before explaining to the werewolves. "We've just started Mum's campaign to become the new mayor of Goreway. She has some great ideas and one of her main priorities will be protecting Skeleton Woods. It will NEVER be a golf course."

"And that's a promise," Mum says in her most authoritative politician voice.

"You certainly have our votes!" Grimmwolf declares.

Leaving Mum to ask them about any changes they'd like to see, I wander over to where Elena is standing with a witch I don't recognize, having just introduced her to Diana and the other witches of the local council.

"Maggie, hi." Elena smiles, gesturing to the blue-haired witch next to her. "This is my aunt, Tabitha."

"Thank you for rescuing all of us," Tabitha says, placing her warm hands around mine as her familiar, a large toad perched on her shoulder, ribbits gratefully at me. "I hadn't intended on spending my trip to England stuck in the monster hunter's prison cell, so it's lovely to be out again. What an honour to meet you."

"It's all thanks to Elena," I inform her, blushing. "If she hadn't helped us find the ring, then none of this would have happened."

"Yes, I told her that I'm surprised she trusted a vampire AND a slayer with the family secret," Tabitha chuckles. "I'm not sure I would have done the same."

"Things are changing now," Elena says, gesturing at all the guests in the party.

"Not necessarily for the better," grumbles Glinda, sitting at Elena's feet, flicking her tail impatiently. "That ogre over there nearly stepped on me. If it wasn't for my excellent instincts, I would have been flattened. What time is our broomstick back to Transylvania?"

"You're always welcome to visit us, Maggie." Elena smiles.

"Thanks, Elena, and I promise to look after Dracula's Ring."

She nods. "It's where it's supposed to be. It is vampire magic after all."

After speaking to Elena's aunt for a while about Transylvania's spookiest spots, I move over to Miles, who is busy admiring Ari's graphic novel, which she finished this afternoon. Bat-Head screeches with joy from my shoulder when she explains that she's now added him in as a character.

"I finally decided on the ending," she says, flicking to the final pages. "I thought that—"

"Whoa!" I interrupt, taking the book from her and closing it. "Don't tell us what happens in the end! You'll spoil it!"

"Fine," she laughs, picking up a cup from the drinks table. "But I wouldn't worry too much. That's not the *final* ending."

"How can an ending not be final?" Miles asks, frowning.

"When it's the first of many," she announces. "I've decided this will be the first book in an entire series."

"A series! Brilliant!" I exclaim.

"We have had a *lot* of adventures," Miles reasons.

"Way too many to fit into just one book," Ari concludes.

"Have you told Sharptooth?" I ask, glancing over to where she's dancing with the zombies. "She's going to be so excited, she might explode!"

"Not yet, but I will," Ari promises, before taking a few gulps of her drink.

Her eyes widen and she suddenly spits it out over Miles.

"ARGH!" he cries, his clothes now splattered with red stains.

She grimaces, putting the cup back down and wiping the red dribble off her chin.

"Sorry," she says, with a shudder. "I just drank ketchup."

Trying my best not to giggle too much at Miles's grumpy expression, I pass them some napkins.

"Thanks again for helping me with this adventure," I say as they clean themselves up. "I couldn't have done any of it without you."

"You don't have to thank us for helping you, Maggie," Miles insists, wiping at his T-shirt. "We're your friends."

"You've got a lot of responsibility on your shoulders,

especially with that thing," Ari adds, gesturing to Dracula's Ring. "We'll always be here to help."

I grin at her and pull them into a group hug, Miles still desperately trying to get the ketchup out of his top and muttering about how he hopes it won't stain.

Deep in conversation with Marrok across the way, Mr Frank catches my eye and I head over to say hi.

"Did you hear that Marrok has been made captain of the school football team?" Mr Frank informs me. "I was just congratulating him."

"Miles told me earlier!" I say happily. "We'll all be there to cheer you on at your first match next week."

"Thanks, Maggie," Marrok says. "I hope Miles wasn't too disappointed; I know he was hoping to be captain, too."

"He said there was no question it should be you. Besides, I think he's got his work cut out in his new role as coach of the vampire football team," I chuckle, glancing over to Maggothead and Nightmare, who are wearing the new sports kit we bought for them.

Ari designed it – it's all black, of course, with the team's emblem, a red bat symbol, on the front, their names printed on the back, and, as per the vampire rules, each shirt has a mini cloak attached to it. Maggothead is currently wearing his football shirt the wrong way round so his cloak falls down his front, and Nightmare is still insisting on wearing the shorts on his head. I spot Bat-Grouch sitting on the branch of a tree just above their heads, watching them with disdain.

"Yeah, I think Miles may be quite busy getting the vampire team into shape," Marrok laughs. "But I look forward to beating them during the non-human football league we're going to organize. Bat-Grouch has agreed to put together a schedule."

"I'm sure he's thrilled at the prospect."

"Thanks for everything, Maggie," Marrok says, his eyes twinkling at me. "Thanks to you and the vampires, our pack has finally found its home." He hesitates, adding in a low voice, "Although I'm not sure we're going to listen to Count Bloodthirst's housewarming advice and replace electricity with 'good, old-fashioned' candlelight."

When Marrok is dragged away by the zombies to teach them how to howl at the moon, Mr Frank admits that he's been thinking about how to improve his role as my slayer guide.

"How would you feel about extra lessons outside of school on folklore and supernatural creatures? Perhaps Ari and Miles could join, too?" he suggests. "We can take some time to go through that vampire magic spell book, too."

"That's a great idea!" I say, already excited to learn more.

We watch Marrok as he throws his head back and lets out a howl that echoes through the trees. The zombies attempt to do the same, but it comes out as a sort of series of grunts, although Marrok continues to encourage them.

"Things may be good for now," Mr Frank observes. "But who knows what else is out there?"

Later, while everyone else is dancing in the light of the flaming torches, Sharptooth sidles up to me and pulls at my sleeve.

"Maggie, do you have a moment?"

"Of course!"

"Great." She picks me up and throws me over her shoulder before I know what's happening. "Come with me!"

She jumps into the air and I drop my cup of lemonade, watching it plummet to the ground as we soar up into the trees. Landing effortlessly on a branch, she puts me upright and steadies me as I get to grips with the fact that we're right at the top of one of the tallest trees in the woods.

She helps me slowly sit down on the branch and I grip it so tightly my knuckles go white, peering over my dangling legs to see the dots of people below. The ogre waves at us, his head nearly scraping the bottoms of my shoes, while Bat-Ears and Bat-Head dodge around his head as they flutter up to join. They both land next to us and then, wrapping their wings around themselves, topple forwards in perfect synchronization, to hang upside down and rest.

"You're good with heights, aren't you, Maggie?" Sharptooth asks, plopping down next to me and offering me a drink from the carton of beetroot juice she has in her pocket. I graciously turn it down.

"Yes." I gulp, hoping that this branch is a sturdy one. "Although humans wouldn't usually be this high without some kind of safety harness on."

"That's okay," Sharptooth says, sipping on her straw. "I'm your safety harness. I won't let you fall."

She squeezes out the last of her drink and then puts the carton back in her pocket, before gesturing outwards at the view. The moon is shining brightly down on the canopy of trees, the stars twinkling across the vast night sky.

"Wow," I say breathlessly, realizing I'd been so shocked at being so high, I hadn't taken in the sights.

"I know," Sharptooth agrees. "I wanted to show you what it's like up here, because it's thanks to you that I found this spot in the first place."

I glance at her in confusion. "It is?"

"When you first came to Skeleton Castle, I'd never met a human before. And talking to you about human books and human music and human food and human hobbies made me realize that there was a big world out there, beyond Skeleton Woods. So I came up here at night to take a look."

She shoots me her wonky smile.

"I know that you're a slayer and I'm a vampire," she concludes, "but I'm very happy that you're my best friend, Maggie Helsby."

I grin back at her. "Me too, Sharptooth Shadow."

We fall back into silence. As a host of monsters party together beneath us, we stay up in the trees, gazing out at the top of the woodland as it stretches before us.

A swarm of bats screech in chorus as they take flight from Skeleton Castle, soaring freely across the night sky, their fluttering wings glinting silver in the moonlight.

EPILOGUE

"Maggie," Mum calls up the stairs, "I hope you're doing your maths homework and not reading about vampires!"

Sitting cross-legged on my bed, I glance up guiltily from the book I'm studying.

"Of course I'm not reading about vampires," I call back.

Bat-Head gives me a pointed look from where he's crouched on my desk, about to take a drink from the egg cup of water I keep for him there.

"What?" I hiss at him. "I'm *not* reading about vampires. I'm reading about vampire *magic*. That's completely different."

Bat-Head doesn't look convinced.

"We'll have dinner in a bit, your dad is stuck at work. An ogre needed an emergency root canal." Mum sighs, adding, "We have warned them about snacking on boulders."

"Okay, no problem!"

"And when you've finished your homework, I could use some help choosing the final design of my mayor campaign posters. Ari has sent over a selection."

"I'll be down in a minute," I promise.

I hear her walk away from the stairs and go back to reading about the legends surrounding Dracula's Ring, something I've been doing a lot since the party a week ago.

"Listen to this, Bat-Head," I announce, tapping at the top of the page. "It says here that the protector of the ring is completely connected to it once they've been chosen. So its magic is engrained in me now. Isn't that crazy? It's part of who I am, just like you are."

Bat-Head lifts his head from the egg cup and starts to choke and splutter.

I sigh, putting the book down and swinging my legs off the bed to cross the room to my desk.

"What have I told you about drinking too fast?" I remind him, tapping his back with my finger. "You always get hiccups when you do."

As he coughs, a burst of red flames comes shooting out of his mouth.

I scream, jumping backwards.

"Everything okay up there?" Mum shouts from the kitchen.

"Uh … yeah, everything's okay!" I quickly call back.

"Are you sure?" Mum checks, sounding concerned.

I stare at my bat as he hiccups again, spitting out a few leftover red sparks and singeing the corner of my incomplete maths homework.

"Absolutely!" I assure her. "Everything is completely … normal."

Bat-Head slowly swivels his head to look at me in shock, plumes of smoke rising from his nostrils. A smile creeps across my lips.

"Looks like we need to go back to the library, Bat-Head," I say quietly, the blood-red ring on my finger shimmering as it catches the light. "I may have one or two more questions."

Acknowledgements

Huge thanks to Lauren, Sarah, Arub, Jessica, Aimee and the talented team at Scholastic – I'm so grateful to you for all the hard work that's gone in to produce this book; thank you for bringing the second story in Maggie and Sharptooth's adventures to life.

Special thanks to my agent, Lauren, to Justine and everyone at Bell Lomax Moreton. Your encouragement is invaluable and I feel so lucky to have you always cheering me on! I'm excited for all the future projects we have to come.

To my family and friends, thank you for your endless support, and big thanks to my dog, Bono, who is always by my side as I write.

As ever, the biggest thank you goes to my readers, without whom I couldn't continue doing the job that I love. Thank you for picking up this book, I hope it makes you smile. May the bats be with you.